ASSAULTED PRETZEL

ASSAULTED PRETZEL

Laura Bradford

CHIVERS

British Library Cataloguing in Publication Data available

This Large Print edition published by AudioGO Ltd, Bath,
2013.
Published by arrangement with Penguin Books Limited

U.K. Hardcover   ISBN   978 1 4713 4874 7
U.K. Softcover   ISBN   978 1 4713 4875 4

11834543

Printed and bound in Great Britain by TJ International Limited

For my family, with all my love.

CHAPTER 1

Claire Weatherly was just reaching for a slice of Ruth Miller's second-to-none Shoo Fly Pie when she heard it — the slow rolling rumble of an approaching storm that threatened to put the kibosh on the treat she'd been hankering for all week. Shielding the plate with her body, she dove her fork into the gooey goodness and —

"You did *what*?"

"I made some calls. Gathered some numbers. There's no comparison."

"I didn't tell you to make those calls!"

"You didn't *tell* me? Are you *kidding* me?"

Poof! The fork in her hand, the pie on her plate, and the feel of the autumn sun on her face were gone. In their place was the whisper of moonlight across the bottom of her comforter and the very real sound of two people arguing in the room across the hall.

She willed her eyes to close and her

thoughts to return to the food festival that had seemed so real only moments earlier, but she couldn't make it happen. The approaching storm in her dreams had shown its true colors.

Rolling onto her back, she stared up at the ceiling and searched for faces to accompany the angry voices. The constant comings and goings in her aunt's century-and-a-half-old Victorian necessitated a gift with names that Claire simply didn't possess. Still, she tried, cycling her way through the various guests who inhabited the rooms around hers . . .

Was it Doug and Kayla Jones?

No. Those were the honeymooners in Room Two. Arguing was the farthest thing from their radar . . .

The Grandersons?

No. That was the elderly couple in Room One whom Diane had been hosting at the inn every fall for the past sixteen years. Sleep was a far higher priority for the Wisconsin duo than fighting . . .

Claire struggled onto her elbow and wiped the sleep from her eyes. Room by room she mentally moved her way around the second-floor hallway.

Was it Melinda Simon, the young public relations executive who'd checked in along with her boss and his wife?

Sure enough, the visual accompaniment to the ever-rising voices in Room Six took shape in Claire's mind, spewing out a positive identity in short order.

Rob Karble — president of the world-famous Karble Toys — and his wife, Ann, had checked into Sleep Heavenly shortly after Claire had returned from work that evening. Friendly enough during dinner, the couple had opted to skip Diane's hot fudge brownies in favor of a long walk along the streets of Heavenly. When they returned some ninety minutes later they'd seemed happy.

Obviously, something had changed since they'd returned from their walk and retired to their room for the night.

"But to draft a memo without even talking to me?"

"Would it have *mattered,* Rob?"

"I —"

"You know as well as I do, the answer to that is no. You've had nothing but tunnel vision since you and Melinda concocted this idea."

"Because it's a good one!"

"A good one? I think that remains to be seen, don't you? But either way, my plan makes it even better. Lucrative, even."

"Does it always have to be about money?"

Claire imagined Ann's teeth unclenching long enough to release the laugh that seeped its way underneath her door. "Did that just come out of your mouth?"

"It did."

"Stop the presses, ladies and gentlemen, Robert Karble is questioning whether we need to make a decision based on money!"

Something resembling a snort was quickly followed by Rob's clipped voice. "Look, I've run this show for nearly twenty years now. And in those twenty years I've realized more profits than you could have ever dreamed *because* of the way I do things. So back off!"

"*Back off?* Did you just tell me to back off?"

Uh-oh . . .

Claire threw back her comforter and swung her feet over the edge of her bed. People like the Grandersons and the Joneses came to Heavenly, Pennsylvania, for the peace and tranquility synonymous with the picturesque Amish town. Awaking to a veritable knock-down, drag-out fight wasn't supposed to be part of the experience.

Wiggling her feet into her slippers, Claire stood and made her way over to her door, a host of potential argument-busters flitting through her thoughts. She could knock on their door and ask them to keep it down or she could be more subtle . . .

"What is it with you, Rob? What do you find so fascinating about these people? Why are you trying to be their white knight?"

Slowly, Claire opened her door to reveal the softly lit hallway that traversed the second story of Heavenly's premier bed-and-breakfast. Here, the wooden floors were polished to a warm glow and the walls were lined with period sconces that cast a magical aura across the narrow footway.

"I . . . I'm not trying to be anyone's white knight!"

"Oh no? Then think like the businessman you've always been and send out this memo."

"And if I don't?" Rob hissed.

"If you don't send it out, I will."

"Ann, I swear, if you send that memo, I'll . . . I'll —"

"You'll what, Rob? Yell? Stamp your feet? Puh-lease. You and I both know you're not the one who's in a position to hurl a threat. *I* am."

Claire took two steps forward and coughed — once, twice. And, just as she'd hoped, the arguing ceased in favor of the kind of quiet that would have had her eyes rolling back in her head by now over the perfection that was Ruth Miller's Shoo Fly Pie.

Figures . . .

But maybe, if she was really lucky, she could drift right back to sleep and into the same magical dream that still had her stomach rumbling with hunger despite the full-blown turkey dinner she'd eaten mere hours before bed.

Yup. It was official. She was hopeless. Completely and utterly hopeless.

Shaking her head in self-disgust, Claire pivoted back toward her room only to freeze, midway, as she caught a flash of movement out of the corner of her eye.

Curious to see who else had been roused from their dreams by the Karbles' heated argument, she turned in time to catch a fleeting glimpse of Melinda Simon just before the door to Room Three clicked shut, the hint of a smile on the statuesque blonde's face sending an inexplicable shiver down Claire's spine.

CHAPTER 2

One look at the dark circles under her aunt's eyes and Claire knew she and Melinda hadn't been the only ones roused from sleep in the wee hours of the morning. Even so, a quick check in the mirror before she'd headed down the stairs to help with breakfast hadn't yielded the kind of tension evident in the sixtysomething's face and stance.

Diane was upset. Or, at the very least, concerned. Either way, Claire hated seeing her aunt being anything other than her normal sunshiny self.

Desperate for a way to fix things, Claire stopped beside the basket of fresh-from-the-oven blueberry muffins and inhaled deeply, willing the effects of their mouthwatering aroma to work their way into her yawn-infused voice. "If I hadn't been so excited about today, I'm sure I would have slept through the noise, Aunt Diane. Truly."

Diane set the ceramic butter crock on the counter beside the muffins and dropped onto a nearby stool, releasing a weary sigh as she did. "That's sweet of you to say, dear, but, considering Mrs. Granderson was ruminating about the ruckus with the new bride across the hall this morning, you'd have been the only one, dear."

So much for wishful thinking . . .

She pulled a second stool from beneath the counter and sank onto its cheerfully upholstered cushion, her hands quickly giving way to the temptation that was her aunt's baking. "I know my only experience with the Karbles was at dinner last night, but they didn't strike me as the type to fight like that, you know?"

Diane's bifocals slipped down the bridge of her nose only to be pushed into place with a defiant shove. "It was a disagreement, not a fight. I just wish they could have had it at a different time and in a different place. I mean, they have so much to be excited about right now . . ." With a wave of a hand, her father's oldest sister returned to her feet and the quietly efficient pace that was as much a part of her makeup as the gray-streaked hair and heart-shaped face. "But it's over now and that's all that matters, right?"

Claire took a bite of muffin and considered her aunt's words. "Do you think there's any chance we'll see a resurrection of the argument over breakfast?"

"Since the two of them headed out of here about twenty minutes ago, I'll say no. And with the reception they're sure to get in town today, I think everything will be fine by the time they return."

She took a second bite, glancing at the clock on the microwave as she did. "At least they left together, right? That has to be a good sign."

Diane breezed around the kitchen, gathering the necessary plates and cups needed to serve a hearty breakfast for five of Sleep Heavenly's seven registered guests. "Actually, they headed in separate directions — Mrs. Karble for her morning run, and Mr. Karble toward parts unknown with a notebook in one hand and a camera in the other. But they did kiss before they left so I'll take *that* as the good sign."

Popping the last of her muffin into her mouth, Claire stepped off her own stool and grabbed the necessary silverware and napkins to round out her aunt's place settings. "Do you think there's any way I could wiggle my nose and have us skip over breakfast and go straight to the festival?"

Bingo! The smile she'd been waiting to see since she walked in the room finally spread its way across Diane's plump lips followed by the face-lighting sparkle that Claire equated with some of the best parts of her childhood. "If I thought that would work, dear, I'd be wiggling along with you. And *I* actually know what's in store. *You've* only heard whisperings." Diane pushed her way through the swinging door that separated the kitchen from the dining room with Claire hot on her heels. "All that is good about living in Heavenly will be on display in a twenty-booth radius today. *With* food."

Claire felt the excitement welling up inside as she headed around the table in the opposite direction of her aunt, stopping in front of each empty chair to fold a napkin and arrange the inn's best silver in preparation for the morning meal. "Esther is dying for me to try something called Schnitz and Knepp. She says I'm going to love it."

Diane stopped midstep and closed her eyes, a peaceful expression playing across her face. "Mmmm. And she's right. You will."

Taking the remaining stack of plates from her aunt's hands, Claire made her way back around the table, depositing one at each spot as she went. "What is Schnitz and

16

Knepp, exactly?"

The woman padded back into the kitchen only to return with a platter of her famous French toast and a gravy boat filled to the brim with maple syrup. "*Schnitz* is the Pennsylvania Dutch word for dried apple slices. For that particular dish, it's cooked with pieces of ham. *Knepp* is a kind of round bread dumpling. A thick sauce is part of the mix and, well, it's delightful."

The answering rumble of her stomach was quickly drowned out by her aunt's warm welcome to each of the guests as they emerged through the open doorway on the far side of the room. It was nine thirty and time to focus their attention on the couples who had chosen to make Sleep Heavenly a part of their visit to the heart of Amish country. Some, like the Grandersons, had been to Heavenly before, their reservation at Diane's bed-and-breakfast as much a given each year as any holiday ever was. Others, like the honeymoon couple who gazed into each other's eyes as they claimed their spot at the large mahogany table, were there for the first time, blissfully unaware of the power the simple town and its people was about to wield on their hearts.

But Claire knew. Because while she hadn't been part of a couple when she arrived in

Heavenly eight months earlier — quite the contrary, in fact — she, too, had been unprepared for the lasting impact Heavenly, Pennsylvania, would have on her life.

Still smarting from the breakup of her five-year marriage to Peter, Claire had come to Heavenly at Diane's urging. Within weeks she knew she'd found her new home — a place where the simplicity she'd always craved was not only at her doorstep but knocking at her heart as well. Less than six months later, she signed on the dotted line of a rental agreement that allowed her to open her very own gift shop — Heavenly Treasures — and become a true member of the community that had unknowingly given her back the gift of hope.

She'd found it in Diane's quiet and steadfast support.

She'd found it in the warmth of her new Amish friends — Esther King and Eli Miller.

She'd found it in the joy of starting fresh on little more than a dream.

She'd found it in the courage Jakob Fisher displayed every day in his decision to return to a town where his Amish roots would forever impact his work as the local police detective.

And she'd found it in the unexpected

friendship she'd forged with Eli's older brother, Benjamin.

Yes, her aunt was right. Whatever had sparked the disagreement between the Karbles during the night was sure to be erased the moment they ventured into town. Heavenly just had a way of doing that for people . . .

"Was everything okay last night, Ms. Weatherly?"

Claire shook the fog from her thoughts and forced her focus onto the woman standing over Virginia Granderson with a pitcher of freshly squeezed orange juice. Somehow, someway, the tension that had hovered around her aunt like a can't-miss storm cloud only twenty minutes earlier was gone, in its place the sunny smile and encouraging words that were synonymous with Diane Weatherly.

"Everything was fine, Virginia. Just a difference of opinion like so many of us have from time to time." Diane filled the elderly woman's glass and then stepped to her right. "Miss Simon, did you have a good rest?"

Melinda Simon, the one mate-less guest at the table, leaned to the side to afford Diane an unobstructed path to her glass. "Actually, that was the first uninterrupted eight hours of sleep I've had in weeks."

Claire drew back. Eight hours? There was no way . . .

Pushing a strand of blonde hair behind her ear, Melinda took a moment to look around at each guest before training her light blue eyes on Claire and Diane. "I guess it's what my dad always said — a vacation, whether working or otherwise, is good for the soul."

"So is marrying one's mate," Doug Jones said before linking hands with his new bride, Kayla.

"That, I'll have to take your word on," Melinda joked. "For now, though, I'll just be happy with the sleep."

For a moment, Claire considered questioning the young executive on her claim, but, in the end, she let it go. After all, what difference did it make whether the woman admitted to hovering in the doorway while her boss and his wife engaged in a verbal battle on the other side of the hall? Maybe Melinda didn't want to get involved in her boss's personal life. Maybe embarrassment was at work. Either way, it really wasn't any of Claire's concern.

"So is everyone heading over to the Amish Food Festival this afternoon?" Diane asked before swapping the pitcher of juice for the coffeepot in Claire's hands. At the collection of nods her inquiry yielded, the innkeeper continued. "The festival is always a highlight for our town, but this year I suspect it will be better than ever with all the celebrating."

Claire set the orange juice down on the serving table and retrieved the sugar and creamer. Following behind her aunt, she stopped beside each freshly poured cup of coffee and added the desired ingredients, her curiosity suddenly in overdrive. "Celebrating?"

Diane filled the last upturned mug and placed the pot on the end of the table, her excitement palpable. "Miss Simon? Would you like to share the news?"

Melinda paused her fork above her plate and studied Diane intently, the young woman's confusion evident in everything from her scrunched eyebrows to her narrowed eyes. "News? What news?"

"About Karble Toys' new Amish line."

Claire looked from Melinda to Diane and back again, her aunt's words catching her by surprise. "You're making an Amish toy line?"

Before Melinda could answer, Doug released his wife's hand and sat up tall. "Are there even enough Amish kids in this country to make a line like that viable for a company as big as Karble?" he asked. "I mean, I'm all about inclusion and everything but isn't that a bit of a risk from a business standpoint?"

"It's not for Amish kids." Melinda set her fork down on her plate and pushed her chair back from the table. "It's for regular kids. And for the parents of those same kids who are tired of all the passive playing that comes from today's electronic world. It's a way for them to introduce their kids to the basics from their own childhood. Which is why I named it the Back to Basics toy line."

"Back to Basics," Claire repeated slowly, the image of children bypassing their talking toys in favor of kitchen sets and wooden jigsaw puzzles making her nod along with her words. "Back to Basics . . . Wow, I like that. But, those toys are already available. Here, in Heavenly."

"Heavenly is one town. These kinds of toys will be of interest to children everywhere," Melinda said.

"But Daniel Lapp offers a catalogue people can order from whether they're in Heavenly or not." She heard the increasing panic in her voice and looked to her aunt for some sort of understanding. Didn't Diane get why the Back to Basics line was bad for the Amish?

"But Karble Toys is big enough they can mass-produce and do it much cheaper."

Diane smiled at Doug. "That's true, Mr. Jones, but that's not what they're doing. Karble Toys is going to utilize Amish folks from right here in Heavenly to make the toys and —"

Melinda stood. "Everyone needs to remember that the Back to Basics line is still very much a work in progress. And if I've learned anything since this notion was tossed out during an unexpected brainstorming session three weeks ago, it's that nothing is a definite until it's a definite. And even then, it's not a definite."

A long, low whistle escaped between Doug's pursed lips, rivaling the echo of Claire's excited clap. "I imagine that kind of work could make a real difference for the Amish in this area."

"Oh, it will!" A mirror of Diane's smile slipped across Claire's face. "Every new source of income for the Amish is a blessing."

"I thought the Amish stuck to farming," Kayla mused.

Claire leaned between the honeymooners and added a teaspoon of sugar to each of their mugs before addressing the new bride.

"Unfortunately, when their population is doubling every twenty years or so, the availability of land decreases, forcing them to turn to other ways in which to make money."

"Like making toys . . ." Virginia mused.

"Yes. And by selling their handmade goods in stores like Heavenly Treasures." Claire glanced around the table one last time and then set the sugar and creamer back on the serving table. "Essentially, they'll do just about any trade or task people are willing to pay them to do."

Diane disappeared into the kitchen only to return with a plate of piping hot sausage. "We even have a member of the Amish community right here in Heavenly who raises white-tailed deer."

Doug's brows rose. "For the meat?"

"For the antlers they shed each year." Diane made her way around the table once again, placing a slice of sausage on each plate she passed. "Pharmaceutical companies pay good money for those antlers, which they'll then grind up and put into various medications and health food supplements."

A second and longer whistle filled the room. "I had no idea," Doug said. "I just assumed they all farmed."

"Most people do." Claire took the empty sausage plate from her aunt's hands then took in Melinda Simon, who was still standing awkwardly behind her chair. "So this Back to Basics line was your idea then, Melinda?"

Slowly, the woman raised her gaze to meet Claire's. "You could say that."

"Man, I'd give just about anything to be the brains behind something like that at work one day." Doug rested his fork beside his plate and reached for his coffee. "I mean, to know that everyone is so pumped for something *you* came up with . . ."

"Oh, sweetie, it'll happen one day." Kayla Jones leaned her head into her husband's shoulder and looked up at him with utter worship. "You just have to come up with the right idea and —"

A snort from the other side of the table brought a hint of red to the newlywed's cheeks and turned the collective focus of the table back on Melinda. "*And* hope that your boss doesn't have any atoning to do. Because if he does, it doesn't matter how great your idea was. He'll kick it *and* you to the curb like you're yesterday's trash."

CHAPTER 3

If it were any other day, the virtual silence along Lighted Way would have sent Claire into a tailspin of worry. But today it was okay. Welcome, even.

The absence of cars and their Amish buggy counterparts along the cobblestoned thoroughfare meant the festival she'd been hearing about since the day she moved to Heavenly had finally arrived. And while the excitement around town had begun building over the past month, Claire's could be traced back even longer — to the moment she opened Heavenly Treasures and had met her new employee, Esther King.

Esther had been Claire's first real connection to an Amish community she'd previously viewed only from the windows of Sleep Heavenly. Back then, when she'd been trying to find her footing after the divorce, she'd often found herself drawn to the window seat in her room, the cool pane of glass a soothing tonic for her latest tear-induced headache. Those moments, by the window, had taught her a lot of things about herself but nothing more profound than the pull she felt in her heart every time she saw a horse and buggy meander down the road toward a world synonymous with simplicity and peace. A world so very different than the one she'd shared with Peter, where his work and his dreams trumped everything else, including her. It had been at that same window, with Diane by her side, where she'd first uttered aloud her desire to own a specialty gift shop of her very own. And it was at that window where Diane's encouraging words and loving arms had convinced Claire that *her* dreams were important, too.

Several weeks later, with a very different crop of tears in her eyes, she'd hung the shingle bearing Heavenly Treasures' name outside the simple white clapboard building positioned halfway down Lighted Way. But as wonderful as the realization of that dream was — and continued to be — it paled in comparison to the friendships she'd made because of the store — Amish friends who'd opened their minds and their hearts to Claire and made her feel as if she was someone special.

Which was why, instead of accompanying

Diane to the annual Amish Food Festival in the fields below Lighted Way, Claire was standing in front of the one building on the whole street that was actually open for business. Unlike many of its white cinder block counterparts in neighboring towns, the exterior of the Heavenly Police Department fell in line seamlessly next to the shops and restaurants that bordered it to its left and right. Like those establishments, the police station boasted the same white clapboard siding, the same wide front porch, the same tastefully written shingle above the front door.

Yet there was one irrefutable difference that set the police station apart from its neighbors. Here, the Amish who traveled the street in their buggies, worked in the neighboring shops and restaurants, and displayed their wares in so many front windows were noticeably absent.

Save, of course, for one.

Squaring her shoulders, Claire tugged open the door of the police station and ventured inside, the contrast between the sunny exterior and the fluorescent-lit lobby making her blink a time or two.

"Can I help you?"

"Is Jakob — I mean, Detective Fisher available?"

28

The balding dispatcher glanced down at something on his desk and then peered up at her over the half wall that separated the inner workings of the police department from the waiting area. "He is. Do you have an appointment?"

She pushed aside a strand of auburn hair that had escaped from her ponytail and shook her head. "No. But if he has a moment, could you tell him that Claire Weatherly is here?"

At the dispatcher's invitation, she took a seat, her heart beginning to thud in her chest at the task in front of her. On one hand she knew it was the right thing to do. On the other hand, she knew Jakob wasn't going to make it easy.

"Miss Weatherly?"

Shaking her head free of the debate raging in her thoughts, she stood and made her way back toward the desk. "Yes?"

"Detective Fisher said you can come on back." The man pointed to the door to his left, instructing her to open it as he buzzed her inside. Once there, he gestured her down the familiar hallway that boasted a handful of cubicles and a half dozen or so offices. When she reached Jakob's door, she knocked on the open frame.

In a flash, Jakob was on his feet, covering

the distance between his desk and the door in several long, easy strides. As he walked, his amber-flecked hazel eyes trained on her face and raised the silent greeting with a side order of knee-weakening dimples. "Claire, what a nice surprise." She felt her hand disappear inside his and marveled at the way his touch always managed to send an electric charge through her body, every single time.

"It's good to see you." At the unexpected waver in her voice, she scooted around his broad frame and motioned toward the chair across from his desk where she'd sat on several occasions. "Can we talk for a few minutes?"

"Of course." He made his way back around his desk and waited for her to sit before he did the same. "Is everything okay? I haven't seen you around much lately."

She was about to question his inquiry but left it unspoken as the reason behind his words assembled itself in her thoughts. She'd been so busy with the shop the past few weeks she hadn't been able to take Jakob up on his suggestion of a walk or a chat over coffee. Then again, if she was honest with herself, she knew she hadn't been too busy for either one. What she *had* been was nervous.

Because as much as she tried to believe her mantra about wanting to take care of herself rather than get involved in a relationship, she knew, deep down, that wasn't entirely true. She had feelings for Jakob; she just wasn't ready to examine them in the way they needed to be examined. And until she was, she needed to keep him at arm's length.

"I'm fine. Good, actually." She willed herself to push past the sudden bout of mental soul-searching and focus on the reason for her being in his office. But before she could speak, he moved on to yet another question.

"Is everything okay at Sleep Heavenly?"

For the briefest of moments she actually considered telling him about the argument that had awoken her during the night and the way Melinda Simon had lied about her role as witness, but, in the end, she opted to keep the incident to herself. It wasn't her place to air the laundry of Diane's guests.

"Everything is good there, too. Aunt Diane sends her love."

Jakob ran a hand through his sandy blond hair and flashed a shy smile. "I'll have to stop by one of these days and say hello."

"She'd like that." She scooted forward in her chair, searching for a way to present her case in a manner that would make him listen rather than protest. "But that's not why I'm here."

He laughed. "I kind of figured that." At the sudden warmth in her cheeks, he leaned forward across his desk, locking his gaze with hers. "So what can I do for you?"

"I was hoping maybe you'd consider coming to the festival with me today."

There. She'd said it.

Instantly, Jakob's smile disappeared along with his eye contact and overall jovial mood. "I can't do that, Claire."

She watched as he pushed back from his desk and rose to his feet, his hands clenching and unclenching at his sides in a motion she'd come to realize was the detective's way of dealing with stress. "But why not? You live in this town, don't you? You work in this town, protecting its people, don't you?"

"That has nothing to do with anything, Claire, and you know it."

She, too, rose to her feet, thwarting his second lap around the midsize office. "Aunt Diane says that almost all of Heavenly comes to this thing every year — which means that it's the *English* who are walking around enjoying the food."

"Food that's made by the *Amish*." He

shifted his weight from foot to foot, the urge to keep pacing virtually dripping from his pores.

"The Amish are around you in this town every day, Jakob. Why does this festival have to be any different?"

And, just like that, the stress and the apprehension that had been so visible in the detective's face and stance were gone, in their place an unmistakable pain and sadness. Her heart ached for the man.

"Because everyone in Heavenly's Amish community will be working at the festival." His shoulders sank along with the strength of his voice. "Including my entire family."

"But you see Esther whenever you come into my shop," she reminded, gently, as an image of Jakob's niece formed in her thoughts. "And, Martha even spoke to you in my shop that one day."

A flash of something resembling joy flickered across Jakob's face at the memory before disappearing behind reality. "My sister said three words to me that day, Claire. *Three words.*"

She took his hand in hers and gave it a gentle squeeze. "But at least she said them, Jakob. And she said them *to* you. Which means there's a chance."

Yanking his hand from hers, he spun

around and retraced his steps back to his desk. "Look, I'm thankful that I can peek into the window of your shop and occasionally get a wave in return from my niece, I really am. And although I've only heard my sister say three words to me in the sixteen years since I left home, I replay those same three words in my head every single night before I go to sleep. But a tentative wave — given only when Esther is sure no one is looking — and three words from someone I haven't seen since doesn't really mean anything in the grand scheme of things."

She stayed where she was but didn't give up. "Yes it does. Don't you see that those things happened because Esther and her mom were given a chance to see you again? To see the kind and generous person you are despite your decision to become a police officer?"

Silence filled the space between them as Jakob seemed to consider her words and she readied for further battle. Finally, though, he spoke, his voice a poor disguise for the anguish she still saw in his eyes. "I'd give just about anything to see my mother again, to see with my own eyes that she is doing well. I'd love to see my brother, Isaac . . . see if he's grown into the fine young man I knew he'd become when we took him in after his mother's death. But they cannot speak to me. I know this. It is a consequence for my leaving after baptism."

It was a fact of Amish life that still bothered her, yet it was one she knew she had no business judging. Instead, she let her heart lead her mouth and hoped it would be a step in soothing some of the hurt she knew Jakob carried with him every day of his life. "If you really want to see that your mom is well and that your brother has become a good man, then come to the festival with me. Come knowing that there won't be any conversation, but that you'll be able to see what you need to see with your own eyes. And come knowing that you're not alone."

His left eyebrow inched upward. "Not alone?"

She took a deep breath and let it seep out from between her lips. "For starters, if you come with me, I'll be by your side. And" — she heard Esther's whispered confession in her thoughts and prayed it was the right moment to share it aloud — "more importantly, you're not alone in wanting a glimpse of your loved ones."

Jakob stepped back and dropped into his chair. "Excuse me?"

Step by step, she made her way around

his desk and squatted down beside him, the slight tremble in his hand making her eyes burn with emotion. "I'm not the only one who wants you to come today, Jakob. Esther does, too."

"Esther?"

"Yes, and *she* told me that Martha has started talking bout you with her."

Covering his mouth with his hand, Jakob's eyes widened as Claire continued. "Esther said her mother only speaks of you when they are alone. The conversation always comes on the heels of Martha asking whether Esther has seen you about town."

Jakob's hand slipped downward. "My sister asks about me?"

Claire reached up, took hold of Jakob's hand, and held it tight. "She told Esther that her mother — *your* mother — prays for you every night. And that your brother, Isaac, drives his buggy past the station from time to time hoping to catch a glimpse of you but never does."

She took the opportunity Jakob's stunned silence afforded to make her final point, hoping against hope he'd see things the way she did. "This is your chance to see them, Jakob. And it's their chance to see you."

"My father will not approve."

"Your father doesn't necessarily have to

know. And if, by chance, he sees you, he can turn away. That's his choice. And maybe your mother and your brother will do the same — I don't know. But if what Esther says is true, I don't think that would happen until they'd taken a good long look."

"A good long look," Jakob echoed in a whisper.

Claire nodded and then squeezed his hand one last time. "So? What do you say? Will you go with me? Esther has been talking about Schnitz and Knepp for weeks now and I'm going to burst if I don't get to try it. *Today.*"

A slow, tentative smile made its way across Jakob's face, ushering in the briefest of dimple sightings. "We can't have you bursting now, can we?"

"Does that mean what I think it means?" she dared to ask.

His answer came by way of the button on the side of his desk phone that linked him to the dispatcher's desk. "Garrett? I'm heading out to the festival for an hour or so. Raise me on my cell if you need anything."

CHAPTER 4

They weren't even halfway down Lighted Way when the potpourri of delectable aromas wafting up the hill from the annual Amish Food Festival kicked her sense of smell into overdrive. And with her aroused sense of smell came a quickening of her pace and a protest from her companion.

"Did you enter us in a race I don't know about?" Jakob mumbled as he elongated his stride beside Claire. "Because the festival isn't going anywhere for the next several hours, you know."

"True. But if you'd been hearing about something since the moment you moved here the way I have, you'd be hankering for a chance to experience it for yourself, too." That said, she knew the same thing that pulled her forward had to be weighing on Jakob's footfalls at least a little. Slowing her steps to a more manageable speed, she cast a look in the detective's direction, all hint of the man's heart-stopping dimples gone. "It's going to be okay, Jakob."

"And if it is, it'll be fleeting. Like it was when I first saw Esther . . . and then Martha."

"Fleeting?"

Jakob slipped his hands into the front pockets of his khaki slacks and shrugged. "Seeing Esther, and then Martha, for the first time a couple of months ago was a dream come true. But the euphoria only lasts so long before reality kicks in. Momentary eye contact is great when it first happens. But when it doesn't go any further than that, the hope kind of fades."

She cast about for something to say to refute his claim but there was nothing. Like it or not, Jakob had earned his excommunication from the Amish community by his own choosing. It didn't matter that he'd left to be a police officer or that he lived a good life. He'd made his choice and he'd done so *after* being baptized.

She didn't agree with the mind-set, but it wasn't a teaching she'd been raised on, either. The only part that still baffled Claire from time to time was why Jakob had chosen to leave his out-of-sight, out-of-mind police job in New York to come back here, to Heavenly, where the constant reminder of everything he'd lost was around virtually every corner.

A slow-moving vehicle at their backs made them both turn, their hands rising into the air in unison at the familiar face piloting the small bus down the cobblestoned street. Keith Watson pulled to a stop beside them and slid his driver's side window open. "If I hadn't just had my eyesight checked not more than three weeks ago, I'd think I was seeing things with the two of you walking down the street just now.

"I mean, do you see this place?" His meaty hand directed their attention to both sides of Lighted Way and its closed-for-business signs. "If this food festival happened more than once a year, my business would be dead in the water."

And Keith was right. The tourists who flocked to Heavenly each year were the sole reason many of the town's businesses existed. Without them, Keith wouldn't have people paying for his tours through Amish country, her aunt wouldn't have guests paying for rooms, and Claire wouldn't have the gift shop that had put her back in control of her own hopes and dreams.

Jakob stepped off the curb and over to the bus, extending his hand toward the middle-aged man who'd gotten himself off the

40

unemployment line by creating Heavenly Tours. Although still in its relative infancy, the bus tour was gaining in popularity with each passing season. The addition of some behind-the-scenes stops that afforded his customers the opportunity to walk through a working Amish farm and watch with their own eyes as Daniel Lapp, an Amish toy maker, engaged in his craft had netted Keith the kind of word-of-mouth business that made all the difference in the world.

"It'll be back to normal before you know it." Jakob closed his hand over Keith's and gave it a firm shake before motioning back at Claire with his chin. "You should do what Claire is doing and enjoy the day off. There's nothing like Amish cooking to chase away your worries."

"Actually, that's why I'm here. I'm going to park the bus in the field and try as many dishes as I can just so I can give my opinions on them when my customers ask. Besides, food always goes with a celebration, and Heavenly certainly has something to celebrate these days."

Claire touched the edge of her hand to her forehead to shield the sun from her eyes and smiled. "So you heard, too?"

"I sure did. Best news I've had all month." Jakob looked from Claire to Keith and back again. "What are you two talking about? What news?"

The bus rolled forward ever so slightly as Keith shifted into park. "My tour stop at Lapp's place — which is by far my most popular stop to begin with — is about to get even more exciting now."

"Oh?" Jakob mused.

Stepping off the curb alongside Jakob, Claire nodded. "Karble Toys is getting ready to launch a new line of toys made by the Amish."

"And they're going to do it right here in Heavenly," Keith finished triumphantly.

Jakob whistled. "Are you kidding me?"

"No." Claire took a deep breath and proceeded to fill the detective in on the pending deal that she, herself, had just learned of that very morning. When she was done, she couldn't help but release a little squeal. "Can you imagine what something like that is going to do for Daniel and Sarah Lapp, as well as people like your broth—"

Realizing she was about to divulge a connection she wasn't sure she was supposed to divulge, she changed direction. Quickly. "Like Isaac Schrock and all of the other Amish men who will be needed to help fill the kind of orders Karble Toys gets?"

"It'll make all the difference in the world,

especially with farmland difficult to come by in these parts nowadays." Jakob cupped his hand over his mouth only to let it slip the rest of the way down his face. "How come I haven't heard this before now?"

"Just heard it myself this morning," Keith said. "Seems the head honcho of Karble is in town to talk specifics. And if the word on the street is correct, he had his first meeting with Lapp and Schrock at Heavenly Scented Brews last night."

"Which explains why Rob Karble turned down Aunt Diane's dessert hour last night." Claire couldn't help but laugh at the unexpected revelation. "She'll be mighty relieved to hear his refusal was based on business rather than the menu."

"How's Daniel with all of this?" Jakob asked, directing his question at Keith.

"You mean Lapp?" Keith removed his hat and scratched the top of his balding head. "Well, from what I heard at the coffee shop this morning before they closed for the festival, he's on cloud nine on account of Sarah being pregnant with number six and his love of making toys." Glancing at the leather strap on his left wrist, Keith nodded in their direction and shifted the bus into drive once again. "Guess it's time to let you folks be on your way. Maybe I'll see you

43

around the festival."

With the gentle guidance of Jakob's hand at her back, Claire stepped back onto the sidewalk, the excitement over the festival stronger than ever. Even Jakob, who had been exhibiting such apprehension about the annual affair prior to Keith's stop, seemed almost eager to get where they were going.

Shop by shop they made their way down the rest of Lighted Way until they reached the end of the sidewalk and turned left, their feet halting in unison as they did. For there, in the field below, was an unending sea of people milling about, laughing and eating and visiting with one another.

She felt her mouth gape ever so slightly. "Wow."

Jakob was silent beside her for several long beats as he canvassed the crowd, the suggestion of a smile playing at the corners of his mouth. "It hasn't changed one bit," he finally said in a voice that bordered on a whisper.

Leaning against the side of Gussman's General Store, she studied Jakob closely, noting the way excitement lit his eyes while tension ruled his upper body. "So you came to this when you were a kid?"

"Came to it? Nah, Martha and I ran our

own booth. And when Isaac came to live with us, he helped, too."

"You made food?"

Jakob nodded, his gaze still making its way back and forth across the crowd like the detective he was. "Technically, Martha made the food and I took care of the selling part. But that's because she made the best homemade salted pretzels you could ever imagine. Got the recipe from our grandmother but did something to them that made them even better. Every year people lined up to buy those pretzels, and every year we made a killing."

"I bet your Dat was thrilled," she said, pleased with herself for remembering the Pennsylvania Dutch word for father.

But if Jakob noticed, he didn't say. Instead, the animation that had made the amber flecks in his eyes sparkle just moments earlier disappeared, the tension previously confined to his upper body making its way into every nuance of his face.

She pushed off the building and took a step toward the detective. "Jakob, I'm sorry, I didn't mean to —"

"Dat was not thrilled. He never was. He only pointed to Benjamin and speculated how much more *he* must have brought home to *his* family."

The familiar flutter in her chest at the mention of Benjamin Miller took root and she willed it away. Now was not the time or the place to let her confusing feelings for the dark-haired, blue-eyed man take over.

Not that there ever was a good time or place. Benjamin's life as an Amish man jettisoned her flutters into the land of wasted time. Yet they still came. Every single time.

Jakob's voice morphed into the one Claire had come to equate with Esther's grandfather, a voice the detective turned to often, whenever he shared one of the more difficult memories of his childhood. "You should spend more time with Benjamin, son. He has turned his sister's pie stand into the talk of the festival."

"The talk of the festival?" she echoed. "I'm surprised he'd say that. I thought the Amish didn't boast like that."

"They don't. But that didn't stop Dat from implying." Jakob fisted his hands at his sides only to release them in conjunction with a deep, audible breath. "No. I'm not going to go there today."

Her stomach dropped. "But you said you'd come. Please, Jakob."

He closed his eyes briefly, opening them once again as he shook his head at her. "No. I mean I'm not revisiting my past today.

Not the bad parts, anyway."

Relief flooded her from head to toe and she reached out, tucking her hand inside the crook of his arm. "Then let's go. I've got some Schnitz and Knepp to try."

His deep, husky laugh warmed her from the inside out, a feeling that rivaled the Benjamin-induced flutter in its own right and only served to increase her level of confusion even more.

Their shoes parted company with cobblestone and then concrete in favor of dirt as they made their way down the hill and onto the official festival grounds, their proximity to each other growing uncomfortably close as the crowd swirled around them.

"Where should we go first?" she shouted over the roar of a crowd made up of English and Amish alike. From what she could see so far, most — but not all — of the folks in straw hats and head caps were situated behind wooden booths, their hands busy exchanging food for money with festival-goers. Some, though, were simply walking around or shuttling more food between the line of buggies on the western side of the field and the owner's particular food booth.

With nary a response, Jakob grabbed hold of her hand and zigzagged her through the maze of booths before coming to a complete stop in the center of a wide clearing. Then, lifting his finger ever so slightly, he guided her eyes to a booth some ten or so yards from where they stood, his voice choked with emotion. "She's still selling them . . ."

She studied the handful of English people waiting their turn for whatever delicacy that particular booth was offering and then let her gaze shift upward, to the hand-painted words across the wooden upper beam.

Salted Pretzels. $2.00

Turning, she looked from Jakob to the stand and back again. "That's Martha's booth?"

His head stopped midnod, the expression on his face telling her everything she needed to know. Yet still, she glanced back at the pretzel booth.

Sure enough, there was Martha, handing a paper-wrapped pretzel to the mother of an all-too-eager youngster on the customer side of the makeshift counter. To Martha's left was Claire's employee and friend, Esther — the strings of the young woman's head cap noticeably tied in the presence of her mother.

Claire smiled.

Esther was proud of her Amish upbringing. Proud of her choice to be baptized. But, every once in a while, the nineteen-year-old showed a slightly rebellious streak in everything from letting the ties of her head cap dangle across her shoulders to pumping Claire for details of life in New York City.

Seconds later, her focus still trained on Esther and Martha, she saw a third person step forward inside the booth. This face bore no resemblance to that of the family member on either side of him or the one still standing, motionless, beside Claire.

"Isaac?" Jakob mumbled beneath his breath.

She reengaged Jakob's hand and gave it a reassuring squeeze. "Yes, that's Isaac."

Claire had met Isaac Schrock one afternoon several weeks earlier when he'd come into Heavenly Treasures to drop off a few consignment items for his sister, Martha. A quiet man, he'd come and gone with little fanfare, waving to Esther on his way back out of the shop.

When he'd gone, Esther had filled in the blanks for Claire, explaining that Isaac had been taken in by Jakob and Martha's family when they were seventeen and fourteen and Isaac was just four. Isaac's mother had come to Heavenly from an Amish community in Ohio or Indiana shortly after Isaac's birth. The widow had raised him on a tiny farm down the street from the Fishers until the day she died, leaving Isaac an orphan quickly claimed by Jakob and Martha's parents.

At Jakob's slight stagger, she moved her hand to his shoulder, following his wide-eyed gaze back to the pretzel booth and the unmistakable look of stunned recognition on Isaac's narrow face.

Slowly, tentatively, Isaac backed away from his position between his sister and niece and made his way around the confines of the booth, his jaw slightly slack, his feet leading the way with purpose.

Claire's heart began to pound in her chest as her gaze ricocheted between an approaching Isaac, a slowly moving Jakob, and a stunned Martha who had looked up at that exact moment and seemed to register what was about to happen.

Swallowing over the lump that rose in her throat, Claire silently willed Isaac to go with his heart rather than heed the pull of the Ordnung. For as limited as her knowledge of the Amish still was at that point, she knew that if Isaac truly thought about what he was about to do, he'd turn and walk the other way.

But knowing that and even preparing for it did little to ease the ache she felt in her heart as Isaac suddenly disappeared into the crowd, his change in intent and direction soliciting a garbled and barely audible protest from Jakob's lips.

CHAPTER 5

He tried to brush off the almost-reunion with Isaac and enjoy the rest of the festival, but Claire knew it was just an act. Jakob may have been able to muster a smile for the English residents of Heavenly who stopped to shake hands with the detective over the next hour or so, but it was a sentiment that never made it to his eyes.

Or his cheeks.

She'd tried to convince him the change in Isaac's direction wasn't what he'd thought but, rather, the result of the sleeve-encased arm that had reached out and pulled Jakob's brother into the crowd. But it didn't matter. Jakob was convinced it was no accident, pointing to the epidemic of whispering that had begun to rise up among the Amish contingent on the heels of the ill-fated encounter.

"I shouldn't have come," Jakob muttered in her ear as they made their way through the center of the festival, all thoughts of Schnitz and Knepp on hold. "My being here just put Isaac and Martha in a bad position."

"But if he was pulled aside for something completely different — like maybe to help a friend or . . . I don't know . . . give some advice — then all of this is a moot point, Jakob," she pleaded. "Why do you assume it's a slight on you?"

Jakob stopped, midstep, and peered down at her, his eyes hooded. "I'm not saying it's a slight on me. I'm saying that Isaac came inches away from making a mistake that could have had him shunned and it would have been my fault."

"You're his brother."

"I'm also his brother who made a commitment I quickly broke."

She touched his shoulder with what she hoped was an understanding hand. "You were their brother first. Not even the Ordnung can change that fact."

Before Jakob could respond, her whole body lurched forward only to be anchored back to her original spot by a pair of strong, yet callused hands. "I am sorry, ma'am, I did not mean to bump you."

The deep voice, along with the telltale fluttering in her chest, told her who was behind her even before she turned. "Benjamin, how are you?"

She felt Jakob stiffen beside her but opted not to let that rattle her. The issue between Jakob and Benjamin was theirs to deal with, not hers.

"Claire. I did not see you standing there."

"It's a festival, Ben," Jakob snapped. "There are people everywhere. Which means looking in a direction other than the one you're walking isn't exactly advisable."

Benjamin paused, clearly torn on whether to engage Jakob, but in the end, he merely took Claire's hand in his and held it gently, his deeply penetrating blue eyes trained squarely on her face. "I was looking down, troubled by the news, and I did not see you. I am sorry."

Jakob held up his hands. "Look. This was not Isaac's fault. I shouldn't have —"

"It is no one's fault," Benjamin said as he grasped his clean-shaven chin between his thumb and forefinger. "There was no reason to think Mr. Karble was not honest."

"Mr. Karble?" Claire echoed. "You mean Rob Karble, the toy guy?"

Benjamin's black hat moved with his nod. "That is the one."

"But isn't he teaming up with Daniel Lapp to design an Amish line of toys that

54

will be made here in Heavenly and sold nationwide?" Jakob stepped closer to Benjamin, tightening up their conversational circle. "That's got to be good for everyone, no?"

"If that is what happened, yes. But plans have changed. Now we learn they will make Daniel's toys on an assembly line far from here."

Claire sucked in a breath. "But I thought Rob Karble was here for meetings with Daniel."

"It was during the meeting in Daniel's workshop this morning that he got what he needed."

"Got what he needed?" Jakob shifted his weight across his widened stance, crossing his arms as he did. "What does that mean?"

"It means he took pictures of Daniel and Isaac's work so his company can make their toys. Isaac even showed the plans for his roller tracks."

"But he's going to pay them for their ideas at least, isn't he?" Claire insisted.

"That is not what I have heard."

"Did you just say Isaac?" Jakob stammered. "What's he got to do with Daniel's toys?"

"Isaac works with Daniel in his toy shop. It is one of his toys that brings Mr. Karble here. He is not happy at the news. No one is."

For a moment, Claire simply stood there, soaking up everything she was hearing against the mental soundtrack of a predawn wake-up call that brought any and all unease it had originally caused back to the surface.

Was *this* what Rob and Ann Karble had been fighting about during the night? And if it was, why did it sound like the toy guru himself was in favor of the project if this was what he'd planned all along?

It made no sense.

"Is it possible Daniel misunderstood?" Jakob finally asked.

"Daniel did not know. He came here happy. But the letter changed that."

Claire forced her focus onto the present — one that included the handsome Amish man in front of her, and the handsome detective beside her. "What letter?"

Stretching his head upward, Benjamin scanned the crowd around them before motioning to someone off to their right. "There are many copies. I know Eli has one."

Eli Miller, Benjamin's younger brother and the object of Esther's affection, quickly joined them, his hand clutched tightly around a rolled-up piece of paper. His smile at Claire was followed by a nod at Jakob. If Eli's acknowledgment of the detective bothered Benjamin, he didn't let it show.

Progress . . .

"Eli, please show Claire the letter."

Eli quietly unfurled the paper and handed it to Claire, his quick-to-boil temper that had gotten him into trouble so many times in the past quickly rising to the surface. "Karble is a crook!"

"Eli!"

At Benjamin's reprimand, Eli clasped his hands behind his back and stood ramrod straight, his posture pulling taut on the suspenders that held up his pants. Claire flashed an understanding smile in the young man's direction and then turned her attention to the interoffice memo in her hands.

Good afternoon, Karble employees,

In Karble Toys' ongoing effort to be a trendsetter in today's marketplace, we are going back — to a simpler time when toys were about playing and laughing and engaging one's mind, hands, and imagination.

That's why we're on the cusp of rolling out a brand new line that will bring kids back to the kind of playing they should do.

Wooden kitchen sets, wooden jigsaws, wooden rocking ponies, and so much more. Authentic wooden toys designed by those who never lost sight of what playtime should mean.

We're calling it our Back to Basics line and it will be manufactured at our Grand Rapids facility.

Although we have much to do before the first toy rolls off the assembly line, I'd like to celebrate this new endeavor with a day off for all Karble Toys' employees next Friday.

With regards,
Rob Karble

Jakob released a long, low whistle beneath his breath. "Where did you get this?" he asked Eli.

"I do not know. But there are many copies here. This one came from Samuel Yoder, after he took Isaac aside and showed him." Eli swiped the back of his hand across his forehead, narrowly missing the brim of his hat. "Isaac is very upset. Esther said he did not return to the pretzel stand again after he showed them the letter."

Claire pulled her focus off Eli long enough

to take in her immediate surroundings. Sure enough, the smiles on the Amish vendors seemed more forced than they had when she and Jakob had first arrived. The Amish who weren't working behind a booth were still milling about, but they were confined to clusters with at least one member of each group holding a copy of Rob Karble's memo in their hand.

"I do not think the people of Heavenly will buy such toys." Eli tucked his thumbs behind his suspenders and rocked back on his heels. "They will know what Mr. Karble does is not right."

Swinging her gaze back to the men, it took every ounce of restraint she had not to dispute Eli's claim, the young man's innocence a blanket of protection she wasn't willing to rip away at that moment. When people lived in such an insular world, they couldn't truly comprehend the big picture. And in Eli's world, greed was a foreign concept.

At least that's what she tried to tell herself. But she knew better.

So, too, did Benjamin and Jakob, and the hatted men wearing an uncharacteristic worry on their faces. They knew the truth. They knew that having Amish-inspired toys mass-produced by a huge company with shelf space in every big-box toy store across the country would virtually annihilate any mail-order business Daniel Lapp currently enjoyed.

Did Eli truly not get that?

"We must go, Eli. It is time to check in on Ruth." Benjamin clapped his hand atop his brother's shoulder and gestured his chin toward their sister's pie booth in the distance. Then, with a quick nod to Jakob, he smiled at Claire. "It is good to see you, Claire. Very good, indeed."

She felt Jakob's eyes studying her as the Miller men walked away, and she prayed her mixed-up feelings for the Amish man weren't visible to the naked eye. If he detected anything, though, he didn't let on, and for that she was grateful. If she didn't understand what was going on inside her heart where Benjamin and Jakob were concerned, how could she expect anyone else to understand?

Eventually, Jakob spoke, his words bringing a welcome diversion from a topic she wanted to avoid at all costs. "In any other place and with any other person, Karble would be facing charges right now. But the Amish won't do that even if they should."

Her shoulders slumped under the weight of Jakob's words and the memory of Eli's face. "Do you really think Eli is oblivious to the damage mass production will wreak on Daniel's business?"

Jakob shook his head. "No. Eli gets it. He's just trying to keep his temper in check and that's a good thing."

Claire couldn't help but agree, even smiling a little at the obvious pride in the detective's face. For although he would probably never have a real relationship with his niece, Esther, his quiet words of encouragement toward the young man who would surely be Esther's husband one day helped — even if neither man would ever admit to the other's existence.

They fell into step once again, the pervasive mood around them taking the joy out of a festival Claire had been anticipating for months. "I guess the decision to ship the jobs to Grand Rapids could have been worse," she mumbled.

"How do you figure that?"

"If Karble had the Amish making the toys first and then took the work away, the disappointment would be even higher, don't you think?"

"I guess. But even now, with this, Daniel and Isaac and all of the other men have to be upset. Work like that could have meant so much. But even if they are upset, they won't show it for long. It's not the Amish way." Jakob stopped beside a booth devoted to bread and lowered his voice. "But it'll be there. Trust me on that."

She tried to nod, to acknowledge what he was saying, but it was hard. The smell of freshly made bread was a killer. "Mmmm . . . Do you smell that?"

He laughed. "I do. But you can't have any bread or it'll fill you up so much there'll be no room for your Schnitz and Knepp."

Jakob was right.

"So where is this must-try food booth I've heard so much about?" She looked to her left and then her right before turning a questioning eye in Jakob's direction. "Do you know?"

He straightened up tall and looked over the heads of the people around them. Seconds later, the dimples she adored so much were in place beside his heart-stopping smile. "I see it. C'mon." Tucking her hand inside his arm, they set out across the festival grounds to a series of booths that dotted the northernmost border, his running commentary about the Amish delicacy making her mouth water. When they were mere steps away, though, he stopped, turning to her, wide-eyed. "What happens if they're all out?"

"All out?" she echoed. "Does that happen?"

"All the time."

She looked back toward the booth they just left and sighed. "I suppose I could have some bread then . . ."

"Nah, I'm just kidding. The Amish don't run out. Not at this festival, anyway."

She pulled her hand from its spot inside the crook of his elbow and used it to swat at him. "Hey . . . now that's not nice. Not nice at —"

A loud scream from somewhere behind the Schnitz and Knepp booth cut her off midsentence, its bloodcurdling pitch chasing all signs of mischievousness from Jakob's demeanor.

"Jakob? What is that?"

He didn't stick around to answer. Instead, he took off running in the direction of the sound, with Claire hot on his heels. Step by step they wove their way through the unending sea of wide-eyed festivalgoers, the sound of their feet on the hard-packed earth impossible to hear over the terror-filled shrieks.

Moments later, he stopped, his hand shooting out to his side in an effort to keep her from going any farther. Peeking around his solid frame, she sucked in her breath as

Esther — who stood hunched over the fully supine and lifeless body of Rob Karble — finally burst into tears.

CHAPTER 6

Claire hated to see people cry. It didn't matter who, when, or why. Simply seeing another person's sorrow bothered her. It always had.

But sitting there, on the steps of Heavenly Treasures, as tears streamed down Esther's cheeks and onto her pale blue dress and white apron, Claire knew she'd never felt more helpless. The every-few-breaths hitch to the young woman's head only made it harder.

"Shhh, it's okay. *You're* okay." Claire reached out and tugged the strings of her friend's head cap until they dangled free, hoping against hope the move would unleash the fiery, determined side she knew was hiding just below the surface. "There's nothing you could have done, Esther, to change what happened."

Lifting her head ever so slightly, Esther turned her puffy and red-rimmed eyes on

Claire. "B-but h-he w-was d-d . . . d-dead."

There was nothing she could say to dispute Esther's words.

Ron Karble was dead — the victim of what appeared to be a fatal blow to his right temple. A half-eaten pretzel found inches from a blood-soaked rock gave both a glimpse of the man's final bite of food and the weapon that likely took his life.

The *who* behind the crime, though, was still a mystery.

She moved her hand still higher and tucked a wayward strand of Esther's brown hair back under the simple cap, her heart twisting at the overwhelming sadness that had replaced shocked horror on her young friend's face. "Jakob will figure out who did this, Esther. I know he will."

"B-but who . . . who w-was that man?" Esther swiped the back of her hand across her damp cheeks and sniffed. "And why w-would some . . . someone h-hurt him like that?"

Claire looked out at the autumn sun as it began its slow descent over Heavenly, the calm and peaceful October in stark contrast to the scene she knew was playing out in the field behind the shops on the other side of Lighted Way. The discovery of the toy manufacturer's body behind the Schnitz and Knepp booth had brought a quick and definitive end to the festival.

Within moments, the Heavenly PD swarmed the grounds and began dividing necessary tasks designed to clear the area around the victim's body, interviewing any and all people who may have been in the vicinity of the crime, and assisting in the investigation, including directing the medical examiner's van around the temporary booths that dotted the surrounding area and removing the camera the victim had worn around his neck.

When it became apparent that Esther knew nothing beyond the heart-stopping fear of having stumbled across a dead body, Jakob had urged Claire to take his niece somewhere where she could cry it out.

And cry it out she had, twisting Claire's heart more and more with each subsequent sob.

"His name was Rob Karble and he was the president of Karble Toys — a great big company that makes just about every kind of toy you can imagine and then sells them in stores from coast to coast."

Esther sniffled again, her voice shaky between hitched breaths. "H-he was the man who stole Uncle Isaac and Mr. Lapp's plans, wasn't he? Th-the one who was going to have the Amish make his toys and then ch-changed his mind?"

"That's the one."

"B-but who would want to . . . to kill him?" Esther whispered.

Claire propped her elbows on the step behind them and stared up at the sky, the faces of potential suspects standing in for the stars that were still an hour or so away. "Who *wouldn't* want to after he pulled the stunt he pulled?"

The second the words were out of her mouth, she wished she could recall them. Not because they weren't true but because the vast majority of the men parading their way through her thoughts were Amish.

Pulling her upper body straight on the step beside Claire, Esther jutted her chin outward. "But killing is wrong! For any reason!"

Oh, how she hoped Esther's fellow Amish had the same depth of conviction. But Amish or not, they were human. And humans could only endure so much before they snapped. The question was whether that snap would take the form of mental chastising, clenched fists, angry words muttered within the walls of an empty barn, or a moment of haste that would change a person's life forever.

To Esther, she simply agreed. Any speculation to the contrary would only start the tears again.

The *clip-clop* of an approaching buggy made them both look to the right, the identity of the men behind the horse making Claire perform a quick check on the status of her ponytail while Esther hastily retied the strings of her head cap.

"Eli will see I have been crying," Esther whispered. "I do not want him to know."

Reaching to her left, she rested a calming hand on her friend's arm. "Eli will understand. You've been through a terrible ordeal and you handled it as well as you, or anyone else, could. You've nothing to be ashamed of, Esther."

Eli's horse released a snorted exhale as the open-top wagon came to a stop in front of Heavenly Treasures. Holding his hat atop his blond hair, Eli jumped down from his seat beside his brother and ran over to Esther.

"Esther. You are okay."

For the first time since finding Rob Karble's body, Esther's young face broke out into a smile, the woman's eyes trained on nothing but those of the man she loved. "I am okay, Eli." Then, pulling her right hand from his protective grasp, she wiped at each of her eyes before forcing her smile to go still wider. "I am sorry you have to see me this way. I . . . I must look silly."

Eli looked from Esther to Claire and back again, his voice dipping to a whisper that stopped just short of being inaudible. "You look beautiful, Esther."

Not wanting to infringe on the young couple's private moment, Claire stood and made her way toward the wagon. As she approached, Benjamin jumped down from his seat and met her halfway, the worry in his eyes not much different than what she'd just witnessed in Eli's.

"Claire? Are you okay?"

She managed a smile of sorts while simultaneously hooking a subtle thumb in Esther's direction. "I'm fine. But Esther? She's had a rough go of it." Following the path of her own finger, she stole a glance at Eli and Esther, their heads bent close together while Eli provided the kind of comfort Esther desperately needed. "Though, now that Eli is here, I think she's going to be okay."

Her heart fluttered in her chest as she turned back to Benjamin and found his penetrating blue eyes studying no one but her. "Did you see his body, too?"

Slowly, she inhaled, the image of Rob Karble lying faceup on the ground with a still-bleeding head wound fresher in her mind than she realized. "I did."

His strong hands, callused from his work in the fields yet surprisingly soft at the same time, reached for hers, the unexpected feel of his skin against hers leaving her momentarily breathless. "And you are sure you are alright?"

She shrugged. "I didn't like seeing that, but I was more concerned for Esther and how quickly I could get her out of there. Fortunately, Jakob did everything he could to speed up that process."

"That is good."

"I'm sure he'll need to question her further once the body has been removed and he gets into the nitty-gritty of his investigation, but for now she gets a much-needed break." She stole yet another glance in Esther's direction. "She was really upset."

"Jakob will find who did this."

Claire drew back, surprised by the conviction she heard in Benjamin's voice. "You sound so sure."

"Jakob is a good detective."

For a moment, she wished she had some sort of recording device that would enable her to play Benjamin's words back for Jakob to hear. If she did, then maybe they'd go a long way toward erasing the hostility the detective still harbored for his childhood rival.

"But it will not be easy for him."

"What won't be easy for him?" she asked.

"Knowing who did this." Benjamin released her hands and rubbed his face, the motion drawing her attention to the worry lines she hadn't noticed at first. "You saw the letter. You saw the way it upset so many. Jakob must question many people to find the answers he will need."

"You mean Amish people, don't you?" Her mind had already gone there, of course, but to hear that Benjamin's had as well surprised her more than she realized. "They'll talk to him, won't they?"

At Benjamin's weighted silence, she closed her eyes briefly. "Can't they see that by giving Jakob the cold shoulder all they'll be doing is hurting themselves?" Then, without waiting for a response, she turned her attention back to her young friend. "Esther? Are you okay? Do you want me to walk you home?"

"I will take Esther home . . . if that is okay with Esther."

Even in the gathering dusk, Claire could see the tinge of red that sprang into Esther's cheeks as the young woman nodded her agreement. It was a moment of sweet innocence against a backdrop that had brought a cold, hard reality to Heavenly's collective doorstep. The question as to whether a member of Esther and Eli's community had precipitated that reality, though, was one Claire simply didn't have the heart to entertain anymore that night. Tomorrow would come soon enough for all of them.

"Then I guess I'll see you back here tomorrow morning?" she asked, earning herself a smile and an emphatic head nod from her one and only employee. Then, turning back to Benjamin, she flashed what she hoped was a friendly smile despite the yawn she had to work to stifle. "Thank you for bringing Eli to see her. She needed that more than anything I could have given her."

"Eli is not the only one who wanted to come."

She backtracked her way to the steps of her store to retrieve her purse, then returned to stand beside Benjamin. "Then I think it was very nice of you to want to check on Esther as well."

"I was concerned for Esther, too, but it is you I came to see."

"M-me?" she stammered.

"Jakob told me what happened. He told me you saw Mr. Karble's body, too. I do not like that you had to see something so troubling."

The man's words alone were enough to get the flutter in her chest going all over again. But when she coupled them with the tender look she saw in his eyes, the flutter became so strong she actually had to look away to catch her breath.

What was wrong with her? Benjamin was Amish. She was English. Anything she thought she saw on his face had to be in her imagination, didn't it?

"How are you to get home?"

Inhaling deeply, she looked back at him, the tenderness she'd surely imagined in his eyes quickly replaced by reality. Benjamin was her friend. Friends showed concern for one another. His being there was about friendship and nothing more.

"I'll walk. It's not all that far."

"I will walk with you," he stated firmly.

She waved aside his suggestion. "No. Please. I'd rather you and Eli see Esther home. She needs the rest."

"Eli will see Esther home and then come back for me. I do not want you walking alone when one who kills is still walking free." Before she could send up a second protest, he gestured toward the end of Lighted Way that led to Sleep Heavenly and the English side of town. "Besides, it is a nice evening. Good for a walk."

While she tried to sort her feelings about the man's offer, he pulled his brother to the side and told him the plan, to which Eli quickly agreed. Any opportunity to spend time alone with Esther was a good one where the youngest Miller boy was concerned.

When he was done, Benjamin and Claire began walking, the sound of their footsteps nearly silent against a night that had given way to the beginning notes of a crickets' chorus. One by one, they passed each of the shops along Lighted Way until the cobblestoned street bowed to blacktop and the English homes that denoted the western side of Heavenly. Here, the modest one- and two-story homes all boasted driveways and garages with at least two cars parked outside. Lamps, glowing computer screens, and flickering television sets were visible behind curtains, painting a picture of life inside that Claire had always thought was normal. And she still did in many ways. But since moving to Heavenly, she'd also come to realize that normal didn't necessarily mean best.

Now, she found herself strongly favoring moments like this — where comfortable silence fed her soul in a way no mindless television program or time-stealing website ever could. The fact that she felt more centered and more at peace on a regular basis these days was surely not a co-incidence.

She considered sharing that thought with Benjamin but opted, instead, to keep it to herself. After all, comparisons were mean-ingless when one only knew a simple life.

"That is a lot of lights."

"We use a lot of electricity on this side of town," she joked.

"But that is more."

Following the path made by his now outstretched hand, Claire focused her at-tention on the familiar Victorian just around the next bend in the road. Sure enough, Sleep Heavenly was ablaze with light while its side parking lot played host to two Heavenly police cars.

"Oh no . . ." Feeling her heart begin to pound, Claire took off in a sprint toward her aunt's inn, Benjamin matching and then surpassing her steps to the front porch and the wide-open door beyond.

When they reached the front hallway, she broke left, the sound of her aunt's tear-choked voice pulling her feet up the steps two at a time. "Aunt Diane? Aunt Diane? Where are you?" she shouted. "What's . . ." The words died on her lips as Virginia

Granderson stepped out of the room she and her husband had been assigned and beckoned Claire inside.

"Diane is in here. With us."

She followed Virginia into the room, stopping midway to the bed at the sight of her precious aunt and the twin tears that rolled down her round face. "Diane. What's wrong?" Instinctively, she dropped onto the Grandersons' bed and draped an arm around the woman. "Are you okay?"

When Diane didn't answer, Virginia filled in the picture. "The Karbles' room was ransacked."

"Ransacked?" she repeated with a voice that was too loud for the confines of a room now inhabited by five adults. "What do you mean, ransacked?"

"We — meaning Diane, Wayne, and myself — came home from the festival maybe three hours ago?" At her husband's nod of agreement, the sixtysomething woman continued. "We spent an hour or two just sitting over a pitcher of iced tea and talking about all of the wonderful food we tried. When we were done, we all came upstairs to freshen up for dinner and that's when your aunt noticed that the Karbles' door was open."

"It was a mess," Diane finally said, her voice strained and tired. "The mattress was ripped open, the drawers were all taken out of their dresser and dumped over, the interiors of their suitcases were ripped . . ." Diane buried her hands in her face, releasing a tortured sigh as she did. "Nothing like this has ever happened here before and I feel horrible. I . . . I don't know what I'm going to tell them when they get back."

She felt her stomach lurch. Diane didn't know? Was that even possible? Quickly, she glanced up at Benjamin, noting the surprise in his face as well. But before either of them could say anything, Diane went on, her words muffled behind her softly wrinkled hands. "I called the police right away and they've been taking pictures for the past thirty minutes. I heard one of them say Jakob would be here shortly when he is done at the festival grounds. I just hope he's here when the Karbles return because I'm sure they will be angry and want the kind of answers I'm at a loss to give right now."

Again, Claire looked at Benjamin, the quiet concern she saw in his eyes giving her the courage she needed to share the part of the story Diane needed to know, especially when it was obvious even to Claire that the two events were most certainly related.

"Diane." Leaving her left arm still draped around Diane's back, Claire sought the woman's now clasped hands with her right, covering them gently and offering a little squeeze. "Rob Karble won't be coming back to the inn."

Her aunt's face crumbled. "But he has to know that something like this has never happened in my inn before!"

She took a deep breath and tried again, this time cutting straight to the chase. "Diane. Rob Karble won't be coming back because he's dead."

Diane's gasp was echoed by Virginia and her husband, with Virginia recovering fast enough to ask the litany of expected questions. "Dead? But . . . how? When?"

Claire opened her mouth to speak, but it was Benjamin who ultimately answered, his words blanketing the room in a stunned silence. "His body was found near the end of the festival. He was murdered."

CHAPTER 7

Claire emptied the last of the quarters into their spot in the register and glanced up at the clock.

9:40.

Twenty more minutes and she could officially throw herself into a day that would have her greeting customers, fielding questions about the Amish, helping match people to a particular gift item, and carefully wrapping purchases for their journey home. They were tasks she always welcomed as a small-business owner who relied on tourists for survival. But at that moment, her eagerness for the day had very little to do with sales and the bottom line, and everything to do with needing a distraction.

Sure, she'd tried to find and maintain a sense of calm for Diane and the rest of her guests the night before, but, in all fairness, there was only so much a person could do when faced with a murdered guest, the ransacked room of that particular murdered guest, and the late-night arrival of that same murdered guest's wife.

A snorted exhale through the open side window startled her from her thoughts and she shut the drawer, the answering rattle of the coins inside failing to trigger the smile it normally did. "You can do this, Claire," she mumbled. "You can pretend like everything is normal."

A soft tap at the shop's back door saved her from engaging in an unending litany of self-debate, and she headed in that direction. Fortunately for her, the sight of the Amish man standing on the other side of the storm door was able to accomplish what the sound of the coins hadn't, adding a side order of flutter to boot.

"Benjamin, hi! I figured that was your horse I heard in the alley just now." Leaning forward, Claire pushed the door open with one hand and waved Eli's brother in with the other.

His normally stoic cheekbones lifted upward in a smile reminiscent of Ruth, his sister and Eli's twin. Ruth Miller ran Shoo Fly Bake Shoppe, the wildly popular Amish bakery next to Heavenly Treasures. The two stores were separated at their sides by a narrow alleyway just large enough to accommodate a buggy visit from whichever Miller brother stopped by the bake shop to look after Ruth at any given point in the day.

"You are well this morning?" Benjamin stepped into Heavenly Treasures' stockroom and turned to face Claire, his dark blue eyes searching her face with an intensity that only served to increase the flutter factor. "You were able to get rest?"

Rest. That was such a subjective term, wasn't it?

Had she been able to shut her door and retire to her bed at some point during the night? Yes. But only after Ann Karble had stopped screaming and been settled into a spare room on the first floor, the police had gotten everything they needed from the ransacked room, and Diane had finally wept herself into something resembling sleep. Had she actually been able to close her eyes and drift off? Not if the dark circles that had lined the bottom of her eyes in the mirror that morning were any indication.

To Benjamin, though, she gave a quick and shallow nod before redirecting the conversation. "I have to thank you for both your calm and your help last night. I'm not sure what I would have done without you there."

"It was the least I could do. All of that

was too much to leave you and your aunt to handle." Benjamin peeked out the screen door at the horse he'd tethered to the hitching post beside the bake shop's back door and then stood up tall once again. "I only wish I could have helped to right such heavy furniture in Mr. Karble's room so you do not have to worry about such things."

She closed her eyes against the image of the guest room across the hall from her own, the period pieces her aunt had so lovingly collected in the years leading up to the grand opening of the inn tossed about like they meant nothing. But when she heard Ann Karble's screams echoing up the stairs from the parlor below, she forced her eyes open. "The officers needed to leave the room exactly as it was found until their investigation is complete. And until Jakob can get in there, it can't be released."

"When he does, you will let me know so I can help?" Benjamin asked. "I do not want you moving such heavy things."

"I'll let you know. Thank you." But even as she said the words, she knew the status of Room Six was the least of everyone's worries.

A man had died. A man who had angered many, many people, including some both she and Benjamin called friend.

The jingle of bells in the shop's main room cut through her reverie and guided her attention to the hands of her wristwatch. 9:55.

Shrugging, she turned on the two-inch heels of her boots and strode into the showroom, Benjamin following at a respectful distance. "Good morning, welcome to Heavenly Treasures . . ."

The more formal greeting died on her lips at the sight of Jakob standing just inside the shop's front door with a camera in one hand and a pair of gloves in the other. "Jakob . . . uh, hi."

The detective mustered a weak smile for Claire then tipped his head ever so slightly at Benjamin. "Ben. Good. I was hoping to track you down at some point today."

Before Benjamin could reply, Claire moved still closer to Jakob, the uncharacteristic droop to the man's broad shoulders sending her antennae pinging. "Jakob? Are you okay?"

"Long, long night. Sorry I couldn't get to Diane's before this morning but things were just too busy at the fairgrounds and then back at the station once we were able to locate the victim's wife."

"Where was she when everything was happening?" she asked before her brain had a chance to catch up with the inherent nosiness of the question. "Wait. I don't really expect you to answer that."

Jakob waved her worries aside and stopped at the counter in the center of Claire's shop, setting the camera and the gloves down as he did. "Seems she went into Breeze Point to do a little research at the library and then to an office store to mail some things. She found out about her husband when she called his cell and I answered it."

She shivered at the notion of such a call. "Did you tell her on the phone?"

"Of course not. I told her who I was and asked her to come to the station." Jakob lifted his hand to his face and exhaled slowly. "Officer Melnick brought her back to the inn when we were done talking and . . . you can probably take it from there."

Once again, the memory of Ann's cries from the bottom of the stairs looped their way through her thoughts, reminding her of the distraction she desperately needed work to provide for the next seven or so hours.

"Did you see her when you went to the inn this morning?" Benjamin asked from his spot somewhere behind Claire.

"No, she was still sleeping. Diane had made up a room for her on the first floor so

I was able to spend time in the room she'd shared on the second floor with the victim without rousing her unnecessarily."

"Don't you find it rather ironic that those of us who didn't even know the man couldn't sleep in the wake of his murder, yet his own wife could sleep so soundly she didn't hear the detective assigned to her husband's case coming and going this morning?" She hadn't meant to share the observation aloud but sleep deprivation and stress tended to wreak havoc on one's good sense.

"I suspect her ability to sleep is due to heartache and depression more than any-thing else."

And, just like that, Claire found herself feeling like a monster for uttering such a statement in the first place. Jakob was right. She couldn't even begin to fathom what Ann Karble was going through at the mo-ment.

Before she could apologize, though, Jakob wiggled the rubber gloves onto his hands and motioned for Claire and Benjamin to join him behind the camera's viewfinder. "I could use a little help in identifying some of the pictures taken on this camera yesterday."

"Is that the same camera that was around Rob Karble's neck when we found him?"

she asked as she moved in beside Jakob and waited for Benjamin to do the same.

"Yes."

Benjamin remained in his spot between the counter and the stockroom door. "I do not understand why you need me to look at pictures."

She felt Jakob tense in response. "Because I'm trying to figure out what the victim was doing in the hours leading up to his death. If I can, maybe I'll be able to catch a killer and put him away where he can't hurt anyone ever again."

A momentary pause was soon followed by the sound of Benjamin's work boots against the thinly carpeted floor. When the man was situated just behind the detective's other shoulder, Jakob pushed a button to the side of a small screen to reveal a crystal clear shot of ham, apple slices, and dumplings, alongside a large salted pretzel. The angle of the shot indicated the person shooting the picture was also the person holding the plate — a person Jakob identified as Rob Karble based on the attire the man was wearing when his body was discovered.

"That is Martha's pretzel and Hannah Yoder's Schnitz and Knepp dish," Benjamin stated in his usual matter-of-fact tone. He turned to her and smiled. "Did you like it,

Claire?"

"I never got to try it," she replied. "That's what we were on the way to try when we heard Esther's screams."

Esther . . .

Oh, how she hoped Esther was feeling better after a good night's sleep. Finding Rob Karble's body behind the Schnitz and Knepp booth was —

"Wait!" At the feel of both Jakob's and Benjamin's eyes on her, she pointed to the screen, her own eyes trained on the subtle details around the plate of piping hot food held aloft over a dirt field that had seen its fair share of foot traffic and lazy festival-goers. Details that put the time the picture was taken not all that long before Esther had found the body.

"This must have been taken shortly before he died," she mused as she drank in the position of Rob Karble's shadow in relation to the corner of the Schnitz and Knepp booth barely visible in the upper right-hand corner of the shot.

Jakob nodded. "Since it's the last picture he took and it shows him having eaten at the very booth closest to where we found him, I'd have to agree."

She leaned still closer to the screen as Jakob worked backward through the last few hours of Rob Karble's life.

There was a picture of Martha's pretzel booth . . .

There was a picture that showed the main thoroughfare of booths through the center of the festival grounds — the image capturing everything from curiosity to utter joy on the faces of people who never realized their photograph was being taken . . .

And there was a picture from the hill above the grounds that took in the festival as a whole — the Amish and English intermingling with one another effortlessly.

Claire swallowed and glanced at the ground, the momentary break from the screen affording an opportunity to rein in the emotions that were threatening to hinder her desire to remain upbeat. But it was hard.

It was hard to look at such happy photographs from an event that so many people — including herself — had looked forward to for months, knowing it had all come to an end in such a tragic way. Murder wasn't supposed to happen in Heavenly at all. It most certainly wasn't supposed to happen for the second time in as many months.

It wasn't right.

It just wasn't right.

"Now this is where you might come in,

Benjamin." Jakob's words pulled her focus back to the camera and the first image they'd seen so far that wasn't taken at or around the festival. "Any idea what this building might be?"

Sure enough, the camera lens had caught a side view of a small wooden structure that wasn't much bigger than a large shed. Only this particular building was painted white and boasted a flower box outside its solitary yet decent-sized window.

"That is Lapp's Toy Shop."

"Are you sure?" Jakob asked.

"Yah. I am sure." Benjamin swept his hand toward the screen. "He built that window box at Sarah's request. Sarah is very good with flowers."

Jakob nodded and then pushed the button that took them to the picture taken just prior to the exterior shot. "And this? What can you tell me about this, Ben?"

She studied the image along with Benjamin, her focus on the elevated wooden track and its matching wooden car while Benjamin merely crossed his arms and rubbed a hand along his jawline. "That is easy. That is Isaac's roller track. It has a double track so children can race their cars. It is one of the toys Mr. Karble was to have in the new toy line. One that was to be built here, in

Heavenly, under Isaac's supervision."

"Under Isaac's supervision," Jakob mumbled beneath his breath before shaking his head and bringing yet another image of a toy onto the screen in front of them. This time, he didn't say anything — no question, no muttering, nothing. Instead, he merely waited for Benjamin to speak.

"That is a wooden jigsaw puzzle that Daniel first made for his son Joshua. It is different than English puzzles because it is a puzzle, itself."

It took Claire a moment to understand what Benjamin meant. But upon closer scrutiny she got it. The entire giraffe was a puzzle — a puzzle that could stand up as a figure when the child was done, unlike the more traditional picture puzzles the English tended to have.

Jakob pressed the button again and again, slowly cycling through toy picture after toy picture until they reached an outdoor shot. Leaning forward, Claire took in the rock wall with a tree-bordered clearing on one side and a gently rolling brook on the other. "Oooh, that's pretty," she said as she looked from the screen to Jakob and back again. "Where is that?"

Without taking his attention off the screen, Jakob spoke, his words simple and succinct despite the emotion evident behind them. "That is Miller's Creek where it begins high on the hill."

She turned to Benjamin, noting his nod. "*Miller's* Creek? As in *your* Miller?"

"It is said that my great-grandfather found that creek and that is why it is called Miller's Creek. All I know is that it is not far from a place I like to go. A place I have shown you as well, Claire."

She felt Jakob stiffen at the implication and she rushed to explain, the memory she shared meaning far more to her than she allowed her words to express. "Shortly after Walter Snow was found dead in the alley next to my shop a couple of months ago, I was out walking, needing a place to slip away and think. Benjamin rode up in his buggy and offered to show me his thinking place." At the feel of Benjamin's gaze on the side of her face, she continued, her own voice suddenly raspy at the memory of sitting on a rock gazing up at stars with the Amish man. "Only I never saw a creek either time I went there."

A beat of awkward silence was broken by Jakob. "We used to catch frogs in that creek after the chores were all done."

"We? You mean you and Martha?" she asked.

"No. Ben and me."

Before she could make sense of what she was hearing, Benjamin's hand moved toward the screen once again. "What is that?"

Jakob's shoulders snapped to attention. "What's what?"

"That paper and those cups."

Sure enough, on closer inspection, a stack of papers was visible atop a large, flat rock just to the left of the stone wall. Moving his finger to the top of the camera, Jakob zoomed in closer on the image, the previously nondescript stack of paper now revealing basic drawings and simple measurements housed between two paper coffee cups.

Pressing the zoom one more time, the drawings became crystal clear.

"That is the plan for Isaac's roller track."

Jakob met Benjamin's eyes and held them steady. "Are you sure?"

"You can show the picture to Isaac if you must, but I am sure. He showed them to me when he made them."

Claire looked back at the plans so obvious now in the image's magnification. "But why would Rob Karble have a picture of them in his camera?"

"Perhaps he stole them," Benjamin mused.

It was a simple sentence yet one that

resulted in drawing a faint gasp from her lips and a spine-chilling response from Jakob's. "And perhaps someone stole them back."

CHAPTER 8

If Jakob sensed her studying him, he gave no indication, his complete focus somewhere other than Heavenly Treasures, or, perhaps, even Heavenly, itself. Something was off about the detective. Something that made her want to ask yet had the simultaneous effect of warning her off any and all questions.

Maybe it was the fact that the dimples that normally came so easily hadn't made an appearance even once.

Maybe it was the dull, troubled look in his eyes.

Maybe it was his uncharacteristic silence as he stood there, by the side window, staring out at the alley that had long been vacated by Benjamin and his buggy.

And maybe it was because, deep down, she knew what was wrong. It was kind of impossible not to on account of what she knew about the detective's past.

"You don't think your brother had anything to do with the murder, do you?" Claire finally asked if for no other reason than to draw him out and let him know she was there and ready to listen.

Slowly, Jakob turned, his eyes hooded, his shoulders drooping downward. "Until I saw him at the festival yesterday, I hadn't seen Isaac in sixteen years. I can image what kind of man he has become based on the boy he once was, but I can't know for sure."

"How old was he when he came to live with you and your family?" Though she knew details from what Esther had told her, she had yet to ask Jakob directly until that moment. "Had you known him long?"

Jakob closed the gap between the window and the counter, his gaze now fixed on the memories that began to pour from his lips. "Isaac was a newborn when his mother showed up in Heavenly. She'd lost her husband in a farming accident in Indiana and she wanted a change. She came here, with Isaac, and never remarried. Instead, she supported the two of them with the quilts she made and the preserves she canned. Then she became ill and asked my mother and father to look out for Isaac when she passed. They obliged. Isaac was four."

"Was it hard for him to adjust? Losing his mom like that?"

"Mary Schrock was a strong woman." Jakob leaned his forearms atop the counter next to the camera. "She prepared Isaac for the change as she was dying. He accepted it as God's will. As we all did."

She tried to take it all in, to process it as the factual account it was, but the part of her that felt people's pain found it difficult to let go, especially as it pertained to a four-year-old boy. "I can't imagine what that would be like at that age — not having pictures to look at to remind you of your loved one."

"The picture is in here," Jakob said, touching his heart as he did. "And Mary gave my mother letters to share with Isaac as he reached different stages — his baptism, courting, marriage, fatherhood, et cetera. Knowing he had those to look forward to was enough for him."

She opened her mouth to speak but closed it as Jakob continued, his words veering off and taking them down a very different path. "One way or the other, Isaac will have to be a part of my investigation. His work with Daniel Lapp alone sets up a connection between him and Karble. And now, with what Benjamin said about the picture of

Isaac's roller track plans, it's even stronger."

"So you ask the questions you need to ask and you move on." But even as she uttered the thought aloud, she knew it wasn't that simple. Because for Jakob to ask the questions, it meant he had to have verbal contact with his brother — something Jakob longed for, yet lost the right to have the day he walked away from his Amish life.

"Talking to the police is not something the Amish relish. Talking to *me* is even worse," Jakob shared from behind the relative protection of the hand that he'd draped across his eyes. "When I came back here to take this job, I saw it as a way to be close to my family even if I knew the dynamic could never be the same. Yet since I've been back, all my presence has done is put my family in a really bad position. First, with having to question my niece when Walter Snow was murdered. And second —"

"If you could see the look on Esther's face whenever you walk down the street, you'd know that she respects you," she blurted out, anxious to put an end to at least a smidgen of Jakob's self-inflicted browbeating. "And when you stop outside the shop and wave to her, she looks like a kid on Christmas morning."

Jakob's hand slid down his face to reveal a

raw pain that made Claire ache from head to toe for the man standing mere inches away. "But she can never know me, not without risk of being shunned. My coming here, my desire to be in her life if even from a distance, has put her in that position."

"You're wrong, Jakob."

"What is wrong is my being here. My presence puts Martha, and Esther, and, now, Isaac in an awkward position. It was selfish of me to do that to them." He pushed off the counter and gathered the items he'd brought. "I think it's best for everyone if I look at taking this job as the mistake it was and resign."

Claire drew back. "Resign? No! You can't just give up and walk away . . ."

Her sentence trailed off as the telltale jingle above the shop's front door alerted them to the arrival of a customer — the normally welcome sound instantly setting her on edge. Exhaling in frustration, she walked around the counter and Jakob only to freeze in place as she cleared both. For there, standing just inside the door, was Esther's virtual carbon copy save for the two decades that separated them in birth and gave Jakob both a sister and a niece.

Martha King was dressed in a dark burgundy dress with a black apron, her hair pulled into a tight bun and secured beneath the white head cap that failed to shield the worry in the woman's face. "Claire. I need help. I need to find my brother. I need to find Jakob."

She heard the gasp from just over her shoulder and knew it was an echo of her own. "Y-you want to talk to Jakob?"

Martha's hazel eyes — so like her eldest daughter's — remained trained on Claire's face without so much as missing a beat. "I must. He is the only one who can help."

And, just like that, the moment she'd been praying for since meeting Jakob was at her hands for the taking.

Jakob's taking.

Noiselessly, Claire stepped to the side to reveal Jakob, who was already placing the gloves and camera back on the counter. Slowly, he crossed to his sister, his voice a moving mixture of uncertainty, surprise, and hope, juxtaposed against a woman who wore the same emotions on her rounded face. "I am here, Martha. Just tell me what it is you need."

Martha took a half step forward only to negate it with a half step back. "I know Mamm and Dat would not approve of me being here. Nor would my husband, Abram. But, Jakob, you are a good man. And a good man protects his brother."

Claire watched as Jakob took the same half step forward followed by an immediate half step backward at Martha's obvious discomfort. It was a dance that was hard to watch, yet one both partners bowed to in recognition of an institution they both understood and respected.

"You mean *Isaac*?" Jakob asked, his focus never straying from his sister.

"Yes, Isaac. I am worried what the English man's murder might mean for him. But I am also worried for Daniel. He and Sarah have been through much the past few weeks. Sarah tries to be strong but it is weighing on her. Such stress is not good for her at this time."

"At this time?" Jakob inquired. "I don't know what you mean."

Claire began nodding even before her mouth became engaged in the conversation playing out in her shop. "Remember? Keith Watson mentioned it yesterday when we saw him on the way to the festival. Sarah Lapp is expecting again. Her fifth, I believe . . ."

"Her *sixth*," Martha corrected, not unkindly. "She lost her fifth in the spring. I am afraid she will lose this one as well if she does not stop worrying about things that are not true. But she was in town this morning. She heard whispers. She saw pointing. And she is frightened for Daniel just as I am for Isaac."

"Why are you frightened for Isaac?"

For the first time since their eyes met, Martha looked down, clearly uncomfortable with Jakob's question. Or, perhaps, the answer she seemed reluctant to put into words.

Claire touched Jakob's back ever so gently and then hooked her thumb in the direction of the counter. "I have a stool behind the counter. Maybe Martha would like a place to sit."

Seemingly unwilling to blink, let alone move, Jakob kept his focus on Martha as if he was afraid any movement or unexpected change of venue would relegate the verbal exchange he was having with his sister to a dream. "Uhhh, okay. Okay, yeah. That would be fine. I — Martha? Would you like to sit?"

At Martha's quick yet definitive nod, Jakob waved his sister over to the stool. When she settled herself onto the cushioned top, he squatted beside her and peered up at her with such awe and such gentleness that Claire had to look away and swallow.

"Now tell me. Why are you so afraid for Isaac?"

"Do you not know?" Martha asked. "Do you not know that toy man was going to make Isaac's toys without Isaac's help?"

Jakob rubbed at the clean-shaven skin along his jawline. "I know. I saw the copy of the memo that everyone was looking at during the festival yesterday. I'm sure it was a shock to Isaac and Daniel if they'd both been led to believe they'd have a hand in actually *making* the toys for the Karble Corporation."

"Shock, yes. For both. But for Isaac it is sadness, too."

Stilling his hand against his face, Jakob looked from Martha to Claire and back again, his sister's words bringing him up short. "Because of the lost work?"

Martha nodded as she filled in the details of her statement. "It was *Isaac* who told him of the toys he and Daniel make."

Unable to hold her tongue any longer, Claire jumped into the conversation, her head desperate to make sense of what she was hearing. "Are you saying Isaac is responsible for bringing Rob Karble to Heavenly in the first place?"

"That is what I am saying." Martha glanced down at her hands intertwined in her lap, struggling to find a way to explain what she knew. "He was excited to bring work here. He was excited to be able to help Daniel in that way. He liked everyone being happy with him for that. But then it all changed."

"Changed how?" Jakob prompted.

"It is hard to get excited about jobs and then know you will not get them. But because Isaac brought that man here, the jobs they already had were to be affected by his decision, too."

In the absence of Esther and her protective streak where her mother was concerned, Claire found herself stepping into the role and trying to make things right. "I'm sure Daniel and Isaac have built a loyal client base over the years . . . people who will continue to order toys through their catalogues."

"Children and grandchildren only play with toys for so long before they outgrow them. That loyal client base, as you call them, will eventually move on to another stage in gift buying," Jakob explained. "And when that happens, a move like Karble's will make their catalogue business dry up."

"An Amish-inspired toy that is made by a machine is very different than an Amish toy made by Amish hands," Claire protested out of hope as much as anything else. To say it out of anything else was simply ludicrous. She was a businesswoman. She knew the cold hard facts behind a move like Karble's.

"For someone like you, Claire, who might notice and care about such things, sure. But for the vast majority of people out there, the two are close enough," Jakob mused. "Toss in the price differential, and you can bet any hemming and hawing over which toy to choose is virtually gone." Then, turning back to his sister, Jakob's matter-of-fact tone softened somewhat. "So was Daniel angry at Isaac?"

"I would not say angry. Daniel Lapp is a good man. Kind." Martha slid off the stool and wandered across the room, her brother's gaze tracking her every step as he, too, rose to his feet. "But he built his toy shop business to what it is now. He brought Isaac in to help him and, now, his business is to be affected by something he did not seek."

"So you're worried that Daniel will be angry at Isaac?" Jakob asked.

Martha stopped beside the collection of painted milk cans she, herself, had sent in to the shop on consignment and slowly turned, her unadorned hands fiddling with the sides of her dress. "No. I worry that you will look to Isaac for what has happened.

Just as Sarah worries you will look to Daniel."

Claire shifted her stance beside the counter to gain a better view of Jakob's face. It didn't take much deducing to know Martha's concern for Isaac and Daniel in the wake of Rob Karble's murder was justified. How Jakob was going to handle that fact with a sister he desperately wanted to reconnect with, though, was the million-dollar question.

A heavy silence weighed in the air as Jakob seemed to mull over Martha's suspicion before eventually giving the only answer he knew how to give. "To tell you Isaac and Daniel will not be questioned in Mr. Karble's death would be a lie, Martha. So I will not say that. But I want you to know that I don't believe either man is responsible. And I promise you that with your help I will not rest until I have proven that to be the case."

Claire held her breath as she stood back and waited for Martha's response. Had Jakob left off the part about his sister's help, Claire suspected a smile would have been immediate on the woman's face. But since he hadn't, her reaction was more difficult to read.

"Can you do that, Martha? Can you help

me eliminate Isaac and Daniel as viable suspects?" Jakob prodded.

One hesitant step at a time, Martha made her way back over to the counter, her soft black ankle boots barely audible against the shop's carpeting. When she reached the stool on which she'd sat only moments earlier, she stopped, raising her gaze to meet her brother's. "I will help. But I do not want anyone to know of this talk, or any talks."

The smile Jakob had been afraid to show at the realization his sister had come to Heavenly Treasures specifically to find him finally spread across his face, undaunted. "I will not tell a soul, Martha. You have my word on that."

Without taking her focus off Jakob, Martha addressed Claire. "Esther is not to know of this conversation."

"But, Martha, she'd be happy to know you talked to Jakob. Thrilled, even. It's all she ever —"

Jakob cleared his throat loudly, successfully cutting Claire off midplea. "Esther will not know. Of this or any other talks we may have."

Visibly satisfied with his response, Martha crossed to the door only to stop mere inches from her destination. "I will bring books to the children's school shortly before lunch. I will walk home past the pond."

And then, just like that, the woman was gone, disappearing down the steps of Heavenly Treasures. Claire gestured toward the front window. "What was that about walking to school and the pond?"

"That is where I am to meet my sister tomorrow morning," Jakob whispered, dumbfounded. "So we can . . . talk."

It was everything she'd been praying for since she'd learned of Jakob's past, yet nothing her aunt Diane ever believed would happen. Bobbing up on the toes of her boots, Claire let loose a little squeal. "Jakob! You did it! You've made a connection with Martha that's going to have the two of you talking again!" She clapped her hands together just as Esther emerged from the back room with a lunch sack in one hand and a copy of the *Heavenly Times* in the other.

"Claire?" Esther peeled her focus from the newspaper and flashed it upward at Claire, an odd expression lighting her tired eyes. "Did I hear Mamm's voice through the window just now?"

She opened her mouth to answer only to close it as Jakob shook her response away. "I . . . I . . ."

"Esther." Jakob stepped into his niece's field of vision and stopped, his usual joy over catching a peek at his niece offset by his obvious need to keep a promise to Martha. "I'm so sorry you had to find Mr. Karble's body the way that you did."

Shocked at seeing her uncle standing mere inches away, Esther quickly smoothed down the edges of her apron and checked to make sure the strings of her head cap were secured. "I did not see who did it."

Jakob nodded. "I read the statement you gave to Officer Nettles while I was securing the scene. I know that you didn't see anything." He retraced his steps back to the counter to retrieve his gloves and the victim's camera, casting a pointed look in Claire's direction as he did. "Well, ladies, I better get back to the station. Got lots to do today."

And then he was gone, slipping out the same door by which his sister had come and gone before Esther's arrival at work.

Not wanting to give Esther time to question Jakob's presence or to repeat her inquiry about Martha, Claire pointed at the newspaper in her friend's left hand, the headline stretched across the front page leaving little doubt to the front-page story. "So how bad is it?" she asked.

Esther allowed one last lingering look at the door before taking in the newspaper, then Claire, and finally the floor — in that order. "It is like it was last time. But this time it is bad for your aunt, too."

"Bad for my *aunt*?" she repeated.

Nodding, Esther flipped the folded paper over in her hand and then handed it to Claire. "I am sorry."

"Sorry? Sorry for what . . ." The words trailed from her mouth as the below-the-fold headline hit her with a one-two punch to the gut.

Sleep Heavenly Guests May Want To Start Sleeping With One Eye Open

CHAPTER 9

Claire smoothed a wrinkle from the white lacy tablecloth Diane had put down for the evening meal and released a quiet sigh. Any hope her aunt had escaped the nastiness in the newspaper was dashed the moment she walked in the back door after work and found the woman hunched and sniffling over a predinner coffee.

When she'd tried to broach the subject of the front page article, though, Diane had waved Claire off, blaming the irrefutable moisture in her eyes to a never-before-heard-of allergy and abandoning her coffee in favor of final dinner preparations that left virtually no room for chitchat let alone a heavy conversation.

"Is everything ready in here?" Diane asked as she came through the door between the kitchen and the dining room. "Water glasses filled? Butter out? Bread basket at each end?"

With a practiced eye, Claire took in each of the tasks, nodding her head as each passed muster. "We're good."

Diane breezed around the large colonial-style table, stopping every two or three chairs to straighten a knife that didn't need to be straightened or reposition a fork that didn't need to be repositioned. "The pot roast is fork tender and the butter is melting into the noodles as we speak. The only thing left to do is transfer the gravy to the two gravy boats and bring it all out to the table."

With barely a breath taken, the woman continued on, the shake in her voice intensifying at the sound of approaching footsteps. "I'll take care of bringing everything in if you'll take care of the greeting."

"But that's *your* job, Aunt Diane," she protested in a hushed tone. "The guests love to see you as they come in from their day and you know that."

"Not today, dear. Today, I think it's more important they see your smile. And if you can engage them in small talk about anything other than the inn, I'd be grateful."

She opened her mouth to argue but resisted the impulse when the first few guests strode into the dining room just as Diane exited through the door on the opposite side of the room.

"Good evening, everyone." Claire forced every ounce of merriment she could muster into her voice. "Wasn't today just the picture-perfect autumn day?"

Wayne Granderson pulled his wife's chair back from the table and waited as she sat down, his head nodding along with her enthusiastic response. "Oh, Claire, Wayne and I took a walk down Lighted Way and out past some of the Amish fields. The sun warmed our backs on the way there, and then felt so wonderful on our faces on the way home . . . didn't it, hon?"

The head that had finally stilled began to nod once again in the man's usual happy but silent way.

"I'd hoped Wayne and I might catch Diane on the porch before she started in on dinner, but no such luck." Virginia dropped her voice to a near whisper and gestured her head in the direction of the kitchen. "She's taking this whole Karble business hard, isn't she?"

At a loss on whether to lie and say everything was fine or to share her own concerns for her aunt's situation, Claire was more than a little grateful when the male half of the newlyweds claimed the seat to the left of his pretty bride and began to talk about their day. The pleasant temperatures and sunny skies had prompted them to pack a picnic lunch and take a bike ride out into the country. But just as Claire began to relax, Doug brought the conversation around full circle when he mentioned their stop at the coffee shop just down from Heavenly Treasures.

"You'd think, in a town like Heavenly, the media would be a little less harsh, a little less about the sensationalism. But, as I'm sure you knew long before you saw today's paper, Claire, that isn't the case, is it?" Doug leaned to his right and planted a gentle kiss on the side of Kayla's forehead before righting himself once again. "I'll have you know, though, that neither Kayla nor myself are the" — he hooked two of his fingers from both of his hands in the air and wiggled them up and down — "unidentified guests who felt the need to make things worse for your aunt."

Virginia pushed her glasses higher across the bridge of her nose and shot a quizzical look in Doug's direction. "Unidentified guests? What are you talking about?"

"The article. In today's local paper." At the second rise to Virginia's left eyebrow, Doug filled in the blanks before Claire could craft a way to change the subject.

"Seems someone staying here saw fit to talk to the local media about what happened in Room Six yesterday — information the reporter then used to cast a good deal of doubt as to the safety and well-being of guests who choose Sleep Heavenly for their lodging when visiting Amish country."

Wayne snorted his disgust, dipping his head forward as he did. "Are you tellin' me this reporter actually thinks this Karble fella's room being ransacked on the same day he was murdered was a coincidence?"

"Two crimes sell more papers than one," Kayla Jones mused before taking a sip from her water goblet. When she was done, she set her glass back down on the table and shot a pointed look toward the empty chairs at the table. "But that still doesn't answer the question as to who spoke to the reporter and said such disparaging things about this beautiful inn."

Diane hummed her way into the room with a platter of pot roast in one hand and a bowl of buttered noodles in the other, a smile plastered across her gently lined face. "I hope everyone brought their appetites this evening because this dinner is a favorite of my guests." Then, without waiting for a response, the woman handed both to Claire and returned to the kitchen for the gravy and the vegetables.

"She's upset, isn't she?" Virginia whispered across the table. "That's why she wasn't on the porch this afternoon, isn't it?"

For a moment, Claire actually considered concocting a story that had her aunt visiting an elderly neighbor or running to the store for a few needed ingredients, but, in the end, she simply nodded. Diane needed support more than anything right now and all four of the guests seated at the table seemed ready and willing to offer just that.

"With any luck, this whole Karble mess will be over soon and Diane's next round of guests won't have to be the wiser." Wayne's eyes widened at the sight of the pot roast platter in Claire's left hand. "Because, I tell you, there's not a hotel around here that feeds you like Diane Weatherly does."

Kayla leaned to the side to afford Claire an unobstructed path to her plate. "Unfortunately, if the Heavenly Times is like most newspapers in the country these days, that story will be accessible to anyone doing a search on Sleep Heavenly."

The fork Claire was using to transfer slices of pot roast to each guest's plate slipped from her hand and clattered against the edge of Kayla's salad bowl. Quickly, she recovered the utensil and glanced over her shoulder for any indication Diane had returned with the gravy. When she was satisfied she hadn't, she spoke quickly. "If it's possible, could we keep the conversation light this evening? Diane is having a hard time with this right now and I hate to see her so upset."

Seconds later, Melinda strode into the room, her long blonde hair secured in a ponytail that hit the midpoint of her back. "Sorry I'm late." Quickly, the public relations executive made her way around the table and sat down in her chair, glancing around at the nearby plates as she did. "What's that?" she asked, pointing to the main platter.

"Pot roast." Virginia grabbed hold of her napkin and unfolded it across her lap. "It's one of Diane's most popular dishes."

"I'm here. I'm here." Diane breezed back into the room with a gravy boat in each hand. "The gravy is nice and bubbly and it's extra delicious over the noodles . . ." The woman's voice faded away as Melinda came into view. "Ms. Simon. I . . . I wasn't sure you'd be joining us this evening."

"Well, I'm here." Melinda shifted her plate to the left and waited for Claire to come around the table with the platter of meat and the bowl of noodles. "Has anyone seen

117

Ann today?"

Slowly, Diane ladled up the gravy and dispensed it across everyone's food, her hand shaking ever so slightly as she did. "I brought a tray of food to her room this afternoon but she didn't want it. The poor dear is beside herself with grief."

"I'm surprised she is staying on," Doug chimed in before rushing to soften his words. "I mean, I would think she'd want to surround herself with family inside the confines of her own home."

Melinda looked up from the piece of meat she was cutting and made a face. "There is no family. Ann's parents died years ago and she and Rob never had any children . . . together."

Seeing the shake in her aunt's hand intensify, Claire took over gravy duty, making her way around the table one final time while Diane fiddled with her apron off to the side and Virginia clucked softly beneath her breath.

"I'm guessing she wants to stay close while the investigation is going on." Wayne chased his last bite of dinner around the plate and then looked up at Claire for seconds. "Diane, I think you've officially outdone yourself with this meal, and that's high praise if I say so myself."

The outer corners of Diane's mouth twitched slightly but stopped short of forming an actual smile.

"I suppose Wayne is right," Virginia mused. "If something awful like that happened to him, I wouldn't go anywhere until I had answers."

"I agree with Virginia." Doug forked up a few gravy-coated noodles and popped them into his mouth. "And then, once she has those answers, I imagine she'll be tasked with trying to figure out who should step into her husband's shoes and run the company."

"Are you kidding me?" Melinda replied while simultaneously buttering a homemade roll from a nearby bread basket. "She'll be trying to figure out how to run it herself."

Doug paused midchew. "Can she?"

"She thinks she can." When the roll in her hand was buttered to her specifications, Melinda took a tiny nibble and then set it down on the edge of her plate. "But running a multimillion-dollar company is actually quite a bit different than hosting a tea for the local gardening club. Meaning, it's more important. With a lot more riding on it than a mention in the lifestyle section of the local paper, that's for sure."

"Mrs. Karble seemed like a smart woman

to me when I spoke with her in the parlor her first evening here," Kayla pondered before taking a quick sip of water. "And besides, when you're married to someone, you invariably hear a lot of behind-the-scenes details about their job. I mean, I heard all sorts of things about Doug's job when we were merely dating. Now that we're married, I imagine I'll hear even more. So who knows, maybe she'd catch on quicker than you might realize."

Melinda pulled her napkin from her lap and balled it up beside her plate, her meal virtually untouched save for a few small bites. "Or maybe the thousands of people employed by Karble Toys will be under the direction of someone who knows nothing about toys *or* managing a large-scale corporation," she hissed before rising to her feet. "And since their only other option is someone with half that knowledge, they're essentially bound for the unemployment line just like me."

Instinctively, Doug's arm snaked its way around his wife's shoulder in protective fashion. "Ms. Simon, my wife was simply saying that —"

"Yeah. I get it. But it's not your wife's livelihood that's on the line now, is it, Mr. Jones?" Without waiting for an answer,

120

Melinda vacated her spot at the table and headed for the parlor door, stopping midway across the room to address Diane. "They say that tragedy has a way of waking people up and making them see all sorts of things, Miss Weatherly. Sometimes it's the need to stop and smell the roses and really appreciate the important people in your life. Sometimes it's the need to be vigilant about your comings and goings. And sometimes it's the need to fix weak spots that allowed the tragedy to happen in the first place."

"Allowed the tragedy to happen?" Claire echoed in disbelief. Then, holding up her hand in an attempt to silence Diane, she continued, her tone a mixture of anger and shock. "Ms. Simon, my aunt is not responsible for what happened to your boss and you know that as well as I do. He was murdered in the middle of the festival grounds more than three-quarters of a mile from here. How you could insinuate she has anything to fix in light of that tragedy is a mystery to me."

Melinda cast her eyes up at the ceiling and slowly shook her head, the gesture more in keeping with an exasperated preschool teacher than a businesswoman employed by a major corporation. "I'm not talking about Rob's murder. That was inevitable. I'm talking about his room being ransacked."

Doug's hand stilled on his wife's back. *"Inevitable?"*

Pulling her focus from the ceiling, Melinda nodded, her ponytail sliding across the silky material of her blouse. "He was on the cusp of making some major moves where the company was concerned. People don't like changes. They resent them."

"Wait. Go back." Claire sifted backward in the conversation a few steps. "So, if I'm hearing you right, Ms. Simon, you're saying the biggest tragedy was the *break-in*?"

"If it seals the fate of Karble Toys it is. And it all could have been avoided if Miss Weatherly, here, invested some of her earnings in a security system or, at the very least, locked the front door before heading off to sample food she's probably tried a million times already."

CHAPTER 10

Room by room, Claire made her way through the inn, her determination to talk to Diane rivaled only by the increasing worry over where, exactly, her aunt had gone.

Based on an eight-month pattern, the postdinner hours usually had the woman in one of three modes — clean up, set up, or chat. Yet, for the first time, it appeared as if the pattern had changed.

"She's gotta be here somewhere," Claire murmured as she looped around the center hallway and started the search all over again. Maybe, when she'd been in the front of the house, Diane had been in the back . . .

Slowly, so as not to miss a telltale sound that would point her in the right direction, Claire made her way toward the kitchen, the lack of running water and ultrasoft humming virtually squashing any chance of cleanup mode. Still, though, she checked, pushing the service entry door open with one hand while fumbling for the light switch with the other.

"Diane?" She blinked as the overhead light bounced off the vast counter space revealing a coating of flour and two distinctly used bread pans. "Diane, are you in here?" But even as she uttered the question aloud, she knew the answer. If her aunt were in the kitchen, there wouldn't be dirty dishes and unkempt countertops.

It just wouldn't happen.

Then again, she wouldn't have expected to see the kitchen looking the way it did within ten minutes of dinner, let alone nearly three hours. Diane was fastidious about her kitchen.

Her mental antennae rising, Claire crossed to the opposite door, flipping off the lights as she headed toward the dining room. Here, like in the kitchen, the normal tasks hadn't been done. Sure, the dinner plates had been removed and the tablecloth replaced — Claire had done those things herself — but nothing had been set up for the next morning's breakfast. Not the china, not the napkins, not the silverware . . .

This time, she didn't worry about the status of the lights, opting to leave the sconces on their dim setting as she turned her sights on the parlor and the conversation she dared hope to find between the innkeeper and the Grandersons. At least then she could chalk up the woman's odd behavior to customer relations rather than the image that was starting to emerge at the base of her antennae.

Like the kitchen and dining room, though, her favorite room in the inn was empty, save for the many touches that had earned it that distinction at first sight. Here, the warm and welcoming touches that dotted the rest of the home culminated in everything from the full-wall fireplace to the floor-to-ceiling bookshelves jam-packed with the kind of literary offerings that beckoned to the reader in everyone. Toss in the sofas and cozy lounge chairs alongside the bay window and it was little wonder why the guests tended to gravitate toward the room at some point during the day regardless of any sightseeing plans on their list.

Claire wandered across the wood-planked floor to the bay window and dropped onto the window seat, her gaze drawn to the gas-powered lamps that dotted the quaint shopping district in the distance. Only this time, instead of reveling in the smile that normally made its way across her face at the sight, she found the worry in her heart intensifying tenfold. It was ten o'clock. The view of Lighted Way from the parlor should be thwarted by the thick velvet drapes Diane always drew closed at nine thirty.

Always.

Something was wrong. Very, very wrong.

Pressing her head to the cool glass, Claire turned her sights toward the grounds surrounding Sleep Heavenly — the edge of the parking lot she could see along the side, the large rambling trees that served as a canopy atop the driveway, the shadow swaying to and fro on the porch swing just visible out of the corner of her right eye . . .

Claire jumped up from the window seat and ran toward the hallway, the smack of her slippers periodically muted along the way by the occasional hooked rug. When she reached the front door, she took a deep breath, willing the worry in her heart to bypass her lips until there was reason to give it voice. To do so prematurely would be silly if the shadow she'd spied from the window was someone other than Diane.

And even if it *was* Diane, it wasn't a crime to take a break before the evening's work was done.

She gave the door a gentle tug and stepped onto the dimly lit front porch, the continued chirp of crickets in the immediate vicinity an indication of her near-silent prowess.

"Aunt Diane?" she half whispered into the shadows. "Are you out here?"

Sure enough, her answer came from the direction of the swing as it was toed to a stop off to her left. "I'm sorry, dear. Did I wake you?"

Claire tried not to laugh at the typical reply. It didn't matter the circumstance, it didn't matter the time or place, if there was responsibility to be taken, Diane Weatherly took it. "I hadn't gone to sleep. I was just painting some picture frames up in my room and lost track of time."

The moment Claire sat on the swing beside her aunt, it began to sway once again, this time propelled by an extra set of feet. "Oh. How are they coming?"

"They look good. But I'm a long way from being ready to sell them at the shop, that's for sure." Shifting to the side, Claire hiked her left calf onto the empty space between them, her lips easily forming into a smile at the sight of the woman she loved so dearly. "When I realized what time it was, I came downstairs to say good night and couldn't find you anywhere."

At Diane's silence, Claire continued, her tone a mediocre masquerade of her true emotions. "I checked in the kitchen, the dining room, and the parlor and didn't see you anywhere until I was looking out the bay window and caught a quick glimpse of your shadow."

"I tried to clean up after the Grandersons retired upstairs, but I just didn't have the energy," Diane said, looking out over the porch railing in the direction of the now pitch-black Amish fields in the distance. "I guess maybe I'm getting older whether I want to admit it or not."

Coming from any other mouth attached to a body that did as much as Diane Weatherly's did on a daily basis, Claire would have had to agree. But coming from Diane, it simply didn't add up. Not by a long shot.

Diane had energy to spare. She'd been that way since Claire was a little girl. A person didn't change that fast. Not at their core, anyway.

Inhaling deeply, she considered how best to approach the elephant on the porch, deciding in the end to face it head-on. "What's troubling you, Aunt Diane? Is it the newspaper article? Because if it is, you've got to know that one less-than-stellar remark doesn't detract a single iota from two decades' worth of rave reviews."

For the briefest of moments she wasn't sure Diane was going to answer, her question hovering in the space between them with nothing to indicate it had even been heard. But just as she was gathering the courage to ask it again, the answer came in raspy and halting bursts. "If it was a poor review of a dinner I prepared, I could weigh that against the hundreds of compliments I got on the same dish knowing it's a subjective opinion. Would it still bother me? I'd be lying if I said it wouldn't. I like to please my guests. But I could rationalize it away as one person's opinion. Same thing for location. What's one person's dream vacation can be a complete bore for someone else. Which, again, comes down to personal taste."

"Okay . . ."

"Today was different, though," Diane continued. "Today I was questioned on *fact*, not opinion."

"Fact?" Claire repeated above the chorus of crickets who'd chosen that exact moment to reach their collective crescendo.

"That's right." Diane tilted her toes down to the porch floor in an effort to bring an end to their rhythmic sway, the resulting cessation of motion casting a harsh glow on the reality that poured from her mouth. "Because no matter how I try to rationalize it away, the fact remains that my way of doing things here at the inn puts my guests at risk, plain and simple."

Claire's mouth gaped open. "Wait. What are you talking about?"

"Twenty years ago, when I opened this inn, I did it because of an image I had in my head. An image of geographical strangers coming together and learning from one another around the dinner table as they would if they were family. Only this family would bring experiences and viewpoints the normal person wouldn't find within their own four walls on a nightly basis."

It was hard not to smile as she considered her aunt's words. So many people she'd met in life stumbled into their careers because of word of mouth, or connections, or even because it was virtually bequeathed to them by a family member. But not Diane. Diane had a way of cutting past all the fluff and finding the part that really mattered.

"And you've done that," she offered once her ears had caught up with her brain. "In spades."

"Twenty years ago, yes. Ten years ago, yes." Diane pushed off the swing and wandered over to the railing that bordered the front side of the porch. "Even as recently as a year ago, maybe. But now . . . the way the world is . . . I'm not so sure."

It took everything in Claire's arsenal of personal restraint not to follow behind her aunt and try to smooth the worry from a face she'd come to equate with genuine happiness. She, of all people, knew there were times in life when you just needed to talk your way through the tough spots. And like it or not, despite the pedestal she'd always put Diane on, the woman was human. Which meant Claire needed to be the sounding board Diane had always been for her.

"I'm not sure I know what you mean," she finally said from her spot on the swing. "What's changed in the past year?"

Pivoting on her sensible soled shoes, Diane leaned against the porch railing and studied their surroundings — taking in the swing, the Adirondack chairs, and the flower boxes packed tight with mums in a near-rainbow of colors. "Everything. The world . . . society . . . *Heavenly.*"

Claire dropped her leg to the ground and sat up tall. "Heavenly? What's wrong with Heavenly?"

Diane's soft laugh filled the night around them. "Oh, my dear, sweet Claire. Do you realize how much you sounded like me just then?"

"Frankly, I consider that a compliment."

Stretching her arm across the back of the swing, Claire rested the side of her head against her upper arm. "But, if you don't mind me asking, why are you saying that?"

"Because this town has taken hold of your heart the same way it did for me twenty years ago."

Something in the woman's tone made Claire's breath hitch. "Y-you almost sound as if you don't love this town as much as you once did."

"No. I love Heavenly every bit as much as I did when I decided to open my inn. In fact, that feeling has only deepened in the years since. But the Heavenly of old didn't have murders. It just didn't."

"Wait a minute. Sixteen years ago, Jakob left the Amish to become a police officer because of a murder that took place right here in Heavenly," Claire reminded. "Granted, it was solved by the time he made the break official, but bad things happened back then, too."

Diane glanced over her shoulder at the lights of downtown and the darkened fields beyond, her words taking Claire by surprise. "But that was the town's first murder in its long history and there weren't any others until this past summer when Walter Snow's body showed up in the alley behind your store."

"And that's over now." She lifted her head off her arm and waved her hand toward Lighted Way. "Everything was back to normal in no time."

"Until the festival yesterday."

There was nothing Claire could say. Arguing facts was an exercise in futility.

Diane pushed off the railing and wandered over to the far side of the porch, the dark blue color of her sweater difficult to discern in the darkness. "But even forgetting all of that, people these days seem to think they can take things that don't belong to them. That they can just waltz into someone's home and help themselves to whatever they want just because they can."

"Aunt Diane, you can't really believe what happened to the Karbles' room yesterday was simply about thievery, can you?"

The fading sound of footsteps stopped and then resumed once again, this time growing louder as they made their way back toward the center of the porch. "What else would you call it?"

"Calculated. Intentional. Planned out. Take your pick." Claire patted the vacant spot to her left. "Aunt Diane, please come sit. It's easier to talk to you when you're not walking all over the place."

"I'm too keyed up to sit, dear," Diane said, plopping down onto the swing and continuing the conversation, anyway. "It doesn't matter what fancy word you give it, Claire. My guests still had their sense of safety violated in *my* inn. They made the choice to spend their vacation here rather than one of the chain hotels in Breeze Point and I let them down."

"Let them down?"

"Of course." Diane clasped her hands in her lap only to disengage them and start fiddling with a loose thread midway down her simple dress. "I've been so busy trying to create this atmosphere of home and family that I've become careless with my guests' safety."

Before Claire could muster a protest, Diane continued. "Every week there are multiple newspaper accounts of criminal activity around the county. Yet, somehow, I thought we were immune from such nonsense here in Heavenly. And because of that naiveté, I let my guests down."

She considered her aunt's words only to discard them against a reality that was being missed. "So what do you think you could have done differently? Locked the front door? Wired in a few surveillance cameras? Installed a home security system? What?"

"All of those, I guess," Diane said, shrugging.

"Do you really think any of those would have mattered yesterday?"

Diane drew back. "Of course. Don't you?"

"No, actually, I don't." This time, it was Claire who stopped the swing and rose to her feet. "Let's say you locked the door. You don't think a *determined* person could come in through, say" — she gestured toward the long windows on either side of the front door — "one of these? Because I do.

"You don't think a *determined* person could cover their head with a hood and look down at the floor as they were passing a surveillance camera? Because I do. And as for a security system . . . you really think, on a day that virtually every resident and police officer in this town was at that food festival, a *determined* person couldn't have been in and out of this place before anyone responded? Because I don't, Aunt Diane, and neither should you."

Even in the dim porch light, Claire could see the flash of hope in Diane's eyes just before a soft clapping exploded from the vicinity of the stairs and made them both jump.

"Hey, it's just me. Jakob." Stepping into the lighted section of the porch, Jakob held up his palms in surrender. "Sorry about that. I guess I got so caught up in what you were saying just now, Claire, that I didn't really think about announcing my presence in a way that wouldn't give you both a heart attack."

Diane unclutched her hand from the front of her chest and managed a wan smile for the detective. "Jakob. I'm so sorry. We didn't hear you . . ."

Jakob's laugh slowed the beating of Claire's heart in her ears. "I'm the one who's sorry. For scaring the two of you just now and for not making things clear where yesterday's break-in is concerned. My failure to do so has obviously made you doubt yourself, Diane, and for that, I'm doubly sorry."

Claire motioned to her aunt while silently acknowledging the way this man spoke to her on a level that had nothing to do with talk of break-ins and murder and everything to do with the alluring mixture of kindness and strength he exuded just standing there in faded blue jeans and a navy blue Henley. "Tell her, will you? She doesn't seem to get what happened here."

Tipping his head in her direction, Jakob

crossed to the swing and sat down, taking Diane's hand in his as he did. "The key word in what your niece just said, Diane, is *determined*. What happened upstairs wasn't a random break-in. If it was, your china would be gone, your guests' jewelry would be gone, and virtually any item of monetary value would be missing. But none of that was taken."

Diane stopped fiddling with the loose thread on her dress and met the detective's eyes. "What are you saying?"

"I'm saying that whoever came in here yesterday came with a purpose. And that purpose had nothing to do with Sleep Heavenly and everything to do with one particular guest who'd chosen to stay here."

"Rob Karble," Diane whispered.

With a nod of confirmation, Jakob moved on. "Whoever it was who did this was on a mission and I don't think there's anything you could have done to deter him or her from that mission." Claire saw the gentle squeeze he offered Diane's hand and swallowed, the sudden need to feel his hand on hers unnerving. "Which is why I'm here. Or, rather, why I showed up on your porch steps just now."

Desperate to fill her mind with something other than the way Jakob's blond hair faded just above his ears or the broad set to his strong shoulders, Claire turned toward the house and began walking. "You need to see Room Six?"

Jakob rose to his feet. "I'd like to, if that's okay. If it's too late, I could come back first thing in the morning. As it is, I didn't even know I was going to stop by until I walked up your driveway."

"Do you think you'll be loud?" Diane asked as she followed them into the front entryway. "My guests have all retired for the evening and I don't want them to be disturbed."

"Nope. I'm looking for something very specific. I have no intention of being loud and what I'm looking for shouldn't take all that long to locate." Jakob stopped at the base of the staircase and motioned his chin to the top. "Which room is Mrs. Karble in?"

"She's in a room here on the first floor but she's sleeping. The shock of everything that's happened has drained the poor thing," Diane explained in true caretaker fashion. "You don't have to speak with her at this late hour, do you?"

"No. Anything I need to ask her can wait until morning."

Twenty minutes later, while Diane was bustling about the kitchen catching up on her premorning prep work, Jakob came down the stairs and met Claire in the parlor, his face grave. "Well, that's all I need. I'm sorry I had to intrude on your evening like this."

She set the paperback mystery novel she'd been reading onto the coffee table and patted the vacant sofa cushion to her right, the burst of happiness she felt as he accepted her invitation warming her cheeks. "Is everything okay?" she asked.

Jakob propped his elbows atop his thighs and rubbed at the skin around his eyes. "When I turned up your driveway this evening it's because I was out walking. Thinking about my sister and Isaac. All I want to do is help them, Claire. So they don't have to worry anymore and . . ."

His voice faded along with his focus, prompting her to touch his shoulder. "Go on, Jakob. Finish your sentence."

His hands moved upward to cradle his head. "I want them to think I'm okay. I want them to think I made a good decision when I left to become a cop. I want them to think" — he stopped, swallowed, and then continued on, his voice barely more than a raspy whisper — "that I'm still an okay guy. An okay brother."

"And that's changed all of a sudden?"

Dropping his hands to his knees, Jakob leaned against the back of the couch and looked up at the ceiling. "I still want those things, want them more than I can ever completely explain. But now, I'm doubting that'll ever happen."

She shifted her body so as to afford a better view of the detective, the urge to reach out and touch his face almost more than she could bear. Instead, she tucked her hand beneath her leg and willed her voice to remain as neutral as possible. "I don't understand. What's changed in the last forty minutes or so?"

A long pause was followed by a labored shrug. "Everything."

"Tell me."

Shifting his gaze to hers, he tried to muster a smile for her benefit but gave up when it became obvious a grimace was the best he could offer. "Do you remember the roller track plans we saw on the victim's camera this morning? The ones Ben said were Isaac's?"

She pulled her hand out from under her leg. "Yes."

"The time stamp on the corner of that photo said it was taken yesterday morning. When I asked your aunt what time Karble came back to the inn yesterday, she said he came back prior to going to the festival. When he did, he had a briefcase in one hand, and his camera in the other."

"She told me that, too," Claire offered.

"Diane also said that within ten minutes, he was back down the stairs and heading out the door for the festival with only the camera around his neck."

"Okay . . ."

"His return to the inn was *after* that picture was taken."

At a loss for what to say, she simply waited for him to continue.

"Don't you see?" he asked. "Those plans should still be in his briefcase or, in the event he removed them before leaving for the festival, *somewhere* in his room up-stairs."

And then she got it. "And they're not, are they?"

"Nope. Not a trace of them anywhere. In fact, there are absolutely no signs there was any contact between Karble and either Daniel or Isaac to be found anywhere."

"Except in the camera," she whispered.

He nodded, slowly. "Except in the camera. Which was on Karble when he was killed."

She tried to make sense of what she was hearing but came up short. "So what, exactly, are you saying?" she finally asked.

"I think I figured out what was driving the determination to get into Room Six."

"The roller track plans?"

Again, he nodded, this time with even more resignation. "That or anything having to do with the Back to Basics line as it pertained to the Amish. I mean, let's face it, if a man with Karble's clout comes to town to make a business deal, don't you think there'd be at least some paperwork to be found?"

She pushed off the sofa with her hands and meandered her away around the room, stopping to straighten a book or move a votive candle every few feet. When she reached the last set of shelves, she turned back to the detective. "And you're thinking the memo that made its way around the festival yesterday is what drove either Isaac or Daniel to come here — while everyone was gone — and go tearing through Mr. Karble's room?"

"It's the only theory that makes any sense so far."

She stared at Jakob. "And the murder? What about that? You can't possibly be considering either one of them for that, can you?"

He, too, pushed off the sofa, his shoulders, his stance, every bit as wooden as Claire's.

"I repeat, it's the only theory that makes any sense so far."

CHAPTER 11

She lifted her face to the warmth of the sun's late morning rays and inhaled slowly, savoring the peaceful Amish countryside spread out around her. No matter how much she adored her shop, no matter how quaint and perfect she found the tourist-friendly section of Lighted Way to be, there was simply no getting around the fact that this side of town was Claire's vision of peace.

Here, everything was different. The pace slowed, storefronts gave way to wide open fields tended by fathers and sons, and the most pervasive sound was silence. A wind-mill off to her right turned round and round with purpose, delivering an alternate source of power to a group of people who saw no need to rely on the outside world for such things. On her left, just beyond a small sheep-tended cemetery with several rows of simple headstones, was a large white farmhouse with a buggy parked off to its side. She didn't really need the various-sized dresses and pants swaying back and forth on the clothesline to know a large family lived inside. That was simply a given with the Amish. But still, she smiled. In this particular home, the mother had obviously purchased a bolt of lavender fabric, as every shirt and dress on the line — whether male or female — was the same color, save, of course, for the darker shade used on her own dress.

Claire followed the bend in the sparsely graveled road and looked ahead to the farmhouse about a quarter mile away. The house, like the one to her left, was large, too, with a recently harvested field just beyond its back door and a small white outbuilding to its side. With any luck, Daniel Lapp would be inside, crafting toys and open to the kind of questions he didn't normally field from Keith Watson's tour bus customers.

She'd planned to work in the shop all day, rearranging the front display window while Esther took care of the customers. But as soon as she walked in the back door and put her stuff on the tiny desk in the alcove she used as her office, she knew she couldn't stay. All night she'd tossed and turned thinking of little else besides Jakob.

The detective wanted nothing more than to reestablish some sort of bond with his sister. And finally, just as it looked as if there might be a chance for real interaction between the two, he's forced to have to look at their brother as a possible suspect in a murder.

A suspect with motive, no less.

What, if anything, she actually thought she'd accomplish by talking to Daniel Lapp was a complete mystery. She just knew she needed to try.

For Jakob. And for Martha.

She looked up as a horse-drawn buggy passed, the orange triangle affixed to its back a reminder to English drivers to use caution when approaching. A little girl in a head cap peeked out at Claire from the buggy's back flaps before disappearing inside with the hint of a smile playing across her cupid bow mouth.

"Good day, Claire."

Startled, she turned to her left to find Benjamin driving a second buggy she hadn't heard approaching. "Hi, Benjamin. I didn't see you there." She stepped over to the side of the buggy and looked up at the Amish man, the Pavlovian flutter virtually instantaneous inside her chest. "How are you?"

"I am good." He loosened his hands on the reins and nodded his head ever so slightly. "You are not working today?"

She turned her head just long enough to take in Daniel Lapp's farm before meeting Benjamin's deep blue eyes once again. "I was supposed to be. But I asked Esther to cover for me while I take a walk."

"You are still troubled about your aunt?" he asked.

There were so many things she was troubled about at that moment she didn't know how to respond. Sure, she was still worried about Diane. Having a mourning woman staying at the inn brought a very different feel to Sleep Heavenly and left Diane seeming almost directionless. But as hard as that was to witness, the stronger worry at that moment had far more to do with the man Benjamin once considered a childhood friend than with anyone else.

"I'm troubled about the whole situation," she finally said after running various responses through her head.

"Situation?" Benjamin repeated as he followed her gaze down the road to Daniel's place. "Ahhh. I share the same worry."

She froze in place. "You do?"

"It is the talk of the town, Ruth says. People believe Mr. Karble was killed in

147

anger and frustration. I can not dispute the anger. I can not dispute the frustration."

"And the killing part?" she whispered.

Silence filled the morning air between them before Claire stole a peek in Benjamin's direction only to find him studying her with an expression she couldn't identify. What, exactly, he was thinking, she couldn't be sure. But whatever it was, it made her stand a little straighter and straighten the hemline of her long-sleeved hunter green blouse atop her formfitting black slacks.

Benjamin cleared his throat and looked away, his hands tightening on the reins once again. "Daniel Lapp is a good man. He would not kill."

Shaking off the sudden desire to run a quick finger comb through her shoulder-length auburn hair, she made herself focus on the conversation and not the man. "And what about Isaac Schrock? Can you say the same thing about him?"

An unexpected pause gave way to his response. "I can."

"Why the hesitation?" she asked.

Benjamin pulled his left hand from the reins and rubbed at his clean-shaven face, an indication to those around him that he was unmarried. His foray into facial hair over a decade earlier had been cut cruelly short by the death of his young bride mere weeks after their wedding. Whether or not he'd ever remarry was a subject Claire had managed to avoid thus far during their months-long friendship.

"I do not mean to hesitate. Isaac is a good man. Hard worker. He has just been" — Benjamin cast about for the correct word before settling on one Claire found more than a little curious — "addle-headed lately."

"How so?"

"He said he would bring a bench wagon to his sister's home. He did not."

Thanks to her ties with Esther, Claire knew that a bench wagon was the way in which the Amish transported church benches between homes. Without the benches, the nearly thirty families that descended on the host family's home for Sunday morning church service wouldn't have anywhere to sit.

"Did he get in trouble from the bishop?" Claire asked.

"No. I did not tell of his mistake. I brought a bench wagon, instead." Benjamin looked again toward the very farm Claire sought and released a quiet sigh. "Isaac has made many mistakes the past month or so. I think he has much on his mind."

She took in everything she was hearing and reconciled it with what she knew. "The notion of his and Daniel's deal with Karble Toys had to be in the forefront of his mind, don't you think? I mean, they had a chance to provide jobs to many of their friends."

"He had much on his mind *before* Mr. Karble was to come here." Benjamin gestured toward the Lapps' farm with his chin. "May I give you a ride the rest of the way?"

Feeling the flutter resurrect itself inside her chest at the invitation, Claire willed her head to answer what her heart could not. "I . . . I think I could use the walk. Besides, it's such a beautiful day, don't you think?"

Her words morphed into a quiet gasp as an unmistakable look of disappointment flitted across Benjamin's face before disappearing behind his usual Amish stoicism. Tipping his hat forward a smidge, he managed a smile that stopped just shy of his breath-hitching blue eyes. "Then enjoy your day, Claire. I hope it is special. Like you."

A lump formed in the base of her throat as his horse continued down the road, the sight of the orange triangle on the back of Benjamin's buggy leaving her a little unsettled. From the moment she first laid eyes on Ruth and Eli Miller's older brother, she'd felt a pull. At first, she'd chalked it up to the almost movie-star good looks the plain Amish dress was unable to mute. The defined cheekbones, emphasized by the slow, genuine smile didn't hurt, either. But it was more than that. Much more.

Benjamin Miller was kind in the way he listened and the way he responded. He led his brother and sister by example. And there was something about him that earned people's respect whether in the Amish community as the leader Esther often described, or in the English world as a caring and thoughtful neighbor.

Even without Diane's not-so-subtle reminders, Claire knew nothing could ever come of her feelings for the widower. He was Amish; she was English. But despite everything her head knew to be true, her heart never seemed to be able to completely let go.

Then again, she also felt a pull toward Jakob. With the detective, it had started in the same place, only instead of movie-star good looks, Jakob's were more of the boy-next-door variety. The boy next door who grew up to be a knockout, anyway.

But just as had been the case with Benjamin, Jakob's looks became all the more appealing once she got to know the man inside. A man who treasured the memories of his family so deeply he was willing to put his own heart on the line just to be closer to them.

She knew where Diane came in on the subject of Jakob thanks to some very different not-so-subtle remarks. And her aunt was right.

Still, Claire was torn.

Shaking her head free of the mental debate, she quickened her pace, anxious to get to Daniel's before the afternoon run of Heavenly Tours' customers demanded his attention. What she was going to ask the toy maker was a work in progress. Many of the questions were probably ones Jakob had already asked. If he hadn't, they were surely on his list. But maybe, just maybe, she would stumble across something he'd missed, something that would allow him to enjoy the act of helping his sister without simultaneously worrying whether that same help would destroy any inroads he hoped to make.

The sound of a diesel engine at her back made her stop and turn, her heart sinking in her chest as she did. Despite her best efforts, Keith Watson and his minibus of Amish enthusiasts had arrived, squashing any hope she had of cornering Daniel.

"Good day, Claire," Keith called as he

paused the bus at the base of the Lapps' turnoff. "Nice day for a walk, isn't it?" Glancing into the rearview mirror he flashed a warm smile at the dozen or so riders who filled the comfortable seats. "Folks, if you haven't had an opportunity to stroll along Lighted Way's shopping district yet, be sure to stop inside Heavenly Treasures. It's a delightful little gift shop with all sorts of Amish-made items from dolls and bibs to quilts and rocking chairs. Miss Weatherly, right here, opened the shop a couple of months ago and it's quickly becoming a favorite among our tourists."

She lifted her hand in a wave to those sitting on her side of the bus and then smiled up at the driver. "Thank you, Keith." Hooking a finger over her shoulder, she willed herself to take the high road. "Heading in to the toy shop?"

At Keith's nod, she stepped onto the bus and looked down the aisle at his customers. "You are all in for quite a treat. Daniel makes his toys in a workshop at the back of his barn, and watching him in action is absolutely fascinating. In fact, that's where I'm headed at the moment, as well."

A wave of smiles made its way through the bus, prompting one from Keith in return. "Then why don't you hop in that first seat right there and I'll take you the rest of the way up the driveway."

Slowly, the bus ambled up the dirt path and came to a stop in front of the white outbuilding depicted on Rob Karble's camera. Opening the door, Keith looked back at his passengers and smiled. "Okay, folks, we're here. Enjoy."

Seconds later, as the first handful of people descended the steps, Daniel stepped outside and nodded a warm welcome to the English tourists. "Good afternoon. Welcome to my toy shop. There are many toys made by myself and by my friend, Isaac Schrock. When you are done, if you would like to see workshop" — he swept his arm toward the barn — "I would be happy to show you."

At the tourists' enthusiastic agreement, Daniel stepped aside to afford them entry into the toy shop. When Claire emerged from the bus behind Keith, the toy maker drew back, his brows scrunched together in surprise. "Miss Weatherly? You take Mr. Watson's tour, too?"

She couldn't help but laugh at the look on the Amish man's round, bearded face. "Not exactly. Keith picked me up at the end of your driveway."

"Oh?"

"She was on her way to see you and it

seemed silly to leave her there." Keith glanced toward the open doors of the barn. "Sounds like Isaac is working now, yes?"

Daniel nodded. "He is."

"Then when my folks are done looking and, hopefully, *buying,* why don't you let Isaac take care of them in the workshop. I know Claire would like a moment of your time." Keith tugged open the toy shop door and stepped inside, the delighted oohs and aahs from inside bringing a smile to Claire's lips.

"People love your toys, Daniel. Adults, children, it makes no difference," she mused. "And from what I've heard from Keith, the chance to get to watch an Amish toy maker at work was just the ticket in getting — and keeping — Heavenly Tours off the ground."

"Mr. Watson's customers are good customers for me, too. And they stay good customers even after they have gone home."

"Which is why that catalogue you have is such a good idea." She peeked inside a small window to the right of the door and took in the line forming at the counter. "Gives people a way to still buy our goods long after their vacation is over."

"You have a catalogue, too?" he asked.

"I'm working on one, as well as a website

where people can order online. Soon, though." She gestured toward the toy shop. "I think you better head in. Looks like you've got quite a few grandmothers lined up to buy presents for their grandchildren right now."

He moved toward the door but paused just shy of walking inside. "Sarah is inside the house. She has been tired lately. I think a visit would do her good. When I am done, we will speak."

"I don't want to intrude." But even as Claire spoke, she knew her hesitation went much deeper than the standard protest. Sarah was already worried about Daniel. In fact, the woman's worry ran so deep it had been one of two factors in why Martha had risked her standing in the Amish community to reach out to her excommunicated brother. To question Daniel about Rob Karble in front of Sarah wasn't a good idea. "Besides, Sarah should be resting in her condition, not entertaining."

"It is no intrusion. It will be a welcome visit."

Long after Daniel disappeared into his toy shop, Claire remained standing in the exact spot she'd claimed, torn between doing what Daniel asked and listening to her gut. If she went into the house to see Sarah, she'd have to keep her questions tame. But if she didn't go inside, she'd appear un-friendly — a persona that was against everything she wanted for herself . . .

Her mind made up, Claire headed toward the neatly kept farmhouse where Daniel and Sarah lived alongside their four children. A fifth child, who'd been due the previous spring, had died just before birth, making Martha's concern for Sarah's stress level all the more valid.

No, she'd keep their visit light and happy, saving her questions for Daniel until just the right moment. It was the least she could do for Sarah and baby number six.

CHAPTER 12

All thoughts of light and happy went out the window the moment Sarah Lapp answered Claire's knock. For stretched across the young woman's relatively nondescript face was the kind of stress and worry you simply couldn't miss. It was there in the lines around her slender lips, and it was there in the dullness of her eyes and the tightness of her jaw.

The only thing that wasn't there was a ready explanation as to why.

"Sarah?" Claire's gaze skipped down to the tiny mound jutting outward from beneath Sarah's black aproned dress. "Is everything alright? Are you feeling poorly?"

Lifting her hand to her abdomen, Sarah glanced down at the floor and swallowed, Claire's answer coming in a barely discernible shake of the woman's head.

"I was at the toy shop just now and decided I'd stop by and say hello." Claire looked around for something to help ease the tension emanating off the woman and settled on the closest thing she could find. She gestured toward the pairing of rocking chairs in the center of the porch. "It's such a lovely day, I thought you might enjoy sitting out here on the porch and visiting with me for a little while."

A little boy, clad in a light blue shirt and a pair of black suspendered pants, poked his straw-hatted head around Sarah's lower body and flashed a shy smile at Claire. Something about the movement snapped Sarah from her fog and pushed the dullness from her eyes.

"Amos, did you feed *all* of the chickens?"

The three-year-old looked up at his mother and nodded solemnly. "Yah."

"Where is David?"

"Making toys. With Mr. Schrock." A burst of respect for his older brother made its way across the youngster's face before disappearing behind the silent question even Claire could read.

"You may go, too, Amos." Pulling her splayed hand from her stomach, Sarah moved it to the top of her son's hat. "But do not get in Mr. Schrock's way. He and Dat have much work to do."

In a flash, Amos was out the door and

down the porch, his bare feet carrying him across the yard and over to the barn in record time.

"I take it he wants to be a toy maker like his Dat?" Claire asked around the smile that stretched her mouth wide.

"He does. But I do not know how much of that is the toys and how much of that is his Dat. Sometimes I think he and David would be excited to collect sticks if that is what Daniel did." Sarah stepped to the side of the doorway and offered Claire the first semblance of a smile. "Please . . . please come in. It will be nice to visit, Miss Weatherly."

"Claire. Please, call me Claire," she reminded as she preceded the woman into the sparsely furnished front room that seemed to be the norm in the handful of Amish homes she'd been inside. From Esther, she knew these rooms were where families would host Sunday church service when it fell to them by way of rotation. The wide-open space easily accommodated the many benches brought in for the occasion and the dozens of Amish families that followed suit.

"I will try to remember and call you Claire." Sarah's simple black boots made soft, gentle sounds against the wood-planked floor as she closed the gap between them. "I have bread baking in the oven that I must check."

Claire lifted her nose into the air and inhaled, the aroma she'd detected from the porch finally identified. "Mmmm, Sarah, that smells wonderful."

When they reached the kitchen, Sarah gestured toward the wooden benches that lined the long sides of the simple wooden rectangular table. "Please sit. This will take just a moment."

Claire settled herself on the bench facing the oven and looked around the plain yet adequate kitchen, noting the presence of many of the traditional staples. Yet in this home — as in all the other Amish homes around them — the refrigerator and stove ran on propane, and the water in the sink was delivered via the wheel she'd seen turning round and round not far from the outbuilding that served as Daniel's toy shop.

She took in the pale green walls adorned only by one clock, a simple shelf with a smattering of plates, and a calendar that depicted a large maple tree adorned in its autumn finery. She knew, from Esther, that the only decorations the Amish were permitted to have were those of the functional variety.

The plunk of metal atop the counter brought her focus back to the oven and Sarah just in time to see the woman's shoulders slump heavily. "Claire, I do not know what to do with all of this."

Leaning to the side just a little, Claire noted the perfect rise and color of both loaves. "Sarah, they look perfect to me . . ."

"I do not mean the bread." Sarah's voice stopped just shy of a whisper as her back remained turned. "I mean about the toy man's . . . *murder.*"

Claire sat up tall, her eyes, her ears trained on nothing but the pregnant woman standing beside the stove with a simple white cap on her head and a mountain of stress atop her diminutive shoulders. "There isn't anything for you to do with all of that, Sarah. Detective Fisher will figure it out."

"That is what I am afraid of." Slowly, Sarah turned to face Claire, tears running down her round face.

"Sarah!" Claire sprang off the bench and pulled the weeping woman into her arms. "Hey, it's okay. Everything is fine."

"It — it is not fine," Sarah stammered. "P-people are — are talking and they are pointing."

"Shhh . . . It's okay." Stepping back, she took hold of Sarah's shoulders and peered into her eyes. "I don't know what's going on, Sarah, but I'd like to help if you'll let me." Then, with gentle hands, she guided the woman over to the bench she'd just vacated. "Sit with me. Talk to me. We'll figure this out, Sarah . . . I promise."

With only a modicum of hesitation, the woman sat at the table and buried her head in her hands. "I do not want Daniel to know I am upset. I do not want him to know what people are saying."

Claire sat down beside the woman and began to rub her back. "If you do not want him to know, I will not tell him. But let's talk this out. You're carrying too much stress right now and it's not good for the baby."

A nod was followed by a sniffle. "I went to town the day after that man . . . that *Mr. Karble* was murdered. I saw them pointing at me and I heard them say that my Daniel would be a suspect because he was . . . *angry.*" Sarah released a breath then pulled her head from her hands to look at Claire. "But I did not think he was angry."

"Do you mean about Karble Toys making the Amish line in a factory somewhere other than here?"

Sarah nodded again. "I saw the letter at the festival just like Daniel did and I was shocked. Like everyone else. But I did not

163

think he would be angry."

"Did he show you the letter?" She removed her hand from Sarah's back and rested it, instead, on the top of the table.

"No. Martha did. She came to my fruit stand and showed me. I knew it was bad, I knew it would make Daniel worry, but I did not think it would make him angry."

"You saw him later on, though, didn't you? After Mr. Karble's body was found?"

"I did," Sarah said. "He helped me pack up my stand and he took me home."

"Did he seem angry to you at that time?"

Tipping her chin upward, Sarah seemed to contemplate the question, her answer coming after a few beats of silence. "No. He did not seem angry. He was tired and worried, but I would not say he was angry."

"Then ignore what the people in town are saying. Sarah, when things like this happen in the English world, it is people's nature to be curious . . . to even speculate on what might have happened." She glanced down at her hands and searched for the best way to wipe the worry from her friend's face. "But you know your husband better than anyone else. If you say he was not angry, then he wasn't angry. Take comfort in that conviction."

"I tried but it was hard. Daniel is my

husband. I do not like people to think such things of him. He is a good man. A hard worker. He is quiet but not anger-filled."

Pivoting her body to the right, she took Sarah's hands in hers and squeezed. "Then know that. Believe that."

"I did. I still worried, of course, as I do not want him to be bothered by this talk of the toy company anymore, but I believed it would be okay," Sarah explained in a raspy, almost garbled whisper.

"Then why are you so upset?" It seemed a fair question in light of the woman's tears, yet as soon as she posed it aloud, she couldn't help but feel she'd crossed some invisible line.

In a flash, Sarah was on her feet, busying herself around the kitchen with jobs that had clearly been done already. Clean counters were made cleaner and spotless floors were swept once, twice.

"Sarah?" she prompted as her internal radar began to ping.

"Daniel will be in for lunch soon."

"Sarah? What's going on?"

The woman paused midsweep, her gaze fixed on the floor. "I can not say."

"But I want to help you and I can't if you don't tell me what's going on." Again, she rose from the bench and made her way over to Sarah only to have her progress thwarted by a hand. "Sarah, please."

"Martha says you are friends with the detective . . . with her brother."

It was a statement she couldn't dispute. "I am. But Jakob is a good man, Sarah. A fair man. And the last thing he wants to do is hurt anyone in this community."

"Do you share everything with him?"

Surprised by the question, Claire drew back. "Jakob is not my boyfriend, Sarah. He is a friend . . . just as Esther is my friend . . . and Martha is my friend . . . and, I hope, you are my friend. I do not share things one friend says with another unless I am permitted to do so."

She stood perfectly still as Sarah studied her closely, the woman's quandary over sharing personal fears aloud as tangible as the broom in her hand. When Sarah did finally speak, it was in a tone so hushed Claire had to bring her ear within mere inches of the woman's mouth.

"The people were right."

"People?" she whispered back.

"The people in town. The ones who pointed and say such things." Removing her hand from the broomstick, Sarah reached into the space between her apron and her burgundy-hued dress and pulled out a sloppily folded piece of typewritten paper. Before Claire could make sense of what was happening, the paper was shoved against her own hand. "They were right, Claire. Daniel must have been angry. Very, very angry. Now, please . . . you must go."

CHAPTER 13

She stepped to the side of the road, yielding the way for Keith Watson and his busload of satisfied customers as they made their way back toward the center of town. The smattering of waves she earned from the left side of the bus managed to register in some dusty corner of her thoughts, but not until the opportunity to return the connection-making gesture was long gone.

"Good one, Claire," she mumbled to herself. "Great way to bridge the gap between the tour and the shop . . ."

Slowly, she released a whoosh of air from her lungs and dropped her gaze back to her feet, the pace with which they were moving more than a little hypnotic. She'd walked this same road not more than sixty minutes earlier with one real task in mind. Yet, here she was, on her way back to Lighted Way, with more questions than ever about Daniel Lapp — questions she'd been unable to ask him in light of Sarah's less-than-subtle desire for Claire to leave.

When he'd come to the house after ringing up Keith's customers, Claire had wanted nothing more than to secure the previously sought moment or two alone with the toy maker. But, Sarah's well-timed stomach clutch, coupled with impressively realistic complaints of feeling light-headed, nixed that.

"What has you so afraid, Sarah?" She listened to the question as it left her lips then cringed at the answer that formed in its wake.

She thinks her husband killed Rob Karble.

Claire stopped and reached into the pocket of her trousers, her fingers closing around the folded note Sarah had shoved into her hand mere moments before Daniel entered the house. For whatever reason, the toy maker's wife had felt the paper was something Claire needed to see. And, based on the sudden thumping in her chest at the notion of what it could be, she couldn't help but agree.

But where did she go to look at it? Right there — where any number of people could pass by at any given moment? The shop — where Esther might see? The inn — where Diane had eyes in the back of her head?

No. At least not yet, anyway. She needed to read the note in private. If it contained something that necessitated a second pair of eyes, she'd worry about that later.

Glancing from side to side, Claire made a mental note of her location. To her right was the Amish cemetery, its sacred feel and lack of trees making it an inappropriate place to sit and read something that could, potentially, be volatile in nature. To her left were a man and his sons, all working hard to harvest the final crop of the season. To veer off onto their property to examine Sarah's note would be awkward at best.

She looked in the direction she'd been headed once again, the final few farms between her and town rapidly diminishing in number. But just as she was preparing to come up with a plan B that had her sending Esther out on an errand, she saw it.

Just up ahead, where the road curved toward town, a narrow path jutted off in the opposite direction, leading the way toward the semisecluded watering hole that had played a big part in Jakob's childhood.

Confident that no one was watching at that exact moment, Claire turned down the trail and into the grove of trees that sheltered her final destination from the eyes and ears of anyone traveling the main road. As

170

she made her way through the trees and out into the clearing, she couldn't help but notice the sense of peace that washed over her despite the worrisome note in her hand. Even if Jakob had never brought her there, she would have recognized the pond and the lone signature tree poised alongside it like a sentry.

It was a scene she saw virtually each and every day with the time of year in which it was depicted the only real variable. On the hand-painted milk can currently displayed in her front window, the tree was bare except for the dusting of snow that covered its branches. On the spatula that hung from the hook above the register, the tree ushered in spring beside the sun-dappled pond. In the painting her customers stopped to admire on a daily basis, the tree provided shade for a single picnic blanket stretched across the ground with promise. And on the coal bucket Martha had brought in just a week earlier, the tree and the pond looked exactly as they did at that moment.

She stopped at the base of the tree and stared up at the burnt orange leaves that rivaled the brightness of the sun. This place that Jakob treasured so much for the memories it gave him with his estranged sister obviously meant as much to Martha. And it wasn't hard to see why. Tucked away from the cares of the world, this place conveyed a feeling of simplicity in everything from its shoreline of flat rocks to its silent but undeniable invitation to splash and play away the summer.

For Jakob and Martha, it represented a time when their lives were easier and their bond unbreakable. For Claire, it represented hope — hope that one day her heart would be whole again. Maybe even ready to give itself over to love for a second time . . .

Closing her eyes, she breathed in the two-month-old image that had her standing in that very spot for her first rock-skipping lesson. The sensation of Jakob's hand around hers as he offered words of encouragement in her ear was still so vivid it nearly took her breath away. Somehow, someway, despite pervasive thoughts to the contrary, something about that encounter had helped her believe she would get past the hurt of her first marriage enough to love again.

When, exactly, it would happen, she didn't know for sure. But she knew it would. And judging by the very real pull she felt toward both Jakob and Benjamin, she knew it wasn't too far off.

She lifted her chin to the hint of a breeze that rustled her hair and the leaves above her with the gentleness of a whisper. When she felt as if she was ready to read the note, she opened her eyes, leaned against the base of the tree, and slowly unfolded the slip of paper Sarah couldn't get rid of fast enough.

At first glance, the page appeared to be a mere duplicate of the one she'd seen just two days earlier. To be sure, though, she read it once again — Rob Karble's inner-company announcement of the Back to Basics line and its tie to the Michigan manufacturing plant exactly as she remembered from the festival.

Confused, she flipped the paper over and stared down at a series of barely legible mathematical computations that had been penciled down the right-hand side. A second and more thorough inspection of the numbers yielded borrowing marks and a handful of minus signs as the one common denominator on the page. The final number — 10,000 — was circled twice.

"Math problems?" she whispered. "What on earth?" Claire turned her attention back to the pond, the shafts of light that sparkled and danced on the surface suddenly dull against a backdrop of questions with no hint of logical answers. Why had Sarah been so intent on giving her this particular piece of paper? How could a series of math problems that could just as easily be found in any third grade classroom in the country serve as proof of Daniel Lapp's emotions where Rob Karble was concerned?

She took a second look at the numbers and tried to make sense of the calculations, narrowing in on the dollar signs she hadn't noticed during the inaugural once-over.

"Okay, so we're dealing with money. Lots of it," she said before rushing to amend her own words. "Or, at least we were in the beginning . . ."

Sure enough, as she continued to study the figures in front of her, a second detail stepped into the foreground. For there, beside the number being subtracted out, was a previously unnoticed and faintly written word that had just as faintly been crossed out.

"Catalogue?" she read aloud before looping back to the start of the word and repeating it one more time for good measure. "Catalogue."

She was just leaning in for a closer look when the snap of a nearby twig made her jump, the sudden and unexpected movement jostling the paper from her hands. Panicked, she dove forward to grab it only to be beaten to the punch by the same breeze she'd found so refreshing not more than five minutes earlier.

"Hey, hey, hey . . . I got it!" Jakob stepped from the outer edge of the grove and sprinted across the clearing toward the pond, the slap of his feet against the hard-packed earth rivaled only by the pounding in Claire's ears. Inches from the water, he made good on his promise, brandishing a triumphant smile in the process. "I'd say *that* was in the nick of time, wouldn't you?"

Without waiting for her response, he held the windswept paper just slightly above her reach and summoned his dimples for the celebration. "Seems you were looking for this?" he teased.

"I was and I am." She hopped upward and retrieved the paper from his hand. "Thanks."

She felt his gaze as she quickly folded the page and stuffed it back inside her trouser pocket. If he connected the paper to the memo they'd seen circulating the festival grounds, he didn't let on. Instead, he merely gestured to the tree and the pond. "So what brings you out here?"

Sarah Lapp is afraid for her husband?

I needed privacy while reading a note that might have something to do with Rob Karble's murder?

She nibbled her lower lip against her

initial instinct for honesty and searched for something that would still be truthful but far less revealing. After all, Sarah didn't want Jakob to see the note. And while there might come a time when Claire would have to overrule that request, now was not that time. She wanted to try and make heads or tails of the mathematical equations first.

"I was out walking and remembered this place." She parted company with the tree and wandered toward the pond and its rocky shoreline. "Remember how you taught me to skip rocks out here a couple of months ago?"

"How could I forget?"

The sudden rasp of the detective's voice warmed her face in a much different way than the shimmering sunlight. Unsure of how to respond, she chose, instead, to scour the ground for the perfect flat rock, locating one a few feet away. She reached down, snatched it from its resting spot, and positioned her fingers the way she'd been taught. Then with her wrist cocked, she pulled her arm backward and sent the rock sailing . . .

One skip.

Two skips.

Three skips.

"Nice!"

Jakob's enthusiasm ignited the smile that spread across her face and ended in a little celebratory hop. "Not bad for only one lesson, huh?" she asked before searching the ground for yet another rock. "I don't usually catch on to stuff like this so quickly."

"Figures."

She paused her hand mere inches above her next rock and looked back at the man. "Excuse me?"

A hint of crimson rose in his cheeks only to disappear behind a well-placed hand and an out-of-the-blue cough.

"Jakob?" She straightened to a stand, the second rock all but forgotten at her feet. "Is something wrong?"

Slowly, he slid his hand down his chin, grimacing ever so slightly as he did. "Sorry. I guess I was just kind of hoping you didn't remember what I'd showed you so that . . . uh . . . maybe I could show you again."

She cast about for something to say, something to lessen the sudden charge that hovered in the air between them, but she came up empty, the louder-than-normal thudding in her chest making it hard to think.

"Nothing like making myself sound like an idiot, eh?" Jakob hoisted his shoulders upward in a shrug and then grabbed hold of a rock he sent skipping across the pond. When the rock disappeared into the water after its fifth bounce, he took another look around the area. "I can hardly believe I'll be seeing her in about five minutes. Even harder to believe it'll be right here in a place I've revisited in my dreams more times than I can count these past sixteen years."

For a moment she was at a loss for what he was talking about, but then, the mixture of apprehension and tenderness she saw on his face brought her up to speed. Today was the day he was meeting Martha. "I hope you can help her. She sure seems worried about your brother and" — Claire swallowed — "Daniel."

"I'm going to do my best. I've lost sixteen years with all of these people but I don't believe either of them would change so much they'd turn to murder." Dropping his voice to a near whisper, he looked both ways before meeting Claire's gaze. "I know this is going to sound awful, but I'm glad she was worried enough to ask for my help. I've waited a long time to talk with my little sister and I miss her. Losing her was like losing a part of me and I haven't felt whole since."

Silence blanketed the space between them as Claire struggled to find just the right words. Never in her five years of marriage to Peter had he ever shared his feelings about anything, let alone done so in such an open and honest way. It was the kind of relationship she'd always wanted them to have, yet never did. As a result, she found herself in uncharted territory where Jakob was concerned.

At a loss, she simply reached out, wrapping her hand around his and offering a gentle squeeze. "Savor it, Jakob. Savor every moment."

"Oh, I will. Trust —"

"Jakob?"

He yanked his hand from Claire's grasp and turned to face the woman whose footsteps were so soft neither Jakob nor Claire had heard her approach. "Martha!" He thrust his hand in his sister's direction only to let it fall awkwardly to his side.

Claire's heart ached for this man who wanted nothing more than to be close to his sister in the way he treasured from his youth. Yet his decision to become a police officer had changed everything. Now, instead of the closeness the siblings once shared, there were only averted gazes and weighted silence.

Anxious to help bridge the gap, she stepped forward, placing a hand of friendship on Martha's upper arm. "Martha, you're doing the right thing, talking to Jakob. He will help."

Slowly, Martha's hazel eyes left their tenuous target somewhere just beyond Jakob's face and trained their focus squarely on Claire. "I am to meet Jakob. Not you."

She drew back at the unexpected rebuke. "I'm sorry, I didn't —"

"Esther is not to know I am here. What I am doing is wrong. I will not put my daughter in a place to do wrong as well." Martha glanced at her brother and lifted her chin in determination. "I will not stay if we are not alone."

Claire rushed to ease any unnecessary worry from her friend's shoulders. "Martha, I won't say a word to Esther! You have my word."

"A word I will have to trust," Martha acknowledged before repeating her stipulation. "I will not stay, Jakob, if we are not alone."

With nary a beat of hesitation, Jakob moved in beside Martha and angled his body to face Claire, the amber flecks in his own hazel eyes uncharacteristically dull. "Claire, I must ask you to go. I am here to see my sister."

CHAPTER 14

She could feel Esther studying her as she went about the busy work of shifting things around shelves that didn't really need to be shifted, and ran a cloth along things that had already been dusted. But it was all she could think to do as she tried to make sense of her feelings.

Deep down inside, she understood Jakob's request. He'd waited a very long time to speak with his sister and he didn't want to put what might very well be his one and only chance at risk. Yet despite that understanding, her heart still ached a little at the dismissal.

One by one, she made her way through the bin of hand-painted spoons, sorting them into odd little piles she undid just as fast.

"Claire? Is everything alright? You seem . . . upset."

"I'm fine, Esther. Really. I guess I just

have a few things on my mind is all." With a practiced hand, she fanned her fingers across the final pile of spoons and displayed them in their original way. "But no worries, I'm fine."

When she was confident she could keep her emotions in check, she turned to face her friend. "What's with your kapp being tied?" she asked as she closed the gap between the spoons and the counter area where Esther stood.

The nineteen-year-old shrugged. "It is supposed to be tied."

She had to laugh. "That never stopped you from letting the strings dangle before," she teased.

"It is time. To act like a lady."

It took everything she could muster not to pick at Esther's statement, pointing out the many ways in which the detective's niece acted like a lady despite untied kapp strings. But she let it go. After all, Esther was right. Amish kapps were essentially prayer veils and wearing them daily was a nod to the biblical command to pray without ceasing.

Still, she'd always found Esther's sweet little act of rebellion innocently endearing.

"That toy makes it hard, though." Esther pointed at a flat wooden doll on the counter beside the register. "I did the tasks you asked me to do while you were out, but when I was done, I played with that toy like a little girl. I am glad Eli did not see. He would think I am not fit to be a wife."

"Not fit to be a wife? Are you kidding me?" She pulled Esther in for a quick hug and then released her with a smile. "Eli knows he has a special woman in you and it won't be long before he asks for your hand in marriage."

A telltale flush rose up Esther's neck and into her cheeks. "He is taking a long time."

"Because he's trying to prove himself worthy." And it was true. He was.

Eli was a hardworking young man who was completely devoted to his twin sister, Ruth, and his family as a whole. When he wasn't next door helping Ruth with Shoo Fly Bake Shoppe, he was working alongside Ben in their family's fields with an enviable determination. But despite his steadfast devotion and stellar work ethic, Eli struggled with a temper that had him asking for forgiveness during many an Amish church service. It was a habit he was working to break as much for Esther and Esther's father as anyone else.

"He does not need to prove himself to me. I know he is a good man," Esther whispered as she scooped the toy from the counter and held it out for Claire to see. "This is called a Jumping Jack. You pull this string, here" — Esther gave a gentle tug — "and the legs and arms move in dance."

Claire clapped her hands then reached for the toy, the arms and legs moving up and down in reaction to her own tug of the string. "Oh, Esther, this is adorable. Where did it come from?"

"From my uncle, Isaac Schrock. He stopped in the alley to speak with Eli and I told him my little sister felt poorly yesterday. He gave me this toy to bring to her." Esther nudged her chin in the direction of Claire's hand and giggled softly. "See? It is hard not to play with it, no?"

She matched Esther's laugh with one of her own as she tugged on the string one last time. "Very hard. Your sister will love it." Looking down at the toy, she handed it back to Esther. "I take it Isaac made that?"

"He did. It is one of his . . . I don't know how to say it properly . . . *special* toys. It is the one he uses to tell of Lapp's Toys."

"Oh. Like a signature toy?"

The doll's appendages moved under Esther's expert hand. "Yes, that is the right word. He uses it on a corner of each of his pages in Mr. Lapp's catalogue."

Her head snapped up. "Catalogue?"

"Yes. You know of it. You have seen it."

She briefly slid her hand inside her front left pocket and fingered the folded note it held, her head nodding along with Esther's words even as her mouth started spewing out questions. "Esther? Can I ask you something? Do you have any idea whether Daniel's mail-order business has been all that successful? I mean, I know he gets orders, and I know it's increased his business, but has it made a *big* difference?"

Drawing the doll to her chest, Esther's eyes widened. "Oh, Claire. It made a very big difference. For Mr. Lapp and for my uncle. It is the reason Mr. Lapp sold off a part of his farm to Mr. Stoltzfus."

"Wait," Claire said. "I don't understand. What does the toy catalogue have to do with Daniel's farm?"

"Uncle Isaac said they sell more toys by mail than they do in the toy shop. People who visit take a catalogue home with them and then order toys for birthdays. And with Christmas coming, Uncle Isaac thinks there will be even more orders. And Mr. Lapp? He says farming takes too much time. By selling land to Mr. Stoltzfus, Mr. Stoltzfus can grow more crops and make more money, while Mr. Lapp and my uncle can spend days making toys."

She mulled over everything Esther said and came up with yet another set of questions. "But you said he sold *part* of his farm, didn't you? That means he could return to the land to earn his way if he needed to, right?"

Esther's head was shaking before Claire had even finished speaking, the reason for the rather simple motion chilling. "Farmland is becoming hard to come by for the Amish. There is not enough land for everyone to farm. It is why so many make money in other ways now. The bigger farms can grow more. Mr. Lapp's farm is no longer big enough to grow multiple crops. Dat thought it was bad for Mr. Lapp to sell, but Mr. Lapp did not ask Dat's advice."

"And if he had no choice but to go back to farming?" Claire asked. "What then?"

"He would have to move to a different Amish community where there is more land. Dat says there is still land in Wisconsin. Up high in New York, too." Esther looked down at the toy in her hand and smiled just a little before setting it back on the counter. "But Mr. Lapp would not go. His Mamm and Dat are too old to move. It is his place to stay and take care of them."

There was no doubt Claire still had much to learn about the Amish and their beliefs, but one thing she did know was that their elders didn't go into nursing homes or retirement communities the way their English counterparts so often did. Instead, they turned their farms over to their youngest son and his family and then lived out the rest of their days in a smaller house on the same farm, helping with the daily work until they were no longer able-bodied enough to do so.

She reached into her pocket a second time, the desire to pull the note out and examine it on the spot more than a little difficult to resist. But she had to. At least for now. There would be time and opportunity to study the figures more closely when she got home that night. If it pointed to a motive for murder like she was beginning to suspect, she'd decide what to do at that time.

Unfortunately, if there was any real basis for the knot of fear now sitting in her chest, doing the right thing would come with a hefty dose of guilt. Especially if it had a pregnant woman's husband trading his suspendered attire for the equally simple prison stripes.

Despite spending a fair chunk of her day away from the shop, the five o'clock closing time still couldn't come soon enough for Claire. All afternoon she'd done her best to stay busy, making lists of needed inventory, assisting customers alongside Esther, and answering the countless Amish-related questions posed by virtually every tourist who came through the door.

"You are glad for this day to be over, yes?" Esther looked up from the register where she was transferring the day's earnings to a yellow envelope and offered Claire a sympathetic smile. "Sometimes I have a day like that, too. But mostly I am just so glad to be here, working with you."

Claire blinked against the threat of tears ushered in by Esther's words and willed herself to end the workday on a positive, upbeat note. She owed her friend that much, especially if she was going to be the one to ultimately set off a powder keg of shame throughout the Amish community.

"I'm sorry, Esther, I really am. Last night was just a really rough night on top of another really rough night and I guess I'm a little more sleep deprived than I realized." She forced her lips into what she hoped was a believable enough smile then took the envelope of money from Esther's outstretched hand. "I'll be better tomorrow. I promise."

It was a promise she probably had no business making in light of the day's revelations, but the need for a burst of optimism momentarily won out over a potential reality she was struggling to embrace.

"Then I look forward to tomorrow. I have missed your smile today." Esther came out from behind the counter only to return long enough to retrieve her little sister's new toy from its resting spot beside the register. "You helped me when I was afraid for Eli many weeks ago. If you let me, Claire, I can help you."

She stared down at the envelope in her hands as a dozen different replies rushed her thoughts. But even before she'd fully considered the merits of each one, she knew, deep down inside, that sharing her fears about Daniel with Esther wouldn't change anything. The only thing it would do was make Esther worry, too.

No, she needed to figure this out herself. Drawing in a breath of courage, she gave in to the one answer she couldn't hold back. "The best way you can help me, Esther, is to remain my friend no matter what."

"I will always be your friend, Claire. That is an easy thing for me to do."

A lump rose in Claire's throat making it difficult to speak. Instead, she simply squeezed Esther's hand and prayed the young woman's words were true.

CHAPTER 15

She inserted the key into the back door of Sleep Heavenly and pushed, the momentary relief she felt at being home quickly wiped away by a deafening silence. Glancing at her wrist, she noted the time, her heart beginning to thud at the confirmation she hadn't really needed.

It was nearly six o'clock.

Dinner was served to the guests promptly at six forty-five each and every evening.

Which meant Diane should be moving about the kitchen preparing dinner the way she had been doing since Claire first came to Heavenly eight months earlier.

Yet no matter how many times Claire turned her ear toward the doorway on the other end of the service entrance, she heard nothing. Not a footstep, not a clank of a pot, not a clink of ice against a water glass. Just complete and utter silence.

Slowly, she made her way through the

vestibule and into the kitchen, the absence of any life merely visual proof for what her ears had already determined. Closer inspection of her surroundings yielded a dozen homemade pot pies waiting on a counter beside an already preheated oven.

A quick scan of the handwritten recipe card beside the hefty portions allowed Claire to place them in the oven and set the timer. With that done, she continued her search into the dining room, the carefully set table smoothing her worries a smidge.

Whatever had come up to veer Diane from her usual tasks had come up fairly recently. Perhaps a guest had needed a new towel? Or maybe a remote in one of the rooms needed a fresh pair of batteries?

Still, she continued from room to room on the first floor of the inn, her need to verify her aunt's well-being driving her feet forward. A faint click off to her left caught her attention and she turned in that direction, the soothing sounds of Diane's voice greeting her footfalls halfway down the hall.

"Thank heavens, I've been looking all over for you, Aunt Diane . . ." The words vanished from her lips as she stopped in front of the now-open door and caught her first glimpse of Ann Karble since the woman's arrival at the inn.

That Ann Karble had been vibrant, poised, and confident, her clothes and her shoes a dead giveaway to the money her husband earned as owner and president of one of the country's largest toy manufacturers. This Ann Karble was but a shell of her former self. The eyes that had been so expertly and tastefully made up at arrival were now puffy and red-rimmed. The cheeks that had sported such a healthy glow were now ghastly white. The body that had hinted at the exercise regimen that had the woman running before dawn only days earlier now appeared fatigued.

Diane grabbed hold of Claire's hand and tugged her inside the room, the door clicking shut behind them. "Oh, Claire. I'm so glad you're here. I've got to see to dinner before the guests come down to an empty table and uncooked pot pies. But —"

She pulled her gaze from Ann's distraught face and fixed it, instead, on her aunt. "I put them in the oven about five minutes ago. They'll be ready at just the right time."

A hasty kiss on her cheek let her know she'd made the right call even before the whispered follow-up commenced. "Thank you, dear. But I need to see to the bread and the drinks, too. Would you mind sitting in here with Ann for a little while? She could use the company." Lowering her voice still further, Diane yanked her head toward the woman on the bed. "I'm growing worried about her and I'd feel better if I knew you were in here with her while I get things finished up in the kitchen."

"Uh, sure. I can do that." But even as she said it, she was well aware of her desire to run the other way. Her day had been wearisome enough all on its own. Trying to come up with ways to cheer up a mourning woman wasn't exactly how she'd envisioned her evening.

Still, as Diane disappeared into the hallway, Claire perched awkwardly on the edge of the bed and offered the victim's wife what she hoped was a friendly yet respectful smile. "Mrs. Karble? I'm so very sorry about your husband. I truly am. If there's anything I can do, please don't hesitate to —"

"Business was so good," Ann said in a voice that was both haunting and broken. "We were rolling out plenty of new toys for the holiday season. I don't know why we had to come here."

Claire hooked her knee upward onto the bed and turned to afford a better view of the brunette, the woman's words not meshing with the argument that had woken everyone from their sleep the night before

194

the murder. "But you *knew* about the Amish line . . ."

Ann's eyes closed momentarily only to reopen and look at Claire. "Of course I knew about the new line. I knew about everything that happened at Karble Toys. It was *my* company, not Robert's."

Her foot dropped back to the ground. "*Your* company? B-but . . . how? I thought it was your husband's."

A part laugh, part strangled cry emerged from Ann's throat. "Because that's what we told people. Even our employees didn't know. Still don't, though that'll change soon enough."

She tried to make sense of what she was hearing but remained silent when she couldn't.

"It was my gift to Robert — the love of my life," Ann continued in a raspy whisper.

"You gave him a company?"

Ann nodded. "My father owned a tiny toy shop when I was a little girl. He made toys in the back room and sold them up front. That store was called Karble's Creations."

"But Karble was your husband's name," Claire protested.

"No, Karble was my name," Ann corrected, weakly. "But since I was my father's only child, there was no one to carry on his name. So when I became serious with Robert, my father was in the process of laying out a new business plan — one that had his little shop springboarding into something much bigger. When he became ill and was faced with the little bit of time he had left, Robert agreed to take my name in marriage and realize my father's dream. I kept a presence over the years, of course, as a nod to my father and his friends who helped finance us at the start, but the day-to-day decisions were really for my husband to make."

"Wow. He did an amazing job." It was a simple statement but true, nonetheless. In fact, if Ann's details were as accurate as she was sure they were, the details of Karble Toys' rise to fame were nothing short of inspiring.

"Yes, yes he did."

Claire pondered everything she'd heard thus far and then asked the first question that sprang into her thoughts. "Did you ever wish you could've gotten some of the public accolades your husband got along the way?"

A comfortable silence hovered between them as Ann slipped into thought. After several moments, though, Ann finally answered, the sincerity in her voice magnifying Claire's empathy for the woman tenfold.

"Honestly, I got such tremendous enjoyment out of watching Robert succeed that it never really crossed my mind. I was so in love with him from the first moment we met that I wanted nothing but the best for him and for our lives together." Ann began to fidget with a string on the comforter as she took a momentary pause. "Our life together was almost perfect."

"Almost?"

"I was never able to give him a child." A long, labored sigh made its way between Ann's trembling lips along with yet another round of heartbreaking words. "Oh, how I wanted to. More than anything, in fact. But it wasn't to be. And now . . . I'm alone. Completely and utterly alone."

Bowing her head forward, Ann began to cry, the movement of her shoulders sending a gentle bounce across the bed. Claire scooted closer and silenced the fidgeting hand with one of her own. Suddenly, this woman who'd been a veritable stranger to Claire just moments earlier could just as easily have been any one of a dozen or so friends she'd had throughout her life — people who'd touched her heart and created a lasting connection.

"I know it feels like that right now. But you will always carry a part of your husband

197

in your heart," she said between soothing noises. "No one can ever take that away from you."

One sniffle was followed by another and still another, but, eventually, Ann's shoulders began to steady. "I . . . I know that. I . . . I just know I'm going to miss looking into his eyes every morning." Working her sleeve over her hand, the woman wiped at the tears that continued to stream down her face, her words coming between little bursts of calm. "They were the most brilliant green I've ever seen. Every time I looked at them, I felt at peace. And I always knew I wanted our child to have those same eyes."

Claire tried to think of something to say but came up empty. Instead, she simply draped her arm across Ann's shoulders and pulled her in for a quick side embrace.

"Now they're gone and the only reason they're gone is because we came here. To Amish country. To enter into a partnership Rob never should've *considered,* let alone try to ink. I mean, when he first told me about his idea over coffee one night, I could see the appeal. Parents and grandparents like the idea of sharing a simpler time with their kids. But, in the long run, all the kids really want is to play with whatever the latest and greatest is at any given moment. Is that sad? Maybe. But it's reality and any businessman worth his salt knows the bottom line is rooted in reality." Slowly but surely, the tears dried, the mounting disbelief in Ann's voice now mirrored in her eyes. "But all Robert could see was that silly little toy he kept messing with all the time. And no matter what I said to try and get through to him, he just didn't seem to get it."

The words streamed from Ann's mouth now as disbelief became tinged with anger. "*Wooden toys?* He wanted to make *wooden toys?* So *make* wooden toys! You don't need the *Amish* to do that. And a man who made the kind of millions Robert did over the past twenty years was smart enough to know that."

Her tirade over, Ann's shoulders lurched forward in utter exhaustion. "I just don't get it," she whispered. "I mean, *why?* Why did he go down this road? Because nothing — no desire for simplicity, no harebrained idea, no stupid little toy — was worth losing the love of my life."

Once again, Claire was left with nothing to say because Ann had said it all.

CHAPTER 16

If Claire closed her eyes and concentrated solely on the faint sounds coming from the windows around her, she could almost pretend all was well. How else could one explain the happy chatter coming from Doug and Kayla Jones as they perused the literary offerings in the parlor? How else could one explain the noises from Room One that suggested Wayne and Virginia Granderson were preparing to retire for the evening once their teeth were brushed and a suitable program had been found on their in-room television?

Yet even as she rested her head against the back of the porch swing and did her best to let its gentle sway calm her, she knew things weren't at all as they sounded.

Ann Karble's room, on the other end of the porch, was pitch-black, the absence of anything resembling life on the other side of the closed curtain a testament to the deep depression that had kept the woman from eating dinner and engaging in any further conversation.

Upstairs, hidden away behind the one unnumbered room in the inn, was Diane, a woman whose smile had stopped short of her eyes ever since the Karbles' room had been ransacked. No matter what Claire tried to tell her, no matter how often Jakob relinquished her from all responsibility, Aunt Diane was still convinced she bore the ultimate blame for the crime.

Down the road in Amish country, things weren't okay for Sarah Lapp, either. And while Claire couldn't be sure what the expectant mother was doing at that moment, she knew it was being done with a heavy heart. How could it not be when you were afraid your husband was involved in a murder?

Not far from that farmhouse was the one where Martha lived. Like Sarah, Martha was also concerned for Daniel Lapp. But Martha's fear didn't stop there. It ran one step further — to her younger brother. In turn, *that* stress had led to a decision that — if discovered — could result in disciplinary measures from the Amish community.

She stared out at the darkness just beyond the porch railing and tried to focus on the parts of her day that had been good. But try as she might, there were simply too many thoughts and too many worries moving through her head to get any real peace out of Esther's smile or the brief alone-time she'd shared with Jakob at the pond.

People she cared about were hurting. Some, terribly. How could she truly expect the sights and sounds of a near-sleeping Heavenly to wield its usual sleep-inducing magic?

In two words, she couldn't.

But, sooner or later, she'd have to sleep. If she didn't she'd be useless at the shop, the inn, and to any of her friends who might need her help. The problem, though, was finding the energy to stop the swing, stand on her feet, and head upstairs to her room.

The *clip-clop* of an approaching horse, however, had her glancing at her wrist and turning it so as to read the time in the muted glow of the porch light.

Ten forty-five . . .

Much too late for someone from the Amish community to be out and about, that was for sure.

Bracing her foot against the floor, Claire brought the swing to a stop, the outline of the now-parked buggy alongside the inn setting her nerves on edge. Something was wrong. It had to be . . .

A tall figure jumped down from the driver's seat and made its way around the buggy, the man's straw hat and hunched shoulders shielding his face from view.

"Hello?" she called out, rising to her feet as she did. "Who's there?"

Less than a second later, the man stepped into the light and tilted his head ever so slightly in her direction, the butterflies his presence sent up in her stomach supplying his name before her eyes could offer their confirmation. "Ben. Hi . . . Is — is everything okay?"

"Yah. But I am not here to talk of me. I am here to see you. To know that you are okay."

She took a half step, half stumble backward. "Me? But, I don't understand."

He took the steps of the porch with ease and gestured toward the swing. "Will you sit with me, Claire?"

When she hesitated, he took her hand and gently guided her toward the swing, the unfamiliar feel of his hand on hers making her more than a little light-headed. "I don't understand," she repeated. "Why are you here? Shouldn't you be in bed by now? I know your day starts very early . . ."

"I could not sleep. I thought only of what

Esther said when she came by Mamm and Dat's house to bring Eli a plate of cookies."

She willed herself to focus on something other than the feel of his thigh alongside hers as the swing began to sway beneath them. "Esther?"

"Yah. She told of your worry and your sadness at the shop this afternoon. She said you did not smile."

She felt her face drain of all color. "She told your parents that?"

"No. She told only me." He studied her closely, the tenderness in his eyes every bit as real as his simple black suspenders. "So please, Claire, won't you tell me what is troubling you? I know I am Amish and that I do not understand everything about your world, but I do have good ears."

"I'm fine, Benjamin. Really. I was just tired today." She ran her hand along the swing's armrest, breathing in the clean night air as she did. "Which is exactly what I told Esther, too."

"Yah. But she believes it is more, and I do, too."

She pulled her hand back to her lap. "I was going to head in to bed in a few minutes. I just wanted a little more fresh air."

"If you were so tired it took away your smile, you would be asleep at this moment."

"And you?" she proposed. "What would you have done if that were the case?"

Benjamin turned his head to look out at his horse, the gentle breeze that lifted her hair unable to reach his beneath the rim of his hat. After several long moments, he looked back at Claire. "I would take the buggy home and look for tomorrow to come."

She didn't need access to a mirror to know his words had brought a flush to her face. Nor did she need the tremble in her hands to know they were treading in dangerous water.

Benjamin was Amish.

She wasn't.

Those two facts, coupled together, were enough to make her stop the swing and rise to her feet, the need to walk around the porch as much about self-sanity as anything else. Yet even as she walked, she could feel the weight of his eyes as they followed her to the front railing.

"I guess I just have a lot of things on my mind is all." There, she said it. Lifting her chin to the breeze, Claire took a deep breath then let it release slowly. "It's been a long week."

"Tell me. I will listen."

She blinked away the sudden burn that

meant tears were near. There were times, when she was busy at the shop or engaged in her day-to-day life, that she actually saw her failed marriage to Peter as a distant memory. And other times, the heartbreak was still so raw it was hard to believe so much time had passed.

Having a man like Benjamin care about her feelings had her walking a fine line between the two. Because while she was grateful for his genuine concern, it also left her wondering how her own husband could have been so uninterested in everything about her and her life.

"Please, Claire. I will listen," he repeated.

Slowly, she turned her back to the distant fields and leaned against the railing, the words coming slowly at first. "I'm worried about Aunt Diane. She seems to think what happened in the Karbles' room is all about a shortcoming at the inn. And it's not. Whoever killed Mr. Karble was looking for something in that room and they'd have gotten in no matter what kind of security measures she may or may not have had in place.

"I've told her it's not her fault, most of the guests have told her it's not her fault, and even Jakob has told her it's not her fault. Yet she doesn't seem to be able to shake this disappointment she has in herself. And, Benjamin? It's painful to watch."

"One day soon she will see."

Oh, how she wished she shared even a tenth of Benjamin's optimism . . .

"What else?" he asked. At her furrowed brows, he rephrased. "What else has taken your smile away?"

Instinctively, her hand dropped to the pocket of her pants and the folded paper inside. She'd been so busy with Ann prior to dinner, she hadn't been able to secure enough privacy to take a second look at the note until after dinner was served and Diane had shooed her from the kitchen. And then, when she finally had the chance to look at the equations more closely, she wished she hadn't.

Because the numbers, coupled with everything Esther had told her in the shop that afternoon, suddenly pointed to a very unsettling place.

"Claire?"

She pulled her hand away from her pocket and waved it in the air in what she hoped was a lighthearted motion. "I'm just worried about my aunt is all. Really."

But even as she offered the most believable placation she could, she knew it fell short. Especially for someone like Benjamin, who seemed to be in touch with everything — his horse, Eli, Ruth and her business, his farm, his life, Claire . . .

Benjamin halted the movement of the swing with his boot and stood, closing the gap between them with only a modicum of hesitation. "Why did you ask questions about Daniel Lapp?"

She swallowed once, twice. "I was just curious about his business."

Reaching out, he placed a gentle finger beneath her chin and nudged it upward until they were eye to eye. "Why did you ask questions about Daniel?" he repeated.

She searched for another way to evade his question or to change topics completely, but the feel of his skin against hers made it difficult to think let alone play games. "Mr. Karble's decision to manufacture the Amish toy line in Michigan must have devastated Daniel."

He dropped his hand to his side but not before sweeping it upward and cupping the side of her face for the kind of split second that felt like hours. "Yah. He had promised toy-making work to a few men. He did not want to go back on his word."

Again, she fingered the note through the outside of her pocket. "It also threatened his ability to make a living in light of the fact he sold a huge chunk of his farm to one of your neighbors."

"Stoltzfus," Benjamin supplied.

"Yes, that's the name."

"Daniel made do before the notion of a new toy line; he will make do after."

She turned her head to the side, her gaze moving from Benjamin's horse and buggy to the ever decreasing number of lights in the homes at the end of the driveway. If she took the note straight to Jakob and she was wrong in her deciphering, Daniel and Sarah would be subjected to unnecessary scrutiny. If she showed the note to Benjamin and got his read on the situation, she was burdening someone else with the same worry that had her sitting out on the porch at eleven o'clock at night instead of fast asleep in her bed.

The only thing left to decide was who could handle the stress more — a potential suspect and his pregnant wife, or the quiet yet reflective man who was standing in front of Claire at that exact moment?

Exhaling an errant strand of hair from her cheek, she reached into her pocket and extracted the memo Sarah had all but shoved in her hand earlier that day. Without a word, she held it out for Benjamin to take.

"What is this?"

"You'll see."

With careful hands, he unfolded the page and stared down at the memo they'd first seen together only days earlier. "I have seen this."

"Turn it over," she whispered. "There's more."

He did as she asked then held the paper up to the light. "I do not see — wait. I see it now. It is numbers." He glanced back at Claire. "These are numbers. But what do they mean?"

"I think they are a loss statement."

"Loss statement?"

"A profit and loss statement," she rushed to explain. "I make one of those for the shop every month so I can see how much I spent and how much I earned. It helps me identify weak places while highlighting the areas that are working."

"Yah. I do that with the farm, too. But I did not know it had a name." Benjamin looked again at the paper in his hand. "This is yours?"

"No, that belongs to Daniel." She lifted her hands to her face and peered at Benjamin across her fingertips. "And if I'm reading them right, I think they give Daniel a pretty substantial motive."

He waited for her to continue, but when

she didn't, he pressed for more. "What is this motive you speak about? Motive for what?"

Pushing off the railing, she sidestepped Benjamin only to double back in his direction after barely straying more than a foot or two. "For Robert Karble's murder."

CHAPTER 17

The sliver of moonlight that slipped its way under Claire's drapes had started at her slippers and slowly made its way to the end of her bed, its farewell to dawn literally just around the corner. From a scientific standpoint, she supposed she should be fascinated by the visual passage of time, but considering the incessant tossing and turning that had enabled her to watch it in the first place, she wasn't.

What she needed was sleep.

Unfortunately, the part of her brain that was supposed to be able to shut off in order to make that happen wasn't cooperating. At all.

Tossing her thin cotton blanket to the side, she swung her legs off the bed and sat up. Lying there, hour after hour, was doing absolutely nothing for her beyond birthing a headache she could no longer ignore any more than the guilt she felt over unleashing her fears on Benjamin.

If she was lucky, the fruit of her amateur sleuthing hadn't affected the man's sleep in the slightest. But, deep down inside, she knew better.

Sure, he'd tried to offer rebuttals to Claire's hypothesizing where Daniel was concerned, but even she knew they were halfhearted. Daniel had motive, plain and simple.

She wiggled her feet into her slippers and pulled her robe from its resting spot at the bottom of her bed, the image of a headache-relieving cup of coffee guiding her every move. When she was fully robed and ready to go, she stepped into the hall and looked both ways, the absence of light beneath the doors of the surrounding rooms reminding her of the need to be as quiet as possible.

Yet, just as quickly as she turned toward the staircase and its access to the kitchen, she turned back, the pull of Room Six in all its taped-off glory winning out over the promise of coffee.

It was hard to believe she'd stepped into this same hallway three evenings earlier to pinpoint the culprits behind an argument that had brought such an untimely end to her last decent night's sleep. And just as happened that time, she found her gaze riveted on the room across the hall from her own. This time, though, the door was wide open with entry denied by a piece of yellow crime scene tape and the internal voice in Claire's head that told her to stay away.

She didn't listen.

Instead, with nary a glance in either direction, she succumbed to the pull that was her curiosity and inched her way over to the tape, her eyes grateful for the illumination provided by the wall sconces lining the hallway from end to end. Their light, while dim, made it easier to survey a room that had yet to be turned back over to Diane.

In the center of the room, as was the case in each of the second floor's additional guest quarters, was a queen-sized bed that spoke to a time when furnishings were tastefully elaborate. Had the sheets and blankets not been ripped off in an intruder's haste, she knew it would have beckoned as a comfortable haven at the end of a long day. To the left side of the headboard was a nightstand. Atop the mahogany surface was an alarm clock, a tipped-over tissue box that had been emptied out across the floor, and a paperback romance novel that gave evidence to which Karble had slept where once the arguing had finally subsided on their last night together.

A dresser along the far wall was missing three of its four drawers. The fourth drawer was extended in a fully open position. Rising up on her toes, Claire peered into its empty depths. The rest of the drawers hadn't gone far, their contents tossed about like the drawers themselves. Socks and shirts that had once been folded were strewn about the room like confetti after a New Year's celebration.

Swinging her focus back to its starting point, she zeroed in on Rob Karble's side of the bed and its own picked-over nightstand. Like Ann's, a tissue box had been knocked on its side, its contents spilling out from the oval opening on top. Next to the box was a man's gold watch that, to Claire's untrained eye, looked to be rather expensive, its continued presence on the nightstand clearly obliterating simple robbery as a motive for the room's ransacking.

She looked back toward the overturned drawer closest to where she stood and surveyed its immediate area, a familiar wooden shape sticking out from under a necktie soliciting a gasp from deep inside her throat.

"Claire?"

Spinning around, she stumbled backward

into the tape, ripping its left end from the wall and creating an undeterred entry point where only seconds earlier there had been none. She glanced down at the tape by her heels and then back up at the woman staying in the room beside her own. "Oh. Melinda. I . . . I didn't know you were there."

"Really? I couldn't have guessed." Flicking her perfectly manicured fingertips in the air, the fully dressed woman punctuated her sarcastic retort with a quick smile before sidling up beside Claire. "So what made you gasp the way you did just now? Because, if I didn't know any better, I'd have to think you saw a ghost or something."

Claire looked again at the necktie and the familiar toy peeking out from beneath its widest point and steadied herself against the edge of the open doorway. "I . . . I don't know," she mumbled.

Melinda rolled her eyes up toward the ceiling, releasing an exasperated sigh in the process. "C'mon, Claire. Of course you do. A person doesn't just gasp like that unless there's a reason."

Slowly, she pulled her hand from the wall and pointed toward the wooden figure that had become the only thing she could see in the entire room. "Do you see that little toy right there? The one peeking out from underneath that blue and gray tie?"

Melinda followed the path made by Claire's finger, her subsequent nod answering the question in short order. "So? What about it?"

She paused to take in the sturdy string and the movable legs, the design and the craftsmanship identical to the toy she'd seen in Esther's hands not more than twelve hours earlier. "Do you know what that is?"

"Of course. It's called a Jumping Jack."

"Does Karble Toys make Jumping Jacks, too?" she asked, although, if she was honest with herself, she was afraid she knew the answer already.

"It was about to." Melinda crossed her arms in front of her chest. "But now? If I was a betting woman? I'd say that's the *last* toy Ann will allow across our production line once she's willed the company."

Claire bit back the urge to set Melinda straight on the true ownership of Karble Toys but opted, instead, to keep the conversational focus where it needed to be for the moment. "The last toy? But why?"

"Because it's that exact toy that brought Robert here in the first place."

"Here?" she echoed in a whisper.

"Yes, here. To this place" — Melinda

spread her arms wide to indicate the inn before dropping them to her side — "and to Heavenly . . . the place where he was murdered."

She shook away the image of the toy guru's lifeless body behind the Schnitz and Knepp festival booth and looked, again, at the Jumping Jack. "So how did he get it?"

"It was sent to him in the mail about four weeks ago." Melinda leaned her shoulder against the wall and drifted off to a different place and time, her words bringing Claire along for the ride. "I'll never forget the moment Daisy brought that package into Robert's office. It was in a padded white envelope that had been addressed in pencil. The boss took one look at it, made a face, and stuck it off to the side of his desk so we could finish a discussion we were having about the upcoming holiday season. When we were done, I headed back to my office down the hall and he got back to the third-quarter reports he'd been poring over all week."

Melinda squared her back with the wall before sliding her way down it and into a seated position with her knees pulled close to her chest. "The next thing I knew, it was six thirty and it was time to head out to meet some of my girlfriends for dinner. So I grabbed my computer and my purse and I headed down the hall past Robert's office. And there he was, sitting in his chair, staring down at" — the woman pointed around the corner and into the Karbles' former room — "that toy. His face was as white as a ghost and he was shaking his head in complete disbelief."

Claire looked from the toy to Melinda and back again, the identity of the person who'd sent the package all but certain in her mind. "So Daniel Lapp mailed that toy to Robert in the hope of garnering some attention for his —"

Melinda's head began shaking before Claire had even finished her sentence. "Not Daniel. The other one."

"The other one? What other one?" And then she knew. Daniel hadn't sent the Jumping Jack to Robert Karble. *Isaac* had.

The Jumping Jack was Isaac's signature toy.

Well, that and his wooden roller track . . .

In a flash, she was back in her shop, standing next to Benjamin and peering at the display screen on the victim's camera — the pictorial comings and goings of the man's last few hours on earth available at the press of a button. One by one she mentally sifted through the pictures they'd seen before narrowing in on one in particular.

"That package changed everything for Robert."

Oh, what she wouldn't give to be standing in front of that camera once again. For if she were, she'd be zooming in on the image of the rock with the roller track plans on it . . .

"And, by the time I went home several hours later, I thought it had changed everything for me, too."

Something about Melinda's words hit pause on Claire's mental rewind. "Wait a minute. At breakfast that first morning, you said the Amish toy line was essentially your idea, didn't you?"

Melinda nodded.

"But it was really Isaac's, wasn't it?"

"Isaac didn't send that toy as a way to drum up jobs for the Amish. He sent it as a way to forge a connection I tried to cover with a toy line." Dropping her knees to the ground, Melinda stared at her running shoes and snorted. "Frankly, it was a brilliant idea — one that, in my opinion, would have had Karble Toys being the talk of every playgroup across the country for the foreseeable future. But once Ann got wind of what we were preparing to do, she started asking questions and Robert let his guilt get the better of him.

"Then" — Melinda pounded the floor with her fist — "wham-O! I was out as product manager in favor of a woman whose only experience with Karble Toys is the amount of money it generates for her and Robert and which boutique or spa she can spend it in once it does."

Claire cupped her head between her hands in a futile effort to follow the woman's ramblings but it was no use. The question she'd asked about Isaac had yielded the kind of answer that made her head spin. Fast.

"How ironic that he essentially demoted me back to public relations while he scrambled to cover his tracks, and *I'm* the one who swooped in and saved his hide in the end," Melinda mumbled as she flexed each foot. "The only thing I can't figure out is whether that qualifies as complete stupidity on my part, or sweet justice."

She tried to keep up with everything Melinda was saying, but it was hard. There were so many things that just didn't make sense. But every time she thought to ask about one thing, Melinda moved on to another until the mountain of questions Claire wanted to ask was so high she wasn't sure where to start.

Dropping her hands to her side, she took one last look into the Karbles' room, the sight of the Jumping Jack toy on the floor beneath Robert's tie helping to assemble her thoughts in a cohesive enough order.

"You said Isaac sent the toy as a way to make a connection with Robert, right?"

Again, Melinda nodded.

"Well, if he wasn't trying to garner attention for the toys he and Daniel make, what other kind of connection could he possibly have been trying to make?"

"A powerful one."

She watched as Melinda pulled her left knee upward again in order to have better access to her sneaker and its half-tied shoelace, the woman's peculiar choice of words making little to no sense. "You realize Isaac is *Amish,* right?"

Melinda finished tying her shoe and then looked up at Claire. "By nurture, yes. By nature, no."

"Excuse me?"

"Isaac is Amish because he was *raised* Amish, not because he was *born* Amish."

Claire cast about for a way to make sense of Melinda's distinction but her mind simply couldn't keep up. "I don't get what you're saying."

Pushing off the ground, Melinda rose to

her feet and addressed Claire as if she were learning disabled and unable to understand the simplest of directions. "Isaac's mother wasn't Amish. She was just unmarried, pregnant, alone, and desperate for a fresh start. Her parents, who were long dead, had grown up around the Amish and she remembered the stories they'd told her about them and their quiet, unassuming, *private* lives — stories that sounded appealing to a woman who felt she had no better choice. So she crafted a story about her husband's passing in an Amish community in the Midwest and her desire to start fresh in Heavenly with —"

"With her new baby," Claire said, completing Melinda's sentence. "Wow. I wonder if the Amish know this . . ."

"They don't." Melinda stretched her arms over her head and then bent at the waist, clearly gearing up for an early morning run. "Isaac only recently found out himself by way of a letter his mother left for him to open on his twenty-fourth birthday."

"But she's been gone for something like twenty years," Claire protested. "Why would she set aside a letter for that long?"

"Because she was twenty-four when she had him and felt he'd understand her choices better at the same age." Melinda pulled one arm to her side and twisted her body to the left and then the right. "Though, being twenty-four now myself, I can't imagine *anything* that would make me choose to live the way the Amish do. I'd go insane."

A swell of loyalty for Esther and Eli and all of her other Amish friends rose to the surface but she stuffed it back down. It was obvious Melinda would be heading out soon and there were too many things Claire still wanted to know about Isaac and Karble Toys. She could defend her friends and their lifestyle at another time.

"I guess I still don't understand why all of this would prompt Isaac to send one of his Jumping Jacks to the head of a major toy manufacturer if he wasn't trying to secure work for himself and his neighbors."

Melinda braced her hands against the wall and set about loosening the muscles of her calves. "It's like I said earlier . . . the toy was an attempt at making a connection. It was something the two of them had in common."

"You mean Isaac and Robert?"

"Yes. Isaac and his father."

She felt her lips part to accommodate the gasp that rose up in her throat and echoed through the hallway. "His *father*?"

"Pretty wild, isn't it?"

She tried to nod, tried to give some sort of indication she wanted to keep talking, but it was hard. Although she didn't know Isaac well, news of his make-believe Amish roots was tough to comprehend. He looked like an Amish man, conducted himself like an Amish man, and spoke like an Amish man.

Then again, he was Amish now. He'd made the choice to be baptized in his late teens. Melinda's revelation really didn't change that. Or did it?

"Did Robert know about Isaac before the package?" Claire finally asked.

"He had no idea. He was in his early twenties himself when he met Isaac's mother during a spring break trip from grad school. They enjoyed each other's company but made the mistake of letting their respective friends pressure them into a situation neither was ready to engage in. As soon as their evening together was over, they knew they'd made a mistake. They parted ways and never saw or spoke to each other ever again."

"And then he gets this package and automatically believes Isaac's claims?"

Melinda shrugged. "The guy's Amish. He wasn't asking for money, wasn't asking for anything. He just wanted to reach out to a man he'd only just learned about himself. That, plus math, was enough for Robert."

"Why did he tell you?"

"Because I happened to walk by as he was trying to make sense of Isaac's letter."

It was so much to take in and process at one time, but she did her best, storing what she'd learned thus far in the back of her mind and seeking as much additional information as possible. "So if that Jumping Jack was sent only to forge a connection with the father he never knew he had, then how did Robert end up here? In Heavenly? How did the whole Back to Basics toy line come about?"

Melinda let go of the wall then hooked first her left, and then her right arm behind the back of her head for what Claire suspected was one of the woman's final stretches. "Once he got over the shock of learning he had an adult son, Robert felt the need to get to know Isaac. He wanted to meet him in person but also knew he wasn't ready to tell Ann. The whole time he was telling me all of this, I was playing with the Jumping Jack. And it dawned on me that toys have changed a lot these last ten years or so. They've become much more passive and aren't really the kind of things that will hold many memories later in life. Next thing I knew, my wheels started turning, and I threw out the notion of a simple wooden toy line. Robert jumped on it, seeing it as a way to get to know Isaac and maybe even help him out a little.

"I asked if I could try my hand at product manager and he agreed. Two days later, I got bumped back to my regular public relations gig so that *Ann* could be more involved in the development of the new line." Melinda took several deep breaths before continuing, her hushed voice becoming less hushed with each passing word. "*Ann*. Ann *Karble*. The woman who shows up at the office twice a week to have lunch with her husband and spends the rest of the time working out, going to spas, and volunteering with all of those organizations that keep full-time homemakers busy and out of their husband's — and his employees' — hair."

She took a moment to absorb everything she was hearing, but it was hard to concentrate on much of anything besides Melinda's growing restlessness. "And he never told her about Isaac?"

"Nope."

"So how did he explain this sudden desire to make an Amish-inspired toy line?" Claire asked.

"He told her he'd always been fascinated with the simplicity of Amish life and felt there were enough others like him to warrant the line." Melinda tapped her finger to her wristwatch and yanked her head toward the staircase, the end to their conversation clearly upon them. But halfway down the hall, the woman doubled back just long enough to toss one last verbal grenade in Claire's direction. "The real question, though, isn't what he told her . . . it's whether she believed him or not."

CHAPTER 18

Claire claimed her spot at the long conference table in Al Gussman's back room and took a moment to smile a greeting at each of her fellow business owners. To her immediate left was Howard Glick, the owner of Glick's Tools 'n More. Beside him was Al, the proprietor of Gussman's General Store and the landlord for most of the buildings along Lighted Way. To her immediate right was Ruth Miller, Eli's twin.

The opposite side of the table played host to Keith Watson of Heavenly Tours, Sandra Moffit of Tastes of Heaven(ly), and Samuel Yoder of Yoder's Fine Furniture.

Al gestured toward the empty chair across from Ruth. "Anyone know if Lapp plans on being here this morning or not?"

"Daniel is home with Sarah. I am here for the toy shop today." All heads turned toward the door as Isaac stepped into the room and crossed to the chair Samuel pulled out for him. "I am sorry if I am late. Please continue."

"We haven't started yet, son. Glad you can be here." Al glanced down briefly at the handwritten agenda in front of him and cleared his throat. "The first couple of weeks of the month seemed to go well around here. The display tables everyone put out in front of their shops on the first two Saturdays seemed to be a nice way to draw folks inside. And, Claire? Those cornstalks you tied to the lampposts with those harvest-colored ribbons were a really nice touch. I saw quite a few tourists using those posts as backdrops for vacation photos."

The chorus of agreement that met Al's words set off a warm flush in Claire's cheeks. "It was my pleasure." And it was. Aside from her tasks at Heavenly Treasures, Claire thoroughly enjoyed her work on the one-woman Lighted Way Beautification Committee. The position combined two of her closet loves — seasonal decorating and being outdoors.

"I can't wait to see what you do for the Christmas season," Sandra said from her spot across from Howard. "Whatever you do, though, I'm sure it will be a draw."

Heads nodded up and down the table only to stop as Al took control of the agenda once again. "Unfortunately, as you all know, business the past few days hasn't been so good for any of us. My wife, Deidre, puts that on the fact that most of the festival-goers have headed home. I suppose there's a chance she's right, but my gut tells me it's what happened *at* that festival that's keeping folks away."

"My gut is saying the same thing, Al." Howard scooted his chair back from the table to accommodate the ever-growing belly that made him a shoo-in as Lighted Way's resident Santa in Claire's eyes. "It's like it was when Walter was murdered a couple of months ago. The curiosity mongers come out in droves to see the spot where it happened, and, in doing so, they keep the tourists away."

Claire peeked down the table at Isaac to gauge his reaction to the topic at hand but saw nothing to indicate the Amish man was even listening.

Keith took a gulp of Al's legendary not-so-great black coffee and grimaced. "Don't you worry, Heavenly will rebound sooner rather than later. People don't stay focused on any one thing for long these days. Give it time. Before you know it, there'll be a scandal in Breeze Point or Haddonville or someplace like that and everyone'll forget all about that Karble fellow. And if they don't, I'll fire off another feature article on one of our shops to the paper. Do that enough, and the good will begin to outweigh the bad."

Isaac's hands dropped to his lap, making Claire's heart ache for him in the process. To discover twenty-four years into your life that your dad is alive only to have him ripped away a month later seemed unusually cruel.

Al offered a grudging nod-shrug combination. "I guess there's something to be said for that line of thinking, Keith, though I wish the one time would have been enough. Can't help but feel two murders in as many months might start to hurt Heavenly's reputation." Turning his focus on Claire, Al nudged his chin toward the end of the table where a chair was normally placed for these meetings. "How's Diane holding up with everything she's had to deal with out at Sleep Heavenly? I didn't get to talk to her when she called to say she wasn't coming this morning. She alright?"

Claire pulled her focus from Isaac and fixed it, instead, on Al, the man's inquiry bringing yet another worry to the foreground of her mind. "Aunt Diane will be okay. She's still blaming herself for the break-in, and that's weighing on her more than I'd like to see. But that's not why she didn't come today. One of the couples staying with us this week wanted to take her to breakfast in Breeze Point. She'll be here next month and —"

"Excuse me, folks, mind if I interrupt for a few moments?" For the second time that morning, all heads turned toward the door. This time, though, it was Jakob, who stood just inside the threshold of the makeshift meeting room Al had set aside in the back of his store.

Rising to his feet, Al waved Jakob over. "Good morning, Detective Fisher. Welcome. Would you like me to set up a chair for you?"

Jakob declined but not before taking a moment to note each and every business owner seated at the table. The fact that the smile slipped from his face when he got to Claire wasn't lost on her. In fact, if she was honest with herself, it hurt. A lot. His odd behavior had come out of nowhere and left her feeling more than a little confused.

"I just wanted to stop in and assure everyone here that we're working around the clock to solve Robert Karble's murder. We know that a crime like this can impact a town on many levels, not the least of which is tourism. But we'll find our man and we'll put this mess behind us. You've got my word on that."

"Then, if all goes well, maybe those of us sitting around this table can stop feeling like our livelihoods are under attack." Howard took a hearty bite of the powdered donut he'd commandeered from the center of the table upon his arrival. "First, there was Walter's whole thing, then there was the toy deal that went awry and threatened a few of us at this table, and now . . . this. Almost makes me think Heavenly got dropped in the middle of a city somewhere."

"It could still happen, you know," Samuel said in the strong yet quiet voice that always made everyone stop and listen to the Amish furniture maker. "Just because that man is dead, it does not mean his company will not still make Amish toys."

"But without Daniel and Isaac's plans to use as guides —"

"Plans, schmans," Al said, cutting off Keith as he did. "How hard would it be to draw up a set of simple toy plans, make them out of wood, and call them Amish?"

"It wouldn't be hard at all," Howard mused. "They wouldn't truly be Amish made, but they could certainly be touted as Amish inspired."

"Karble Toys will not make Amish line. Robert is dead."

Isaac's mumbled confidence was eventually picked up by Keith. "You know something? Isaac is right. Assuming Karble Toys doesn't implode without its leader, *and* they have a public relations genius hidden away who actually *knows* what they're doing, the company is going to want to distance themselves from what happened to Karble as soon as possible."

"Why do you say that, Keith?" Al liberated a donut from the platter in the center of the table and hoisted it into his mouth.

"Toys are supposed to be happy. Murder isn't. The sooner they can push that black mark under the carpet the better. Launching a line of toys that will only serve as a reminder of what happened to the company's former president would bring what happened back into people's minds all over again. Someone with little experience in the business might see Karble's murder as a way to drive business on sympathy. But it wouldn't be long before they realized their mistake," Keith explained. "I'm just disappointed I didn't put two and two together before now."

Al lifted his half-eaten donut into the air and nodded at Keith. "And that, ladies and gentlemen of the Lighted Way Business Owners' Association, is why this guy is our marketing whiz. He thinks much faster and far savvier than the rest of us do."

And Al was right. Keith was a smart man. But Isaac had *come* to the meeting already convinced Karble Toys would abandon its plans for an Amish line in the wake of Robert's murder.

Was that simply because he, like Keith, had a feel for how such an event would play out in the business world? Or was it something more along the lines of a lucky guess?

Or, perhaps, wishful thinking?

"Wishful thinking," she whispered to herself mere seconds before a chill shot down her spine.

"What was that, Claire?"

At the mention of her name she looked up to find Jakob watching her curiously from his position behind Al. "Excuse me?"

"You just said something about wishful thinking."

In a scramble to cover her tracks, Claire quickly plastered a silly expression on her face and topped it off with a shrugged apology aimed at everyone seated around the table. "Oh, I'm sorry. I . . . I guess I was channeling a movie I watched last night before bed. It happens sometimes."

She knew she sounded like an idiot, but she didn't care. It was the best answer she could come up with in lieu of voicing the fear that had come from left field to add a second — and potentially stronger — suspect to the lineup previously reserved for Daniel Lapp.

Claire stepped out of Gussman's General Store and paused on the cobblestoned sidewalk to breathe in the crispness of the autumn day. The meeting had gone well with lots of ideas for the upcoming holiday season volleyed around, but even Claire knew she'd been a rather lackluster member of the monthly-meeting-turned-brainstorming-session.

It wasn't that she hadn't tried to give some input on how best to make Lighted Way reminiscent of Dickens. Because she had. But every time she tried to focus for longer than a moment or two on someone's decorating idea or suggested street-wide promotion, she found her thoughts wandering back toward Isaac. The fact the toy maker had bid a hasty retreat within minutes of Jakob's departure had only made things worse.

Twenty-four hours earlier, she'd been heartbroken at the very real possibility that

Daniel had killed Robert Karble in a desperate attempt to save his livelihood. Now, after everything she'd learned from Melinda that morning and observed on her own in Isaac during the meeting, she couldn't help but feel as if she'd had both the suspect and the motive wrong.

Isaac Schrock certainly had a lot of factors that warranted a turn in the hot seat. He had an emotional connection with the victim — one that could have just as easily been tinged with resentment as anything else. He'd shared his love of making toys with his father and was under the impression that shared connection was going to help not only him but his coworker and even some of the people in their community. And then, while feeling good about the unexpected benefit of reaching out to the victim, he's hit with the fact that his actions were leading the way to a business decision that was poised to hurt the same people that, only days earlier, had stood to benefit.

The man had no doubt been on quite a roller-coaster ride the past few weeks. The only question that remained was whether he'd snapped under the pressure of the twists and turns.

"I take it you and the detective have had some sort of disagreement?"

She looked over her shoulder and smiled at the plump man who'd just emerged from Al's side door. "Oh, hi, Howard, I thought you'd already left." Turning around, she planted an affectionate kiss on the seventy-something man with the burgeoning belly, stubbled chin, and shiny-as-a-new-penny bald spot on the top of his head. "Did you enjoy the meeting this morning?"

The owner of Glick's Tools 'n More tucked his thumbs behind the suspenders he always wore and rocked back on his heels, his wide smile and animated eyes quickly pulling her from the doldrums. "I enjoyed the donuts most of all. But some good ideas came up today, so I guess it was a good meeting, too."

It felt good to laugh, and in that moment she realized just how little laughing she'd been doing since the festival. "I won't tell Al you said that."

"Why? I just said that very same thing to him not more than two minutes ago."

She peeked around Howard's stout frame toward the general store's side entrance. "How did you come out after I did? When I left, the only one in there was Al."

"I thought, seeing as how I ate most of those donuts by myself, that the least I could do was take the plate into that little kitchen Al's got on the other side of the storeroom."

"Well, that was nice of you." And it was. She just didn't need to sound so fervent when she said it. But she knew why she had. Somehow, someway she was hoping Howard's happy-go-lucky demeanor could seep into her soul and get her through the rest of the day.

"So what's wrong, Claire? What's got you and Detective Fisher avoiding each other the way you did when he stopped by at the beginning of our meeting? That's not like the two of you."

She considered protesting his observation, maybe even chalking it up to the fact she hadn't slept all night, but, in the end, she knew it was futile. The problem, though, was how to answer without clueing the good-hearted town gossip in to the fact that Jakob and Martha were talking.

"It's nothing, really. He's just been distracted lately with the murder investigation and everything, and I've been distracted, too, worrying about Diane."

Like a dog who'd suddenly been thrown a bigger, better bone, Howard jumped on her words. "You tell Diane that Howard Glick says that break-in wasn't her fault. Whoever was after that Karble fellow was just finishing the job is all."

"Finishing the job?"

Howard filled his cheeks with air then slowly released it along with a slow, deliberate nod. "Of course. Seems to me that whoever ransacked that fellow's room was just making sure there wasn't any proof left behind tying him to the murder."

"But Robert Karble was murdered at the fairgrounds. How would there be any proof at an inn that's three-quarters of a mile or so down the road from the scene of the crime?"

"I'm not talking about physical proof like fingerprints or bloody shoe tracks or anything like that." More than a little aware of the way she was hanging on his every word, Howard paused long enough to run a hand along his stubbled jawline before stopping to scratch his chin. "What I'm talking about, Claire, is something that links the murderer to his victim."

"Like . . ." she prompted a bit impatiently.

"Like a picture or a letter. Something like that."

Reaching outward, she grabbed hold of the railing that led to the general store's front porch and used it to steady herself against the dizzying effects of Howard's comment.

A letter . . .

CHAPTER 19

It took every ounce of theatrics Claire could muster to unlock the front door of Heavenly Treasures and engage her first few customers with the kind of welcoming smile that came so naturally on any other given day. But with Esther having the day off, she really didn't have any other options. Besides, business had been slow enough the past few days she didn't need to make things worse by being unfriendly.

Still, even as she flashed just the right smile and answered any and all questions in an engaging fashion, she couldn't help but revisit her conversation with Howard. Everything the man had said made perfect sense.

The problem was where that perfect sense pointed. Or, rather, toward whom it pointed.

So much about Isaac Schrock as Robert's murderer fit. And it fit well.

But if she went to Jakob with everything

she'd learned and it turned out she was wrong, the repercussions from opening Isaac's box of secrets could end up needlessly hurting an awful lot of innocent people, including Isaac, himself.

No, she needed to be sure before she said anything. She had to be. Locking up his brother for murder would be hard enough on Jakob. Saddling him with that stress prematurely was unnecessary.

She'd tell him when she had proof.

Or when she verified her suspicion that Isaac's letter was missing from Robert's room.

The familiar snort of a horse via the shop's side window brought her to the screen in time to see Benjamin jump down from his buggy seat and reward the animal with a quick pat to the side of its long face. Judging by the hour, the man was making the first of many stops throughout the day to check in on his sister Ruth and her bake shop. Claire would have found it curious that it wasn't Eli in the alley if not for the fact that Esther wasn't working, either. With any luck, the young couple was finding ways to spend the day together as they moved toward an engagement everyone knew was coming.

When that day came, she knew she'd lose

Esther as an employee. For once an Amish woman married, her attention turned toward the home and the children she'd soon birth. It wasn't a day Claire looked forward to for herself, yet it was one she eagerly anticipated for her friends.

Eli and Esther were good people. They deserved happiness with each other.

Releasing the sigh that seemed to come out of nowhere, Claire turned back to the counter and the temporarily sidelined task of placing price tags on the latest round of handmade items Martha had sent in with Esther the previous day. Pricing was just one of many mundane tasks to do around the shop that day, and the longer she put it off, the later she'd be staying at the store.

"Good morning, Claire."

She looked up from the hand-sewn doll dress in her hands to find Benjamin standing in the open doorway between the actual store and the back room, his blue eyes trained on her face. Setting the dress down on the counter, she used the sides of her chocolate brown skirt to erase the sudden clamminess of her palms. "Benjamin. Hi. I saw you in the alley just now but I assumed you were here to check on Ruth."

A flash of red rose in his cheeks only to disappear with the swipe of a strong, callused hand and a curiously timed cough. "I will look in on Ruth, but I want to see how you are this morning."

She felt the matching flush as it marched across her own face, claiming all attempts at an intelligent reply. "Oh. Okay. Sure."

He allowed himself to take in her day's attire, his gaze moving quickly down the sage green sweater set that looked surprisingly good with the midcalf-length skirt she'd paired with simple boots. When he reached the ground, he returned his focus to her face and the simple high ponytail she'd pulled together as she was walking out of the inn that morning.

"You, you look very . . . pretty. But that does not stop the worry I see in you. Or the worry I feel *for* you."

His voice still held its normal strength, yet, at the same time, it was raspy with an emotion that seemed out of character. It left her scrambling for something to say that could lessen the sudden charge in the room.

"Please do not worry about me, Benjamin. We both have enough on our plate right now without adding things that just don't matter."

"You matter, Claire. To me."

She blinked away the moist haze ushered in by his words. "I . . . I'm fine. Really."

He took a handful of tentative steps into the showroom only to stop just shy of the items she was no longer pricing. "I thought about what you said. About Daniel and his toy business. I do not want to believe he would be driven to sin by money. It is not his way. It is not the Amish way."

Twelve hours ago, she'd have given some thought to arguing Benjamin's claim; the note from Sarah, coupled with everything she'd learned from Esther about Daniel's farm, giving her grounds to at least consider Daniel Lapp for murder. But now, after her talk with Melinda and her own observations at the monthly business meeting that morning, her suspicions were shifting.

To a *different* Amish man.

She allowed herself to meet Benjamin's intense gaze despite the emotion she was still fighting to hold back with a few well-timed blinks. Only now, the confusing feelings his genuine concern and telling words had stirred up were slowly morphing into more of the worry variety. How did she tell him she suspected yet another member of his peaceful community? How did she tell him that a man he knew and respected had come into the Amish community on a lie?

You don't . . .

But even as her heart nixed the notion of

uttering Isaac's name aloud, her head was all too aware of the plaguing questions that needed to be asked and answered. By somebody.

"There is something else — something new, is there not?"

His spot-on assessment of her mental state renewed the threat of tears and started the rapid-fire blinking once again. Never, in her life, had she ever met a man who seemed as if he was able to see inside her soul and know when something was wrong regardless of whatever false bravado she felt compelled to display. Finding him now — and in an Amish form — seemed almost punishing.

"Benjamin Miller is Amish, dear. Forgetting that will only bring you heartache."

She closed her eyes against the mantra Aunt Diane had taken to spouting during their many special talks and willed her heart to embrace the sentiment. Although she found the increase in similar reminders tiresome at times, she couldn't argue the why behind the words. Benjamin touched something inside her, plain and simple. And no matter how many times she denied that fact to her aunt, she knew, deep down, it was true.

So, too, did Diane.

"I am here."

The feel of Benjamin's hand on her arm, coupled with the sincerity of his words in her ear, forced her to open her eyes and focus. "I just learned that someone who is close to people I know is not what he seems. Or, rather, he is what he seems *now,* but he didn't come about it in the way they believe."

Now that the floodgate was open, she began to ramble. "I mean, it wasn't his fault; he wasn't party to the misinformation and didn't even know about it himself until he opened a letter a few weeks ago . . . but he does now and I worry what that knowledge will do for his relationships and what it may have made him do to one that didn't go as he'd planned."

There. She'd said it.

Though, what exactly she'd said was hard enough to remember let alone try to decipher. Even for her.

With obvious reluctance, Benjamin removed his hand from Claire's upper arm and took a long, deep breath, exhaling it just as slowly. "A letter?"

She nodded. "It was written for him more than twenty years ago and . . ." The seemingly generic story crumbled on her tongue as Benjamin shifted from foot to foot in a way that suggested he understood far more of the story than she'd chosen to share.

His response served as confirmation. "You're talking about Isaac, are you not?"

Unsure of what to say, she looked down at the floor.

"I have always wondered about his mother. I think many Amish did. She did not know things she should have known," Benjamin explained before allowing his gaze to fix on a spot somewhere over Claire's head. Geographically he was standing in Heavenly Treasures just as surely as Claire. But in terms of whatever was playing through his thoughts at that moment, he was somewhere very different. "I remember when Isaac's mother came here. I was ten, maybe eleven. She sat on a bench next to me at church that first day."

She waited for him to explain how the woman's choice of church seating had alerted a young Benjamin to something being amiss, but, instead, he went on, citing a few more examples as he did.

"Then, when it was her turn to have services at her house, I went with Dat on the bench wagon the day before the service. When I went to the door to tell her Dat had arrived with benches, she did not know she was to host." Benjamin sidestepped his way to the edge of the counter and leaned heavily against it, the weight of his childhood suspicions coming to roost.

And then she got it. Regardless of which Amish community you lived in, Amish families took turns hosting a Sunday service for their district. It wasn't something confined just to Heavenly. As a supposedly Amish woman, Isaac's mother should have known that.

"But what was it about her sitting with you that you found odd?" Claire finally asked.

"Men and boys sit on one side of the room for service. Women and girls sit on the other." Benjamin paused to study her before going on, his not-so-subtle attempt to gauge her reaction to the tradition catching her by surprise. "I whispered her mistake to her. But even as young boy, I knew something was not right. These were things she should have known."

She willed herself to concentrate on the conversation unfolding between them rather than the flutter in her chest every time he looked at her in the way that he did. "Will Isaac be kicked out?"

Benjamin pushed off the counter, his head shaking side to side almost immediately. "No. Of course not. Isaac was baptized. He accepted the Amish life for himself. He is Amish now just as I am Amish."

She inhaled a sense of relief only to have it disappear against a reality she'd managed to ignore thus far. "You're not going to tell anyone, are you?"

"I do not see why I —"

"Because his real identity stands to hurt more than just Isaac. And she's been through so much already this week that I . . . I can't imagine burdening her with something like that."

Benjamin drew back in confusion. "I do not understand. Who do you speak of being upset? Mary Schrock died many, many years ago."

She opened her mouth to answer but closed it just as quickly. The way Isaac had come to be was not all that unusual any longer. Television programs and newspaper stories had desensitized the English to such accounts, removing much of the surprise to such real-world tales in the process. But for the Amish, the notion of a child growing up amid lies of their paternity was a novelty.

"Claire?" Benjamin prodded again. "Please. I do not understand what you say."

There was a part of her that wanted to tell him everything about Isaac's true paternity and the fears it had stoked in her heart.

But there was also a part of her — a part she hadn't been aware of until that very moment — that wanted to view the world through Benjamin's untainted eyes, instead. After all, it was a far nicer view than the one her world afforded at times.

Knowing she had to give him some sort of answer, she offered the best one she could without telling more than absolutely necessary. "I'm talking about the woman who was married to Isaac's father. Learning of Isaac's existence on the heels of her husband's death might just be the thing that brings on a nervous breakdown."

For several long minutes, Benjamin said nothing. He merely stood there, watching her. And as he did, she realized she didn't mind. In fact, if she was honest with herself, there was something comforting about being in a room with this man. He didn't judge, he didn't saddle her with expectations to be something she wasn't, and he seemed to genuinely care about her thoughts and her feelings.

Eventually, though, he spoke, the accuracy of his quiet assessment more than a little impressive. "Isaac's father was the man from the toy company, yah? The man who was murdered at the festival?"

She tried to nod but wasn't entirely sure

if she'd been successful.

"That is why he came to Heavenly to make our toys." Since he hadn't phrased his comment in the form of a question, she simply remained silent as Benjamin continued connecting the dots. "But it did not go the way Isaac wished. Instead of good, it turned bad."

"Or it would have if Robert Karble hadn't been murdered." She hated that she had to add that caveat to Benjamin's synopsis of the events, but knowing what she now knew about the originating letter, the deal-gone-bad, Daniel's partial farm, and the victim's ransacked room, she simply couldn't ignore its presence.

Silence blanketed the space between them for the second time and she found herself wondering if she'd overstepped. In less than twenty-four hours, she'd all but accused two different Amish men from Benjamin's community of the unthinkable. But just as she was searching for something to say to offset her potentially offending comment, his mouth turned upward in the faintest hint of a smile.

"You need time to not worry. Time to be at ease and to smile. The worry will not go away because you do, but it will be easier to face after some time to take a breath." He swept his hand toward the screen window she'd first spied him from. "I go next door, to the bake shop. Ruth will pack dinner. I will get it . . . and you . . . when the shop is closed. We will have a picnic and smile. When it is done, I will take you back to the inn and you will sleep. We will decide what to do about Isaac and Daniel tomorrow."

"*We* will decide?" she repeated in an emotion-filled voice she could do little to squelch.

"Yah. We will do. Together."

She considered arguing, citing his friendship with both men as a reason he shouldn't get involved, but she couldn't. Because deep down inside, she knew she wanted Benjamin's help in tracking down Robert's killer. He was smart, he was observant, he had access to the Amish in ways she didn't, and he wasn't one to rush to a careless conclusion.

The fact they'd also be spending more time together *as* they pursued the truth was completely beside the point.

Or was it?

Chapter 20

If Claire could freeze the highlights of her time in Heavenly and stick them on a shelf to be relived at will, there was little doubt which ones she'd choose . . .

Her first morning in town.

The day she told Diane she was staying.

The first moment she saw the Heavenly Treasures' shingle above the door of her shop.

And that exact second; sitting on the buggy seat beside Benjamin with a carefully packed picnic basket behind them and the anticipation of their time together lifting her heart in a way she couldn't ignore.

She knew Diane was right. She knew there could never be anything between them of any romantic nature, but still it felt nice. Nice to know her company was enjoyed, nice to know someone wanted to get to know the person she was inside, nice to know her happiness meant so much to another human being.

"I never get tired of the peacefulness I feel every time I travel this part of town," she mused above the hypnotic sounds of the horse. "It's like your way of life quiets the everyday stress of my own."

With a gentle firmness, Benjamin steered the horse off the main road and onto the familiar dirt path that would take them to the top of the wooded hill he'd first shared with her two months earlier. Once they were on the winding trail, he relaxed his hold on the reins and turned to Claire. "Your life is stressful?"

Realizing she'd given a false impression, she rushed to set things right. "No, not in the way you must think. My life is very calm now. I love my quiet time with Aunt Diane, I love meeting the guests who check in to the inn each week, and I love the homey feel of that big, rambling house." She raised her chin and breathed in the clean country air. "And I love the shop. I love seeing all of the items Martha and Esther make, I love seeing my own candles on the shelves and knowing customers enjoy them, too, and I love the friendships I've made with Esther and Ruth and Eli and . . . you . . . *because* of my shop."

"Then I do not understand what causes

the stress you speak of."

She rested her hand on his forearm and did her best to ignore the warmth she felt beneath his sleeve. "Could you stop the buggy for just a moment? I think it might be easier to show you."

With a tug, Benjamin brought the horse to a stop, the chirping of some distant birds and the gentle tap of branches above their heads taking over for the *clip-clop* of the animal's feet. She closed her eyes and savored nature's soothing melody intertwined with the rise and fall of Benjamin's quiet breath. "Do you hear that?"

She opened her eyes at his audible pause. "You don't, do you?"

"I do not hear anything besides the birds and the trees."

"Exactly. All you hear out here are God's noises. In town and over by the inn, it's different. Sure, the traffic sounds aren't as pervasive as they were in New York, but it's still there. Horns still honk on occasion, car engines still rev, doorbells still ring, and lawn mowers still sputter to life." She held her hands out to her sides and motioned toward the absence of those same things around them. "But here . . . where you live . . . it's not like that. I guess that's why I feel my happiest when I'm here. Like I'm closer to God, somehow."

When he said nothing, she looked back at him to find that he was staring intently at her. She felt her cheeks warm in a way for which the last of the sun's rays couldn't take credit.

"You really feel that?" he finally asked, his normally strong voice almost hoarse.

"I feel that every single time, Benjamin." And it was true. She just hadn't intended to sound quite so Pollyanna when she said it.

Suddenly uncomfortable, she hooked her finger over her shoulder in the direction of the picnic basket and made a show of sniffing the air. "Ruth didn't happen to pack fried chicken in that basket, did she?"

A slow smile made its way across Benjamin's face just before he urged the horse to resume its trip up the slow, winding hill. "Yah, I think that she did. That is good, yah?"

She had to laugh. "It is *very* good." She looked behind them at the basket and the folded red-checkered blanket it rested on. "How did she have the time to put that together with everything else your sister does at Shoo Fly?"

"That is Ruth's job. Farming is what Eli and I do."

"Ruth bakes cookies and pies. She doesn't

pack picnic dinners for fellow shopkeepers," she reminded.

"Such picnics are a new idea Ruth has for bake shop. She will pack picnics for visitors to eat at the park. She will be happy to try on us, first."

She clapped her hands together at the news. "Oh, Benjamin, what a wonderful idea. There are so many pretty little spots in and around Heavenly that the tourists will be able to enjoy even more now with an idea like that." She felt the cadence of the horse slow ever so slightly as they moved through the trail's lone covered bridge and emerged into the wide-open clearing on the other side. "Ruth really is a very smart business-woman."

This time, when Benjamin tugged the horse to a stop, it was for real. Jumping down from his seat, he came around the front of the horse to offer Claire a hand down. When she was safely on the ground, he reached into the back of the buggy and retrieved the basket and blanket from inside. "Where should we sit?"

She looked around them, her gaze quickly coming to rest on the large rock where they'd sat to stargaze as summer drew to a close. With the blanket spread out across the top, it would be a perfect makeshift table. She said as much to Benjamin.

Five minutes later, their outdoor table was complete with heaping plates of food and a small vase of fresh flowers Ruth had sent along for ambience. He pointed to one end of the rock. "Would you like to sit, Claire?"

Nodding, she took the place he'd indicated while simultaneously wondering what, exactly, Benjamin had said to his sister about the nature of their picnic. Surely Ruth had to know it was a simple friendship . . .

"You should see your face as I see it right now," Benjamin said. "It makes me think of Eli and Ruth when they were little and Dat had made a toy for them."

She struggled to find words to describe the smile she knew she wore despite the nagging reality that tugged at her heart. "When I was a little girl, I used to dream about going on a picnic with my prince one day."

Benjamin's brows furrowed beneath the brim of his hat. "I am not a prince. I am Amish."

My Amish prince . . .

In an effort to keep things light, she made a face. "I was ten when I dreamed that. But even though I'm older now, the notion of a picnic still makes me happy. Hence, the smile I can feel on my face."

He bowed his head over his plate and offered a prayer before encouraging her to try his sister's food. "I asked Ruth to put in chocolate chip cookies. She said they were your favorite."

She looked up from her plate, the question that had been flitting in and out of her head since he'd first mentioned Ruth finally finding its way out of her mouth. "Didn't Ruth think it was strange you were taking me on a picnic?"

"She did not say."

A second thought struck on the heels of the first, widening her eyes as it did. "You didn't tell her about Isaac, did you?"

"I said I would not." Benjamin worked his way around the chicken bone and then deposited it back on his plate. "Ruth worries like you do."

She stopped midbite of her own chicken and stared at the man. "Ruth suspects Isaac, too?"

"No, she worries about everyone. You worry about your aunt and your friends. Ruth worries about Eli."

"She worries about Eli? Why?"

He reached for a second piece of chicken but paused it just shy of his mouth. "She worries for Eli as we all do. We worry his temper will cause problems."

Returning her chicken to the plate, she reached for one of two bottles of water Ruth had included in the basket. "The two of you don't need to worry about Eli and his temper as much anymore. He will keep it in check because of Esther. He doesn't want to do anything to lose the trust of the woman he wants to marry."

He offered a slow nod. "I believe that, too. And it is as good a reason as any for Eli to grow into a man."

"Then Ruth can stop worrying as much, right?"

"Eli is not all that worries Ruth. She worries for her big brother, too."

Claire looked down at her plate, mentally ticking off the names of each of Ruth's brothers and sisters. When she was done, she met Benjamin's eyes with her own. "But you are her only older brother, aren't you?"

"Yah."

She felt her stomach churn with dread. "But *why*? Are you sick?"

He looked down at his plate and shook his head. "I am not sick."

"Then why is she worried about you?"

Slowly, his chin lifted until his focus was back on Claire. "She worries that I am alone. She worries that ten years have passed since Elizabeth. She worries that I will live a lonely life."

Elizabeth.

Benjamin's first wife.

The same Amish woman Jakob had been in love with at one time, too.

There was so much she wanted to know about Benjamin's first wife, questions that came to her at the oddest of times. Yet, at the same time, they were questions sure to yield answers she didn't necessarily want to hear.

Instead, she searched for something to say that would keep her own hard-to-explain heart in one piece. "Do you worry about that?"

His gaze left hers and traveled to a distant place she could only guess about. "Three or four months ago, I did not worry. But now, I do not know. I think there is worry but it is for choices I did not expect."

"Choices?"

A flash of something resembling pain skittered across his face only to disappear behind stoicism in both word and stance. "Choices I can not make."

She reached again for her water, observing the man on the other side of the picnic blanket as she did. For someone as normally straightforward as Benjamin Miller, his cryptic answers left her feeling confused and ready for a change in topic, even if that change brought them back to the same stressful place she'd been anxious to leave when they set out on their picnic.

"So I know I threw a lot on you this morning about Isaac, but had you given any more thought to the things I said about Daniel before that?"

"Daniel . . ." Another pause was quickly replaced by the man's full attention — both verbally and visually. "I did. But today, after what you said about Isaac, I wonder if there is not a different person who could have killed the toy maker."

Her shoulders drooped under the weight of his words. "Oh, Benjamin. If we're right and Isaac did this, how on earth are we going to tell Martha . . . *and Esther?*" There was so much about uncovering the identity of Walter Snow's murderer that had been exciting, but nothing more so than seeing the subsequent smile on Esther's face. But now, she couldn't help but cringe at the image of having to tell the young woman that her Uncle Isaac had snapped and done the unthinkable.

"I do not speak of Isaac. I speak of a different person."

She stared at him across the mouth of her water bottle and tried to make sense of what she was hearing. "A different person? I don't . . . wait. Are you saying you think someone other than Daniel or Isaac killed Robert Karble?"

For several long minutes, he said nothing. But then, just as she feared he wasn't going to answer, he finally did, the hesitant way in which he shared his thoughts out of character for a man with such quiet and understated confidence. "I do not know much of the English world. But today, while I was in the fields, I tried to think of how I would feel if I learned such news of Elizabeth."

At a loss for what he was getting at, she simply kept quiet, her thoughts racing to dissect his words while her ears stayed tuned for further clarification.

Benjamin did not disappoint. "*I* could not kill at that news, but perhaps someone else could."

She set her water bottle back on the blanket and leaned forward. "Benjamin, please. I'm not following what you're saying."

Dragging a hand down his clean-shaven face, the man released a troubled sigh. "Women kill in the English world, yah?"

She drew back. "Women? Of course. Statistically I imagine men are responsible for far more of the country's murders than women are, but they by no means have a corner on the market. Why do you ask?"

"Today. At the shop. You feared the toy maker's wife would be hurt if she found out about Isaac, yah?"

"Yah — I mean, yes," she quickly corrected. "Ann just lost her husband. She can't possibly handle hearing that kind of news right now. Especially when all she ever wanted was to give Robert a child of their own."

"But what if she had known of Isaac *before* the toy maker's death? Would she still be hurt or would she be angry?"

CHAPTER 21

Benjamin and his buggy were halfway down Lighted Way before Claire finally turned and went inside. She tried to rationalize her decision to linger on the inn's front porch to a few more moments of fresh air before retiring for the night, but it was more than that and she knew it.

Spending the evening with Benjamin had been magical. Simply being in his presence had a way of making her feel as if the last piece in her self-puzzle had been set in place, allowing her to finally complete the picture she'd always envisioned for her life.

Moving to Heavenly had brought her peace. The kind of peace that enabled her to accept who she was and what she wanted for herself.

Opening Heavenly Treasures had been about accomplishing a dream and becoming a part of something special.

Spending time with Benjamin helped

reinforce something she'd only recently started to believe. Suddenly, the notion that she had a lot to offer as a person seemed to be shared with someone else — someone other than her aunt or her employee-turned-friend, Esther.

There was no reason for Benjamin to seek her out the way he did. No reason he needed to care about her accidental sleuthing. No reason he needed to ask his sister to pack a picnic dinner for an English woman. Yet he did. Because he enjoyed her company every bit as much as she enjoyed his. And it felt good.

She shut the door behind her and then stepped into the parlor, the shadows from the many dancing candle flames in the room calling to her with their usual beckoning gesture. One day, she knew she'd buy a small home of her own, but for now the inn was everything she wanted and needed in a home. It was warm, it was inviting, and it was safe.

Like Benjamin . . .

"I see Benjamin Miller brought you home again, dear."

Claire jumped a little at the sound of her aunt's voice, the woman's presence difficult to decipher in the dimly lit room. "Oh, Aunt Diane . . . I didn't see you in here." She hurried across the room and planted a kiss on the top of the woman's head. "What are you doing in here" — she glanced at the open book on the armrest of Diane's chosen chair — "reading?"

"I was. Until I heard Mr. Miller's horse and I realized he was driving you home . . . again. That's when I stopped reading."

Claire lowered herself to the comfortable ottoman that housed her aunt's feet and gestured toward the cozy mystery the woman had selected. "Is it because you need better lighting or is the book not as good as you'd hoped?"

Diane lifted the book off the armrest and flipped it over, a slight smile playing at the corners of her lips as she took in a line or two of the story before setting it in her lap. "It's actually quite good. But it's hard to read when you're worried."

"Aunt Diane, please tell me you're not still blaming yourself for what happened upstairs. Because whoever did that to the Karbles' room would have gotten in no matter what security measure you put in place. They were motivated to get into that room."

With careful fingers Diane removed her reading glasses to afford an unobstructed view of her only niece. "No, dear. The worry I'm talking about is the worry I have when

I think of what you're doing to yourself."

"Doing to myself?" she echoed. "What are you talking about?"

"When you married Peter, I wanted nothing more than to talk you out of that decision because I knew he wasn't right for you. He was too focused on his image and himself to ever see you the way he should." Diane stopped, took a breath, and then continued, the woman's spot-on assessment making it difficult for Claire to breathe. "But I said nothing because you seemed so in love with him and all I wanted was for you to be happy."

She reached out, gently squeezed her aunt's forearm, and then stood, the angst that always accompanied talk of her ex-husband propelling her feet around the room with no real destination in mind. When she reached the thick velvet drapes that hindered her view of the night sky over Heavenly's Amish fields, she turned back. "I'm not sure I really knew who I was then. At least that's the only reason I can come up with for not seeing what was in front of my face all along."

"You are a smart woman, dear. Just look at everything you've accomplished in the past year." Diane swiveled her body around to face Claire. "You found the courage to leave New York and come here, you recognized the difference in how you felt in these surroundings, you crafted a business plan for Heavenly Treasures, leased a storefront, opened the shop, and made new friends. Good friends."

All she could do was nod. Diane was right. Her life was so much better, richer now.

But she already knew that . . .

"I couldn't agree more," she finally said as she wandered past her aunt and over to the floor-to-ceiling bookshelves that adorned the wall opposite the window.

"Then how can you come so far in such a short period of time in those aspects, but be exactly where you were with Peter when it comes to not seeing what's in front of your face?"

She whirled around to find her aunt eyeing her closely. "Diane, I don't have the foggiest idea what you're driving at right now."

"I'm talking about Benjamin, dear."

Her cheeks warmed at the mere mention of his name. "Benjamin?" she parroted.

"From the first moment you laid eyes on him outside Shoo Fly Bake Shoppe, you knew he was Amish. In fact, there's no way you could miss that fact. He wears black pants, black shoes, a simple long-sleeved shirt, suspenders, and a black rimmed hat.

He doesn't have a beard but only because his wife died within six months of their marriage."

She steadied herself against the back of the couch, then made her way around it to sink into its depths. Everything her aunt said was right and it was everything she knew in her head to be right, as well. But her heart didn't want to see those things. Her heart wanted to see Benjamin for something he wasn't.

Just like Peter . . .

Pitching her body forward, she dropped her head into her hands and bit back the sob that was no more than seconds away. "Oh, Diane . . . what am I doing?"

"You're feeling again, dear." Slowly, Diane rose from her chair, crossed the room, and sat down beside Claire. "And that's good. It's what I want for you. But I don't want you to go down a road that is nothing more than a dead end. And that's what this is with Benjamin, dear. It can't go anywhere. For either of you."

"My head knows that, it really does. But, Diane, he *sees* me. He *hears* me. He makes me feel" — she swallowed back the lump that crept its way up her throat again and again — *"special."*

She felt Diane's arms around her, felt

273

their normal warmth and understanding, but for the first time in Claire's life she doubted whether they could make things right.

"Because you are, dear. And Benjamin is not the only one in this town who sees that."

At her answering silence, Diane began to tick off names. "*I* see it. Esther sees it. Eli sees it. Howard sees it. Al sees it. Everyone who ever stays in this inn sees it. *Jakob* sees it . . ."

Disengaging herself from her aunt's arms, she met the woman's gaze head-on. "You always do that. You always bring Jakob into every discussion we have about Benjamin. Why do you do that?"

"Because Jakob is a much more suitable partner for you, dear." Diane folded her hands in her lap and leaned heavily against the back cushions of the couch. "He is handsome, smart, genuine, kind, and more than a little smitten with you."

Claire snorted. "Smitten with me? Uh, no . . . he might be all those other things but he's most definitely not smitten with me."

Diane's eyes widened, affording Claire a look at her own reflection in their depths. "How can you say that? He lights up every time he sees you, you're the only person in this entire town who could actually convince him to go to the festival, and he shows up here much more than he should."

The truth in her aunt's words lifted her spirits momentarily before the reality of Jakob's recent behavior took center stage. Maybe her aunt had been right at one time. But not anymore. She said as much aloud.

"Dear, you can't fault him for becoming discouraged when you haven't given him any reason to think you have feelings for him, too." Diane disengaged her hands from each other and reached, instead, for one of Claire's. "Perhaps he's beginning to think you aren't interested."

She waited a beat to keep from seeming rude and then tugged her hand from inside her aunt's and rose to her feet. "I'm not."

Diane's brows furrowed. "You're not what?"

"Interested." Lifting her arms into the air, Claire let them fall to her side just as quickly. "I'm not interested in Jakob. I'm not interested in Benjamin. I'm not interested in anyone right now." She took a step away from the couch only to reclaim her spot beside Diane as the tears began to fall. "Oh, Diane, what is wrong with me? How can I have feelings for two such different men? Especially when one isn't possible and the other is showing signs of giving up?"

She swiped at the tears as Diane's palm found her back and attempted to rub away the sadness. "Shhh . . . I don't believe Jakob has lost interest. I really don't."

"Then you didn't see him at the monthly business meeting this morning. He avoided making eye contact almost the entire time. And it was so blatant even Howard asked about it." The words poured from her mouth as the stress of the past few days reached its saturation point. "I . . . I wouldn't have thought anything of it if he hadn't dismissed me the other day when we were talking out by the pond. In fact, once Martha showed up, he couldn't get rid of me fast enough."

Diane's gasp alerted Claire to her mistake. "Martha?"

Leaning forward, she dropped her head into her hands and moaned. "Diane . . . please. Can you pretend I didn't just say that? I promised I'd keep it quiet."

When Diane didn't respond, Claire repeated her plea. "Please, Diane? I gave my word."

"Then I won't ask and I won't repeat what you just said," Diane said. "But you have to know the notion of those two speaking is cause for celebration."

"For you and me — maybe. For Martha's family and the rest of the Amish community — not so much. But, either way, I promised I wouldn't say anything to anyone."

Diane pulled her hand from Claire's back and used it, instead, to guide her niece's face up and to the side until they were looking at each other. "Did you ever stop to think Jakob's odd behavior might have something to do with that?"

She blinked against the tears in an effort to clear the hazing effect that made it difficult to truly see Diane in the flickering candlelight. "No. I mean, Jakob knows I've been pushing to see the two of them together ever since I met them. And Martha? She has to know it. How could she not?"

"You could ask him, dear." Diane wiped a stray tear from Claire's cheek with a gentle thumb. "Then, if you find out you've done something to upset him, you'll know. If an apology is called for, you give one and you move on. But by asking, you just may find out his coolness is because of stress or any number of things that are completely unrelated to you. Do that, and maybe you can put an end to that ache in your heart."

"There isn't an ache." But even as she said the words, she knew they weren't true. She was hurting over Jakob's sudden disinterest in their friendship. She'd been kind to him since his arrival in town. She'd been a good friend, and even if nothing more ever came from their time together, it hurt to be treated as if she'd done something wrong.

Fortunately, she didn't have to contradict herself aloud. Diane simply knew. She gathered her wits long enough to say what needed to be said before her throat closed completely. "I love you, Aunt Diane."

The tears that had been confined to Claire's face made a mirrored performance on Diane's. "That makes me a very rich woman, my dear. A very rich woman, indeed." With one last tender touch to Claire's face, Diane stood and made her way toward the staircase and the all-too-short night of sleep that remained before rising to make breakfast for the guests. At the bottom of the stairs, she turned and smiled at Claire. "Ask him what's wrong. Whatever answer he gives, it's better than guessing."

And with that, Diane made her way upstairs, leaving Claire to ponder everything with a clarity that had gotten buried under the stressful weight of the last few days. It was time to pull back and look at everything with a fresh pair of eyes.

Jakob.

Ann.

Isaac.

Everyone.

Rising to her feet, she took a moment to blow out each of the candles around the parlor before striking out in the same direction Diane had just gone. Somehow, Claire had to find a way to sleep. Doing without it for one night had been bad enough. She didn't need another encore.

Step by step she ascended the stairs to the inn's second floor and the privacy her room afforded at the end of the hall. Perhaps a warm soak in the tub would take the much-needed calm ushered in by Diane and transform it into the precursor for a restful night's sleep.

She could hope, anyway.

Yet as she moved down the hallway, she found herself drawn to Melinda's partially opened door and the purposeful tap of a keyboard on the other side. She knocked softly. "Melinda? Can I come in?"

Melinda paused her fingers on the keys and peered out at Claire through the open space. "Uh . . . yeah. Sure." Wrapping her hands around her laptop, Melinda moved the gadget to the nightstand beside her bed and sat up tall. "What can I do for you, Claire?"

She pointed at the still lit screen and the

several paragraphs she couldn't read from the doorway. "You're up late. Working?"

Her inquiry was met with a half nod, half shrug. "Trying to. The boss's murder is proving to be quite a public relations challenge. You know, how to spin it in such a way that Karble Toys is seen as sympathetic."

Leaning against the door frame, Claire studied the strikingly attractive woman she knew was in her midtwenties. "I would imagine that would be pretty easy considering the man was murdered."

"That may have been the case if he wasn't murdered in an area inhabited by people the world sees as peaceful. And *after* the company announced in-house that it was reneging on its word to those same peaceful people."

"Wow. I hadn't thought of it that way."

Melinda gestured toward the screen saver that appeared in place of the document she'd been typing, its image of billowing white curtains parting to provide a panoramic view of the ocean spectacular. "That's why I'm still up at eleven o'clock. Because I have my work cut out for me trying to spin this whole ordeal. If I don't get it just right, I'll be out of a job."

"And if you get it right?" she asked.

"I can write my ticket with any company I want."

Claire parted company with the doorway and took a few tentative steps into Melinda's room. "Your ticket? What ticket?"

"To that." Melinda nudged her chin in the direction of the beach scene that faded into darkness a second later.

"A beach?"

"A beach *house*," Melinda corrected. "*My* beach house." Retrieving the computer from its temporary perch, the woman splayed her fingers across the keyboard once again, her face and shoulders suddenly sporting a look of impatience. "Which won't be my beach house if I don't get back to this press release. It really needs to go out tomorrow."

The statement, while fairly innocuous all on its own, was obviously Claire's hint to leave. Now.

"Oh. Yeah. Okay. I'm sorry. I'll leave you to your work then." Claire turned and retraced her steps back to the door only to stop and turn toward Melinda once again. "Melinda?"

The tapping that had accompanied her short trek to the door ceased long enough for a sigh to become the only audible sound in the room. "Yes?"

"Aren't you a little worried about what'll

happen if Isaac's letter gets out?"

Melinda's left eyebrow rose upward. "Isaac's letter?"

"Yeah. The one you told me about this morning . . . or last night . . . or whenever we were talking out in the hall."

"The only way it would *get out,* as you say, is if I *let* it get out."

Claire took in everything about the woman now sizing her up from the bedroom-turned-makeshift-office, Melinda's not-so-quiet confidence impossible to miss. "What do you mean?"

"I have the letter, Claire. I've had it all along."

CHAPTER 22

For the second night in a row, Claire watched the moon make its way across her darkened room only to be bullied away by the first of the sun's morning rays. She'd wanted to sleep, intended to sleep, but when she finally slipped into her pajamas and wiggled under the covers after her impromptu talk with Melinda, her brain simply wouldn't shut off.

Quite the contrary, in fact.

Suddenly her mental list of suspects in Robert Karble's murder had gotten rather lengthy with each and every member boasting a workable motive.

First, there was Daniel — the Amish toy maker who had been the only person on the list as recently as twenty-four hours ago. The motive Claire had fashioned for him still held water, with money having been the driving force behind the crime.

Rolling onto her side, she retrieved the

wrinkled piece of paper Sarah Lapp had forced into her hand out of fear for her husband and his future. And even now, in the sparse light invited into the room by the curtains she routinely failed to close, the reason for her suspicion was hard to miss.

If Daniel's catalogue business dried up in light of Karble Toys' ability to mass-produce and market its Amish line on a far superior scale, the soon-to-be father of five would be forced to earn his income elsewhere. Unfortunately, the recent sale of more than half of his farmland to a neighbor eliminated his original income source as a viable option.

Had desperation made the normally peaceful man snap?

Next on the list was Isaac with the kind of motive she never could have imagined yet now was incapable of forgetting. She glanced down at the mathematical computations Daniel had agonized over and realized they worked as a secondary motive for Isaac, too. After all, if Daniel's toy shop suffered, Isaac as his coworker would suffer as well. Though, if she had to guess, she'd still stick with betrayal as Isaac's motive to kill.

She rested the paper atop her stomach and stared up at the ceiling. It was painful to imagine the courage it must have taken Isaac to reach out to Robert despite the vast differences in their lifestyle. And then, to have Robert knowingly threaten the livelihood of the very people who'd rallied around his son as a child? Yes, Isaac had every reason to feel betrayed . . .

The letter he'd sent Robert simply underscored his place on the list by simultaneously offering a motive for yet another crime — one that proved futile thanks to Melinda's quick thinking.

Oh, how she'd wanted to ask if she could see the letter upon learning it was in Melinda's possession, but something about the woman's attitude had kept her from making the request. Besides, it really wasn't any of Claire's business. All that mattered was that its fate did a fairly decent job of negating the name Benjamin had added to her list midway through their picnic.

Mentally, she drew a line through Ann's name, the relief she felt in return taking her by surprise.

What was it about Ann Karble that spoke to her so clearly? Was it simply the fact that the widow was grieving and therefore sympathetic? Or was it something more? She didn't know. All she knew was that there was a vulnerability to the victim's wife that made her likable in a way Melinda really wasn't. Ann was mourning. Melinda was viewing the tragedy as a way to secure a dream.

Melinda . . .

With a gasp that echoed its way around her room, Claire bolted upright in her bed. "Melinda?" she whispered aloud as her mental pencil hastily completed its line through Ann's name and went about the task of adding yet another suspect to the list.

Betrayal was a powerful motive for murder. So, too, was revenge. Add the two together and Melinda Simon's name earned itself a double underline and a couple of exclamation points to boot.

The up-and-coming public relations manager had seen a chance to try her hand at product management in the wake of Robert's newly discovered son. Her boss had championed the idea one moment and removed Melinda from the helm in favor of his wife the next. Killing Robert would have been about revenge. Leading the man's multimillion-dollar company back from the clutches of a public relations nightmare would be the ultimate coup de grâce.

She padded around her room on still damp feet and surveyed the outfit she'd laid out on her bed after managing to secure a ninety-minute power snooze and a hot shower. The sleep had come on the heels of the realization that it was time to talk to Jakob. The shower had come when she'd rolled over and looked at the clock and realized she'd slept through breakfast and needed help clearing the fog of exhaustion from her brain.

Peeling the extra-large towel from her relatively petite frame, Claire stepped into her favorite pair of jeans and topped them off with a white button-down shirt. Not a look she'd dare on a day she was manning the shop, but for one that had Esther working the register while she attended to bookkeeping duties in the back office it worked just fine.

A quick search through her jewelry box completed the outfit with a silver pendant necklace and a pair of small hoop earrings. The only part of her prework ritual that still remained was what to do with her hair, until the whoosh of air brakes in the parking lot aided the decision in leaving it down.

She grabbed her purse from her dresser and headed out into the hall, resisting the pull to knock on Melinda's door as she did.

Rome wasn't built in a day. Or so they said. Either way, she had time to mull over her suspect list a little longer before taking her thoughts and suspicions to Jakob. To do so prematurely could prove disastrous to a friendship she both wanted and needed.

"Good morning, Claire. I am so happy you got a good night's sleep. I know you needed that." Diane met her at the bottom of the stairs before doing a double take. "Claire? You look more tired than you did last night. Is everything okay?"

She rested a reassuring hand on her aunt's arm and offered an accompanying smile. "I'm fine. Believe it or not, I actually managed to get about ninety minutes although the circles under my eyes point to none." Without waiting for an answer, she pointed toward the narrow windows that flanked the inn's front door. "I thought I heard a truck or something outside a few minutes ago. Did we get a delivery?"

"No, it's just Keith. He's here to take the newlyweds and the Grandersons on a behind-the-scenes tour of the Amish countryside." Motioning for Claire to follow, Diane turned on her sensible shoes and led the way into the dining room, where Keith was sipping on a cup of coffee. "Would you like to join Keith and me in a cup of coffee as we wait for the others to come down?"

She stopped just inside the sun-dappled room and liberated a leftover croissant from a plate on the nearby serving table. Breaking off a bite with one hand, she paused the flaky pastry a few inches from her lips, much to the chagrin of her growling stomach. "Good morning, Keith."

The driver tipped his balding head in return. "What did you think of that meeting yesterday?" Then, keeping his gaze on Claire, he nudged his chin in Diane's direction. "I was just telling your aunt here how she should have been at Al's to hear all of Sandra's ideas for the upcoming holiday season. They really were spectacular, weren't they?"

She couldn't help but agree. Sandra Moffit had a knack for making things magical just as Keith had one for spreading the word about her latest endeavors. "I loved the idea of the carolers, but my favorite idea of all was the one that has costumed Santas from all over the world roaming Lighted Way and giving out candy. It's just the kind of thing that will appeal to traveling tourists as well as folks who live within an easy drive."

Diane clapped her hands softly. "Oh, how wonderful! It sounds so . . . so magical."

"But wait. It gets better." Keith scooted his chair from the table just enough to afford room to drape his ankle across his opposing knee. "Sandra suggested we put the real Santa Claus in a chair smack-dab in the middle of Daniel's workshop, citing the backdrop as the perfect accompaniment to the coveted Christmas photograph most parents want with their children."

"Now all you have to do, Keith," Claire mused, "is buy a set of those antlers people stick on their cars each Christmas and transform your bus into something kids will beg to ride in on the way to visit Santa."

The idea was barely through her lips before Keith started laughing. "You know, I had that very same idea when I was on the way to pick up my first round of customers after yesterday's meeting. Tried to tell myself I was grasping at straws, but now, after hearing you say it, maybe it's not so silly after all."

"Silly?" Diane echoed. "I think it's brilliant."

"Brilliant, you say?" Claire lifted her hand above her head in preparation for a bow that was quickly curtailed by the sound of footsteps on the stairs.

Rising to his feet, Keith took one last sip of his coffee then returned the empty cup to its matching saucer. "Diane, I thank you for your hospitality, but it sounds as if your guests are ready for their tour and I don't want to keep them waiting."

"Is Ann going, too?" Claire asked as she glanced at Diane. "A drive like that might do her good."

Keith stopped just inside the door. "I thought you said Ann wasn't here."

"She's not." Diane set her own coffee cup down beside Keith's. "She's at the police station with Jakob trying to get answers."

"That's what I thought." Then, meeting Claire's eyes, he hooked his thumb in the direction of the excited voices coming from the inn's front hall. "Would you like to tag along? I could drop you off at the shop as we make our way through town."

"No, I can't ask you to do that."

"Why not?" Diane challenged. "You know Doug and Kayla. You know Virginia and Wayne. And with only an hour and a half of sleep in the past forty-eight, it might be safer to take the ride, dear."

She considered declining, citing the need for fresh air and good old-fashioned exercise as her reasons, but a rapid series of yawns that momentarily rendered her speechless convinced her otherwise. "Well, if you're really sure it's okay, maybe it *would* be better to ride into town with all of you rather than risk falling asleep on the side of the road and being mistaken as Heavenly's latest dead body."

CHAPTER 23

Any concern Claire had over crashing the countryside tour Diane had arranged was wiped away by the warm greeting that met her initial steps onto the bus. The triumphant I-told-you-so look from the man behind the wheel simply provided the additional puff of air she needed to make her way down the center aisle and claim one of the twelve remaining cushioned seats as her own.

Virginia Granderson swiveled around in the front-row seat she shared with her husband and reached for Claire's hand. "Wayne, isn't this a treat! Claire's coming with us this morning!"

Kayla Jones leaned across Doug's lap and wiggled her fingers across the aisle. "Oooh, you'll be able to point out some of the things we've talked about over dinner these last few days."

"Like the Amish farm that's raising the

white-tailed deer for the pharmaceutical company." Doug gently stroked the side of Kayla's face as he, too, nodded his pleasure at Claire's inclusion. "I mean, I've gotta admit . . . that kind of resourcefulness is pretty cool."

Keith's hand adjusted the mirror over his seat to afford a better view of all five passengers and then shifted the sixteen-passenger bus into drive. "They have to be resourceful these days, just like the rest of us do. The difference is that our need to be resourceful comes from things like corporate downsizing and age discrimination. With the Amish — at least in this area — it's because of the lack of farmland."

"Have they lost their land somehow?" Doug asked. "Is that why they're having trouble doing something they've done for years?"

At the end of the inn's gravel driveway, Keith turned left and headed toward town at a slow yet steady pace, the microphone affixed to his shirt collar making it easy for everyone to hear him. "They have the same amount of land they've always had, son, but they also have far more people living here now than they did twenty years ago."

Kayla gave Doug a gentle nudge with her elbow. "That's right. Diane and Claire told us that, remember? I think they said the Amish population is doubling every twenty years."

"With that kind of population explosion there just isn't enough land to go around," Keith said by way of agreement. "So they're forced to turn to other ways of making a living — like carpentry, masonry, shoemaking, deer raising, toy making, et cetera. Basically anything they can do to make a living like the rest of us."

"Ran into a fella down at Glick's Tools 'n More the other day and he said some Amish are raising alpaca sheep for the wool," Wayne shared.

Keith nodded then pointed out the front window to Lighted Way's shopping district. "I'll be taking these cobblestones slowly but you're still going to feel some bumps." Then, with a pointed look at Claire via his mirror, he addressed her directly. "You want me to drop you off in front of the shop? Or do you want to come along with us and I can drop you off when the tour is wrapping up?"

Virginia's smile widened exponentially. "Oh, Claire, stay. Your aunt said the reason you were able to sleep in a little today was because Esther is working. So stay. We'd all love to have you along" — the woman

glanced at Kayla and Doug for confirmation — "wouldn't we?"

Kayla was the first to agree. "You probably know everything there is to know about
the Amish already but we'd love to have you
stay if you have the time."

Claire held up her hands and laughed.
"Oh, trust me, I'm still learning about the
Amish every day." She met Keith's gaze in
the mirror and, at his wink, opted to stay.
Besides, the seat felt mighty comfortable
after a second night of little to no sleep.
"But I'm just going to sit here and listen to
all of you. I can ask Diane or Keith questions any old time."

The bus moved slowly along the cobblestoned street, pausing a time or two as an
Amish buggy pulled out from one of the
narrow alleyways that ran along the side of
many of the shops and cafés.

"The Amish won't drive in cars, right?"
Doug asked.

Instinctively, Claire opened her mouth to
answer only to shut it just as quickly. This
was Keith's tour, not hers, and his answer
lacked nothing. "No. They'll ride in cars,
they just won't drive them. That's why,
when the Amish are going to travel farther
than they want to go by horse and buggy,
they'll hire a driver to take them. They can

also take trains and busses. The only transportation they avoid is airplanes."

Doug gestured toward a buggy parked in front of Gussman's General Store. "How come the buggies around Heavenly are gray instead of black?"

"Gray buggies mean the old Amish order. They're stricter than some of the other orders you might come across elsewhere." Keith steered the bus around a line of parked cars and headed out the other side of Lighted Way, the wide-open fields and scattered farmhouses in the distance beckoning in their peacefulness. "Women can drive the buggies. No license and no inspection is needed. But a while back, the state of Pennsylvania mandated lights be installed on the buggies for the safety of both the Amish and the English."

The bus followed the gentle curves of the road, slowing to a crawl from time to time to afford a better view of whatever Keith was talking about at any given moment. Mile by mile he shared details about the Amish on everything from their homes and beliefs to weddings and funerals. Much of the information he shared was things Claire had learned over the past eight months. But some of it was new to her and, as a result, fascinating.

"I want you all to take a look right here." Keith pointed to a small white building on the driver's side of the bus. "Anyone want to take a guess what this is?"

Claire straightened up tall in her seat and looked across Kayla and Doug's heads to the one-room building beyond — the smattering of bikelike scooters around its exterior soliciting smiles from the women on the bus.

"A school?" Virginia guessed.

"That's right. It's a school." Keith pulled the bus to the side of the road and stopped long enough to add a few interesting facts. "The Amish own private schools. They're all within walking distance of the families they serve. That school right there? It serves roughly twenty-five children in grades one through eight. And since most Amish families have an average of seven children, it takes less than six families to fill a school.

"The families in each district pay the teacher and provide the supplies. The teacher is in her late teens or early twenties and is unmarried. Once she marries, she no longer teaches."

"Do the kids learn the same things our kids learn?" Wayne peered around his wife to get a closer look out the window. "Or are they more sheltered?"

"They learn the cores — math, reading,

writing, spelling, history, and geography. But they don't really get into science. They stop going to school after they've completed eighth grade because the Amish believe that the things taught in high school threaten their culture."

"Do they speak Pennsylvania Dutch or English in the classroom?" Kayla asked.

"In school, Amish children are taught to read classic German and English as a second language. English, though, is what they learn to speak in school. Pennsylvania Dutch is spoken in the home to preserve the Amish culture."

Keith lifted his finger to the window. "See that cupboard there? It's filled with drinking cups for the children. And right there, next to it, you can see the hand pump they use to fill their cups. Can everyone see that?"

Heads bobbed around the bus, including Claire's. Then, as they continued to watch, a pair of little girls dressed in black coats came running out the front door and across the patch of yard between the side of the school and the fence. "And that building those little ones are running off to? That's the school's outhouse."

Five minutes later, they were back on the road, the passing farms and running commentary helping to chase away the last of Claire's sleepy fog. She had to admit, Keith Watson gave a good tour. The fact that a stop at Lapp's Toy Shop was part of the experience only made it better.

Claire took in the rapt interest on the faces around her as Keith continued sharing fact after fact about Heavenly's Amish. "Only one in ten kids decides not to be baptized in their late teens. And if they don't, they're still welcome to have ties with their family for life. But if they are baptized and *then* leave, they will be excommunicated."

A soft tsking sound emerged from the row in front of Claire but was quickly lost against the sudden roar in her ears. Jakob had been baptized before heeding the call to police work. That single decision — which would have been considered com-mendable in the English world — had cost him his family.

She pressed her forehead against the cool glass and closed her eyes. Aunt Diane was right. She needed to talk to Jakob. The friendship they'd forged over the past two months meant too much to her to simply accept his recent snub without question. Maybe she'd read it wrong. Or maybe he was distracted by something completely dif-ferent, like Martha.

"See that cemetery right there?" Keith asked as he again slowed the bus to direct the attention of his customers to the windows on the opposite side of the aisle. "About an acre is set aside in each church district as burial ground for the people of that district. The tombstones, as you can see, are quite humble with only the person's name and length of life noted."

"I saw a picture of an Amish funeral procession once," Doug volunteered. "The line of buggies went on forever."

"They do that. Why, some processions can have hundreds of buggies in them. And that's why the young boys are tasked with using chalk to mark each buggy's proper position in line. The closer the kinship, the smaller the number."

Keith pulled back onto the road and continued driving, his words keeping the current subject close. "Widows wear black for the rest of their life."

"Can the Amish remarry after a death?"

She held her breath as she waited for Keith to answer Kayla's inquiry.

"Yes, they can. Though you see that more if the death occurred early on." Keith continued speaking, but Claire didn't hear the rest of what he said. Instead, she found her thoughts veering off in a direction she knew they shouldn't go, starring a man that had no business being in her thoughts, let alone her heart.

"Just up ahead, you'll see the farm where we'll be stopping. It's owned by Daniel Lapp. Daniel recently sold half of his farm to another Amish man so he could, instead, concentrate on his growing toy business."

At the mention of Daniel, Claire shook all thoughts of Benjamin from her head and focused on Keith and the questions coming from her aunt's guests.

Doug's head rose up above the seat. "Daniel Lapp? Isn't that the man Karble Toys was about to do business with?"

"You mean the man Karble Toys was about to *rip off,*" Keith corrected. "Yeah, that's him. Daniel is a master toy maker, which you're about to see when we stop. He makes rocking ponies, Noah's Ark toys, jigsaw puzzles, sewing boards, pull toys, doll cribs, kitchen sets . . . you name it. And he makes 'em all by hand."

A hush of anticipation filled the air around them as Keith pulled the bus into a narrow turnoff to the side of Daniel's barn and cut the engine. "You should head into the shop first and look around. Then, when you're done browsing, Daniel will take you inside the barn right here so you can watch him working on whatever toy he's making at the moment. It's quite fascinating to see."

Claire lingered behind as first Doug and Kayla and then the Grandersons descended the steps to the gravel drive below. When they'd cleared the bus, she made her way down the aisle to where Keith was checking his watch and making a few notations in a small notebook. "Keith? I have to tell you, that was a fantastic tour. I can see why your business has grown so much in the past few months. You really give a great window into the Amish world."

Keith waved aside her praise but not before she caught the tug of a smile on the left side of his mouth. "My business has grown because of this place. Anyone can drive down a road and spout off a few facts. But stopping here, at a real Amish home to watch a real Amish toy maker in action? That's what has folks like Diane calling me instead of the next guy."

Setting his notebook on his seat, he followed her off the bus and over to the front door of Daniel's shop. "Have you been inside? Seen the toys up close?"

She peeked inside the window beside the door and nodded. "I have. The jigsaws are my favorite. Especially the ones shaped like animals that can stand up when the pieces are placed together just right."

"That is nice to hear, Miss Weatherly, and I thank you."

Whirling around, she came face-to-face with Daniel's assistant toy maker. "Isaac! Hi! I didn't know you were behind me."

The man's narrow and beardless face clouded momentarily. "I am sorry. I did not mean to frighten you. I have come to take visitors to the workshop to watch as I make a giraffe-shaped jigsaw puzzle."

Again and again, despite his attempt at conversation with first her, and then Keith, Claire found herself drawn to the Amish man's emerald green eyes that were so unlike any she'd ever seen before.

Except, of course, on Isaac's father . . .

She nibbled her lower lip inward and contemplated what to say, her thoughts quickly narrowing in on one topic. "Is there any chance you could show us how you make one of your Jumping Jacks?"

Just as quickly as it had disappeared, the cloud that had been Isaac's just moments earlier returned with a vengeance. "I do not make Jumping Jacks any longer."

CHAPTER 24

She lowered her hand to her side as the bus carrying her friends turned onto the main road and headed toward town with one less passenger than it had at the start. The decision to stay behind and talk to Isaac had snuck up on her during the workshop part of the tour and she'd seen no reason to argue. Especially in light of the wide-open shot he'd given her by swearing off his signature toy.

Drawing in a breath of courage, Claire retraced her steps back to the workshop where, only moments earlier, she'd stood with five other people and marveled at the man's toy-making ability with nothing more than the simplest of tools. "Isaac?" she called as she tugged on the heavy barn door and peeked inside to find Jakob's brother hunched over a nondescript piece of wood.

Isaac looked up, his mouth set in a grim line. "Miss Weatherly? Did you leave something behind?"

"No. I . . . I was hoping maybe we could talk for a few minutes." At his answering nod, she pulled the door closed in her wake and pointed at the worktable. "What are you making now?"

He followed her gaze downward, shrugging as he did. "I do not know yet. Something new. Something different. Something that can replace my Jumping Jack."

"But why?" she prodded, her words echoing around the otherwise empty barn that no longer had any need for the cluttering effect that often came with basic farm implements. "I saw the Jumping Jack you made for your niece the other day. It was wonderful. It even had Esther and me playing with it a little, too."

The smile he allowed stopped short of his eyes, giving her a window into the Amish man's pain despite the lack of any discernible response. Trying to figure out what his pain stemmed from, though, was futile. Besides, she'd been guessing and interpreting long enough. It was time to ask the hard questions of the only person capable of answering.

"Why would you stop making something that people enjoy?"

For a moment, she didn't think he was

going to answer, the emotion behind his eyes and the rigid stance he adopted tangible proof she'd hit a sore spot. But, eventually, he spoke, his words giving little away. "They do not bring me joy any longer. Instead, they bring worry."

"How can a toy bring worry?" It was a rhetorical question in many ways since she knew the answer, but she let it stand nonetheless.

"It is that toy that brought the big toy company to Heavenly. It is that toy that made friends look forward to work they have difficulty finding. It is that toy that almost destroyed Daniel's business and mine, as well. It is difficult to find joy in such a toy now."

She allowed her gaze to leave his long enough to perform a quick sweep of the workshop she'd barely noticed while standing alongside the Grandersons and the Joneses not more than ten minutes earlier. Then, she'd been as mesmerized as everyone else at the way Isaac could transform a piece of wood into a toy right in front of their eyes. Now, though, she found herself wanting to soak up everything about her surroundings as if some concrete piece of evidence linking Isaac to Robert's murder was there, waiting to be noticed.

But it wasn't.

Not that she could see, anyway.

"I could understand you feeling that way if it was really your Jumping Jack that brought him here, Isaac. But it wasn't."

He drew back. "Miss Weatherly?"

She took a step closer to the table, her voice dropping to a near whisper. "I can't say for certain, but I suspect you could have sent a handful of dirt and Robert Karble still would have come here."

Isaac plucked a carving tool from a simple holder to his left and began furiously working at the block of wood. "He came because of toys. He was to make Amish toys."

"But why? Because he suddenly woke up one day and thought of the Amish and their history of simple wooden toys?"

He swapped the tool for a piece of sandpaper he didn't need. "Perhaps that is what happened."

Swinging her focus toward the door, she lowered her voice still further. "Isaac, I know."

Pushing the sandpaper to the side, he grabbed for the sculpting tool once again only to let it drop through his fingers and onto the table with a dull thump. "What is it you think you know?"

"I know Robert Karble was your father."

307

She didn't need a sudden infusion of light to see the man's face drain of all color, nor did she need bionic ears to hear the single swallow that preceded the weary slump of his shoulders. With several quick strides, she closed the gap between them and took his hands in hers, the coldness she felt there making her release them and step back in one motion.

"Please," he suddenly implored. "You can not tell anyone. Not Daniel. Not Sarah. Not Esther. Not Martha. Not Jakob. Not anyone. Please."

"They won't think any less of you, Isaac. How could they? None of what happened had anything to do with you. You weren't even born yet."

"My parents were not married. Mamm — I mean, my *mother* was not Amish. How then could I be Amish?"

"Because you made the decision to be baptized. That alone makes you Amish." But even as she offered the reassurance she knew he needed to hear, she couldn't help but wonder if everyone in Isaac's community would feel the same as Benjamin did on the subject.

"But I did not come about it in an honest way." Bracing his hands against the table, he rose to his feet and removed his hat, looking down at it as if it were suddenly a foreign object.

She stepped forward, took the hat from his hands, and secured it onto his head once again. "Did you believe you were Amish, Isaac?"

"Yah."

"Did you make the choice to be baptized all on your own?"

"Yah."

"Then *you* came by your Amish lifestyle and beliefs in an honest way. To torture yourself by considering otherwise not only makes no sense but is also wrong."

He reached up and felt the top of his hat with his callused hand, the slow nod of his head doing little to ease the pain in his eyes. "I know I need to tell. To remain silent will make me dishonest as well. But I do not know how to tell. Last month, I did not know of my father. I believed him dead before my birth. Then I read the letter from Mamm. She tells of the truth and how I am to find my father. I send a letter and Jumping Jack. Because he, too, is a toy maker. He sends a letter back. I send another. He comes to visit with a picture book. He wants to see more toys that I make. I show him my drawings and tell him how I make my toys. We have a good talk, share laughs. We talk of toys and he tells of time we will spend together *making* toys. Then he changes mind. He wants to steal my ideas and hurt my friends. I get angry. Very, very angry. Then Esther screams and people come running. Once again, I am without a father."

"Did you hurt him, Isaac?" she asked despite the internal warning bells clanging in her head.

Bowing his head, the first and only tear she'd ever seen an Amish man shed fell to the ground at his feet. "No. I am Amish. I do not kill."

Isaac's words were still looping their way through her head when she let herself in through the back door of Heavenly Treasures shortly before lunch. The relative quiet on the other side of the wall told her everything she needed to know.

"Quiet day so far, Esther?" she asked as she poked her head into the storeroom. A quick survey of the room, however, yielded no sign of her friend.

Concerned, she turned around and made her way into the tiny office Claire used mainly for bookkeeping. There, sitting at the desk with her head on the metal surface, was Esther. "Esther? Is everything okay?"

In an instant, Esther was on her feet and running a worried hand along her head cap in a desperate attempt to appear neat. "Claire! I did not hear you come in. I . . . I have been watching the store all morning. We had some customers, sold some items."

She took Esther's trembling hands in hers and rushed to reassure the young woman that she wasn't angry. "Esther, Esther. It's okay. You're welcome to come in my office, you know that. But is everything okay? You look a little pale right now."

Esther tugged her hands free only to bring them to her face. "I do? Eli stopped in a while ago to say hello. I do not want him to think I look poorly."

"You look pale, Esther. But that doesn't stop you from being beautiful." She pushed a stray piece of hair inside her friend's kapp and offered what she hoped was a reassuring smile. "Trust me, Esther, Eli was just happy to see you. And I know this because he's always happy to see you."

At the uncertainty that remained in Esther's face, she asked the next most logical question she could. "Wait. Did you and Eli have an argument or something?"

"No."

"Are you feeling sick?"

"No."

"Then what's wrong? And don't tell me there's nothing because I know better." And it was true. In just the short time since meeting and getting to know Esther, she could read the young woman like a book. It helped, of course, that there was only one of three things on Esther's mind at any given time — her family, her crafts, and Eli.

Her family . . .

"Is everything okay at home?" she asked.

Esther's face crumbled. "I do not know, Claire. I am worried."

"Worried about what, exactly?"

"Mamm."

Tossing her purse onto the floor beside her desk, she took Esther by the arm and guided her back to the chair. "What's wrong with your mother? Is she sick?"

"I do not know. She will not say. She asks me to watch my brothers and sisters often when I am home but does not say what she is doing or where she goes. I wonder if she sees the doctor but does not say." Esther brought her hands to her head in prayer and scrunched her eyes closed. "I almost asked Dat yesterday but I did not. Instead, I asked Mamm when she got home. When I told her I almost asked Dat, she sent me out to do chores and would not speak to me again until dinner."

"Maybe she just needed a break. Caring for all those children has to be tiring."

"Not for Mamm," Esther said sadly. "But that is not all. When Eli came in today he said he saw Mamm coming from trail that leads to the pond. The same trail that she could take to the doctor if she kept going past the pond."

"The pond?" she repeated.

"Yes."

Martha wasn't sick. She'd bet her bottom dollar on that one. She'd also bet the reason for Martha's suspicious behavior had everything to do with a particular Heavenly detective and nothing whatsoever to do with some phantom health issue.

"I do not want Mamm to be sick, Claire!"

It took everything in her power not to blurt out what she knew and erase the fear from Esther's eyes once and for all. But she couldn't. She'd given her word.

No, it was up to Jakob to set things right with his niece.

Jakob *and* Martha.

CHAPTER 25

Claire surveyed the table one last time, her gaze lingering on the place setting across from Kayla Jones. "Do you think she'll ever come out for dinner?"

"I checked in on her about thirty minutes ago and she was dressed and moving around." Diane tipped the water pitcher atop Ann's glass and began to pour. "She is trying so hard to pick herself up and move forward but it's difficult. She wants closure on what happened so she can leave, yet I know that when she does, it's only going to bring a whole new wave of pain."

All Claire could do was nod. Her heart ached for the grieving widow and the shock she knew still lay in wait.

"Thankfully, our guests are every bit as worried about Ann as we are and so I know they'll do their best to keep the conversation light. Assuming, of course, she joins us . . ." Diane filled the last two glasses at the table then turned to look at Claire. "Were you able to straighten things out with Jakob, dear?"

She plucked two bread baskets from the serving table and positioned them at opposite ends of the table with a crock of butter next to each one. "I called the station and left a message for him, but he hasn't returned my call."

"He will."

Something about the conviction in her aunt's voice made her laugh. "You sound so sure of yourself."

Diane came around the table and stopped next to Claire, the sound of footsteps descending the stairs necessitating an end to their conversation. "No, I'm sure of Jakob . . . and his feelings for you."

She felt her mouth slack open but shut it fast when Doug and Kayla rounded the corner and entered the room.

"Mmmm. Diane, something smells absolutely wonderful in here." Kayla lifted her chin into the air and inhaled deeply. "Mmmm. What is that?"

Doug brought his palm to his forehead. "Wait. Wait. Don't tell me. It's a hearty and homemade beef stew."

At Diane's nod, Kayla's eyes widened on her husband. "How did you know that?"

"I read the hand-printed menu Diane left in the parlor this morning."

"Hand-printed menu?" Kayla repeated before turning her gaze on Diane. "Do you do that every day?"

Again, Diane nodded.

A smile that began at the corners of Kayla's mouth made its way across her face just before she turned an accusing look on her new husband. "Hey! That's how you've known what's for dinner every night since we've been here! You rat! I was actually starting to think you had some sort of gift!"

"I do," Doug quipped while simultaneously pulling Kayla in for a loving squeeze. "I *read*."

"Ha, ha, ha. Very funny, mister." Kayla shook her head then rolled her eyes at Claire and Diane. "Do you see what I have to put up with?"

"Treasure him. Treasure each other."

All eyes turned toward the door and the woman that had been missing from the table since the festival.

"Ann! I'm so happy you've decided to join us for supper this evening." Sweeping her hand in the space between the newlyweds and Ann, Diane addressed the sudden silence in the room. "Doug and Kayla, you remember Ann Karble, don't you? She'll be sitting directly across from you tonight, Kayla."

Slowly, Claire released the breath she hadn't realized she was holding until that moment. But standing there, watching the young couple from Tennessee welcome the grieving widow with open arms, she couldn't help but feel relieved and proud. Somehow, despite the question mark factor that accompanied every first-time guest to Sleep Heavenly, the inn always attracted kind people.

She supposed some of that came from the nature of their surroundings. Heavenly wasn't a party town. It was a quiet place steeped in the kind of quaintness that made a person feel comfortable. Her aunt simply took that comfort a step further and made everyone who stayed under her roof feel like family to her, to Claire, and to one another.

The addition of Virginia and Wayne several minutes later did nothing to change the dynamic around the table. If anything, the added conversation and friendly smiles they offered Ann lightened the atmosphere even more.

Blinking against a sudden and unexpected threat of tears, Claire followed Diane into the kitchen, where two serving bowls of stew waited. "You always have the nicest people staying here, you know that?" she whispered.

Diane beamed. "God is good, isn't He?"

She took hold of both bowls and stepped through the swinging door Diane held open. "I think Ann needs a night like this, you know? I mean, I know it won't make her forget, but just to hear laughter and feel like a person again for a little while has to help."

"I agree." Diane came around Claire as they reached the dining room's wide entrance and brought her hands together in a quiet clap. "The stew is still quite hot. So enjoy your salads and Claire and I will take care of ladling the stew into your bowls. We've got plenty so please don't be shy asking for seconds or thirds."

Slowly, they made their way around the table, stopping at everyone's place to put two or three heaping ladlefuls of stew into each bowl, the pleasant aroma the meal emitted making Claire's stomach rumble in hunger.

"I'm sorry I'm late." Melinda breezed into the room in a formfitting running suit, stopping midway to the table as Ann looked up. "Oh . . . Ann. I didn't expect you to be here."

"So sorry to disappoint, Melinda."

The slight snap in Ann's voice earned more than a few passing glances in her direction, including one from both Diane and Claire that subsequently ended with them looking at each other.

Yanking her chair back from the table, Melinda slid into it and pulled her napkin onto her lap. "I've been working on the formal press release that should go out to the media as well as our shareholders tomorrow morning. The time for damage control is now."

The timid smile that had graced the widow's face prior to Melinda's arrival disappeared in a cloud of anger. "Don't you think your damage control is coming a little too late, *Melinda*? After all, my husband is dead. No press release is going to change that."

Melinda speared a piece of cucumber onto her fork only to let it go uneaten as she braced both hands on the edge of the table instead. "I'm not trying to change anything, *Ann.* I'm just trying to keep the company Robert built afloat. Talking about this company as his dream, and the toys it makes as his legacy, will keep the focus where we want and need it to be for our continued success."

"I repeat, don't you think your damage control is coming a little too late, Melinda? Because if you're doing your job the way it should be done, there shouldn't be any damage to control."

Melinda's long lashes mingled above narrowed eyes. "Excuse me?"

"This stew is especially good when it's warm," Diane offered in her cheery voice. "And the bread is wonderful for soaking up the leftover gravy base."

Wayne reached for a piece of homemade bread, dipped it into his bowl, and took a bite, his eyes nearly rolling back in his head as he did. "Mmmm. Diane is right. This is really, really good." He waved at the couple to his left. "Doug? Kayla? Give it a try."

Before they could echo the man's attempt at diverting the brewing argument between Ann and Melinda, Ann smacked her hand on the table. "There would be no need for damage control, Melinda, if there was no death. And there would be no death if you hadn't come up with the idea of an Amish toy line — an Amish toy line that brought us here . . . to the place where he was murdered!"

Claire tightened her grip on the serving bowl and tried to think of something to say, but there was nothing. The venom in Ann's voice, coupled with the bitterness behind her words, brought a hush to the room.

"My suggestion is not what brought him

here," Melinda hissed.

Warning bells sounded in Claire's head. If the argument continued, Melinda was going to divulge the kind of news no woman wanted to hear in front of a tableful of strangers.

"Perhaps we should table this discussion until —"

"Oh no? It was *your* idea to make an Amish line, wasn't it?" Ann challenged before casting an exasperated glance in Doug's direction. "An Amish toy line, can you believe that?"

Melinda leaned her face across the table. "An Amish toy line — pitched to the purchasing public as a way to acquaint kids with the kind of simpler toys their grandparents played with — was a genius idea, Ann. *Genius.* The problem came when Robert gave my idea to you. *You,* Ann — the woman who couldn't find her way around a toy store without a personal shopper if your life depended on it!"

Pulling her focus from Melinda, Ann fixed it, instead, on Claire. "Should I tell her?"

Claire swallowed.

"Tell me what?" Melinda challenged.

"Maybe now isn't the time," Claire mumbled. "Maybe the two of you should talk . . . after dinner."

But it didn't matter. Ann was already on a roll and she wasn't about to wait. "Not only can I find my way around a toy store, Melinda, I could give you and everyone else at Karble Toys a crash course."

Melinda's laugh echoed across the room. "Please. You expect me to believe that?"

"I don't care if you do or not. But the fact remains that Karble Toys is *my* company, Melinda. I *allowed* Robert to run it because I loved him. That said, I knew the ins and outs of every decision that was made in every meeting he ever had. Did I make them all? Or course not. I trusted Robert. Though, between the two of us, I never would have hired you for that job even if you were brought in at half the salary of your predecessor. You get what you pay for as far as personnel are concerned."

"D-did you say half?" Melinda croaked.

"Actually, if I remember correctly, you came in at a little less than half, but who's counting? It was still more than I would have paid." Ann scooted her chair back a few inches and then tossed her napkin onto the table. The anger she'd exhibited only seconds earlier was suddenly gone, in its place a resurgence of grief. "Diane, I'm so sorry for —"

"Assuming what you say is true, Ann, how

does it make you feel to know that you stepped in on a project that meant the world to Robert only to mess it up?"

"Mess it up?"

"He wanted those toys to be made here. In Heavenly. By the Amish. It mattered to him more than any other business decision he'd ever made. He gave these people his word and you — in all your supposed business experience — made his word mean nothing." Melinda's attempt at a rapid departure from the table landed her chair against the wall with a thud. "Live with that, Ann. *Live . . . with . . . that!*"

For the second time that week, Claire found herself sitting on the edge of Ann's bed, trying desperately to find just the right words to soothe away a hurt she could only imagine. It was one thing to lose your husband in such an unexpected way as murder; it was quite another to forgive yourself for any angst experienced by the victim prior to the crime.

"Do you think she was right?" Ann asked in a halting voice. "Do you really think my decision to produce the Back to Basics line in-house hurt Robert the way she said?"

Oh, how she wished she could refute Melinda's statement, chalking it up to the woman's youthful ignorance. But she couldn't.

Not with everything she knew about Robert and Isaac.

Still, she had to say something to ease the widow's pain. "Did you love him?" she finally asked.

Ann peeked up at Claire through tear-dappled lashes. "Robert? Of course I did. He was the love of my life."

"Did you tell him that?"

"Every day."

"Then take comfort in that." She tugged the soft fleece blanket up higher on Ann's shoulders and hoped the added warmth would make a dent in the woman's near-constant shivering.

"It's hard. Even before Melinda said what she said, I'd replayed our last argument again and again."

Claire pushed off the top edge of the bed and wandered over to the window that overlooked the inn's extensive and tastefully landscaped backyard. "Ann? Can I ask why you were so adamant the new toy line be manufactured in-house?"

"Cost. Convenience. Liability. All of it." Ann struggled up onto her elbow as she continued. "Robert was at the Grand Rapids plant twice a month checking in on everything. The people on the line up there know what Karble Toys is looking for in terms of quality and durability. The Amish don't."

She turned from the window. "Have you ever seen an Amish-made toy, Ann? There is no better quality or durability."

Dropping back down to the bed, Ann closed her eyes and moaned. "That's exactly what Robert said. Like he was suddenly an expert on all things Amish."

Unsure of what to say, she, instead, said nothing. She was on a slippery slope as it was. If she continued down the current path, she was likely to stir up Ann's guilt once again. And that wasn't Claire's intention.

"But even if they're the most durable toys on the face of the earth, there's no way the Amish could do it as cheaply as we could in a factory. And no matter how you dress it up, Karble Toys is a company. We are in business to make money."

"It must have been hard, though, for your husband to sign his name to that last memo if he was so passionate about the Amish crafting the new line." The second the words were out, she wished she could recall them. But it was too late.

Ann sat up and swung her legs over the

edge of her bed. "He didn't sign it, Claire. *I* did."

She stared at the back of the woman's head as she worked to make sense of what she was hearing. "I saw the memo, Ann. Or, rather, a copy of it, I should say. Either way, his signature was at the bottom of it."

"His *signature,* yes. But he's not the one who signed it, Claire. I did." Drawing the blanket around her body like a cape, Ann sighed. "I showed him numbers, I explained my reasons, but he still wouldn't sign. It was like everything he'd learned since taking the helm of the company had just disappeared in a cloud of . . . I don't know. I just don't get what he was thinking. Or what was driving him to make the choices he was making."

There was a part of Claire that wanted to blurt out the obvious answer, but to do so would mean ripping all remaining ground out from under Ann's feet. That, she couldn't do.

"Part of me wonders if there was something going on between him and that little diva down the hall from his office —"

"Diva?"

Ann bobbed her head ever so slightly. "From the moment Melinda strutted herself in for that first interview, I knew Robert would be pressured to hire her by the single men in the office. But Robert loved me. I saw it in his eyes every day. A person can't fake that."

No, they can't. Not for long, anyway.

Closing her eyes against the image of Peter, Claire willed herself to focus on the here and now. "Tell me about his eyes," she finally managed to say.

The underlying tone of sadness that had lapped at every word the woman uttered all evening disappeared in favor of a wistful quality that had Claire blinking back tears. "Robert had the most beautiful emerald green eyes I've ever seen. So many things pulled me in when we first met — his laugh, his easygoing personality, his intelligence, et cetera. But it was his eyes . . . and the way they sparkled liked gems when he smiled . . . that I'll never forget." In an instant, the sadness was back along with the teeth-clattering shivers. "I . . . I can't imagine living the rest of my life never being able to look into those eyes again."

CHAPTER 26

Claire's head was pounding by the time she stepped out of Ann's room and headed toward the parlor where she knew Diane would be waiting. So many times over the past thirty minutes, she'd contemplated telling the widow about Isaac, but every time she opened her mouth to do so, the little voice inside her head she equated with good judgment would tell her to keep quiet.

Besides, it wasn't her secret to tell. It was Robert's.

And Isaac's . . .

Step by step, she made her way down the hallway, Diane's hushed voice interspersed with that of a male, propelling her feet forward and into the cozy sitting room.

"Oh . . ." She stopped just inside the doorway at the sight of the tastefully dressed man sitting on the couch beside her aunt. "Jakob. I didn't know you were here."

"He just arrived. To see you." Diane's

smile dimmed momentarily in conjunction with a gestured hand toward the hallway. "How is she, dear?"

Caught between uncertainty over Jakob's presence and exhaustion in the wake of her talk with Ann, she opted to slump against the wall rather than join them on the couch. "She's hurting as much as ever. Only now, she's second-guessing things she said and did as well as Robert's true motivations behind the Amish-inspired line."

Diane tsked softly under her breath. "I imagine that's one of the hardest parts of an unexpected death. All those should-haves and could-haves." Pushing off the couch, Diane rested a brief hand on Jakob's shoulder then came around the back of the couch to dispense a good-night kiss on Claire's forehead. "I'm going to head upstairs to bed. The Grandersons are heading out first thing in the morning and I want to make sure they have a hearty breakfast before they leave."

"Good night, Diane." Jakob met Claire's eyes across the couch and then patted the empty cushion vacated by her aunt. "Come sit? Please?"

She left the comfort of the wall but stopped short of accepting his offer. "I don't want to sit. I feel like I've been cooped up for too long thinking about way too many things."

He nudged his chin toward the front window. "We could sit outside on the porch, but that's still sitting . . ."

"Make it a walk and we're good." At his nod, she met him midway across the room and headed out the opposite doorway from which she'd entered.

They made their way onto the front porch and then down the steps onto the sidewalk below. "Do you want to walk toward town?" he asked when they reached the driveway. "Or do you want to go the opposite way?"

Normally, she'd say toward town without so much as a moment's hesitation. But things weren't normal. In fact, the notion of walking in the direction of the Amish only served to reignite the pounding behind her eyes. "Let's save town for another night . . . when an occasional buggy sighting can fill me with peace like it usually does."

"And tonight is different?"

"It is." She knew she was being vague, but she couldn't help it. So much of what was nagging at her heart and mind had to do with Jakob.

"Why?"

It was a simple question, one she should have been able to shrug away, but she couldn't. Not when he raked his hand through his already-disheveled crop of blond hair and followed it with an encouraging and dimple-accompanied smile. "There's just a lot going on right now. That's all."

"Such as . . ."

Realizing resistance was futile, she chose the less personal of the two conversational options. "A couple of days ago, I actually thought I knew who killed Robert Karble. I didn't like who it was but I thought I'd figured it out. He had motive, he had as good an opportunity as anyone else at that festival, and, well, it just made sense."

Jakob lengthened his already long stride in order to keep up with Claire. "Who was that?"

"Daniel Lapp." Even now, with everything she knew about all of her other suspects, it still pained her to say the Amish toy maker's name aloud. "He stood to lose huge with Robert's — I mean *Ann's* decision to move the production line to Michigan.

"But then I talked to Melinda and I —" She stopped in the middle of the sidewalk as the enormity of what she was about to say, and who she was about to say it to, hit her with a one-two punch. Isaac was Jakob's brother. It was up to Isaac to tell Jakob about his connection with the murder victim, not Claire.

"You, what?" When she didn't answer, he took hold of her hand and repeated his inquiry.

The warmth she felt at his touch made her stumble back a little, reminding her of the other discussion they needed to have. "I . . . I began to see that she has her own motive for wanting to see her boss dead."

Nice save . . .

She felt the intensity of his eyes but refused to meet them with her own. Despite having known each other for just over two months, Jakob had a knack for reading her thoughts that made her more than a little uncomfortable.

If he suspected she was holding something back, though, he didn't comment. Instead, he took to her quick shift like a duck to water. "Wouldn't killing Robert put her job in jeopardy if the company folds as a result?"

"Karble Toys isn't going anywhere. But, even if it was, the eyes of the corporate world are on the company right now. Waiting to see how they handle this tragedy. If Melinda plays her cards right, her handling of the press could be her ticket into any number of companies. And really big ones, at that."

With nary a word necessary, Claire and Jakob resumed their walk, the sound of their own footsteps over the next two blocks standing in for their conversation. Eventually, though, Jakob spoke, his voice every bit as strong as it was quiet. "I've been looking at the same two suspects myself, as well as a few others."

Again, she stopped. "Others?"

A streetlamp midway down the next block cast just enough light on Jakob's face for Claire to see the worry etched in the lines around his mouth and to the side of his eyes. And in that moment, she knew.

Somehow, Jakob had found out about Isaac.

But how? Had Isaac told him or —

"I owe you an apology, Claire."

"An apology?" She looked up at him, confused. "For what?"

"For being a jerk at the meeting yesterday. For dismissing you so quickly at the pond before that. It was wrong. Though, I'm not sure how I can do it any other way."

Just like that, Jakob took them down a path she knew they needed to go, yet she was unprepared for the journey. "Do what? Have a relationship with Martha? Because if that's what all of this is, you have to know I've wanted nothing else for the two of you since I was made aware of your ties."

He shifted from foot to foot then put one hand to her lower back and pointed with the other. "Can we go sit over there? In the park?"

She followed his eyes to the neighborhood park that was less than a block away. There, the handful of swings that gently swayed in the late-evening breeze offered a sense of calm she desperately needed. Nodding, she allowed him to silently guide her to an empty picnic table tucked under a tree less than ten feet from the swing set. "I know you've been wanting me to have a relationship with my sister. You've made no bones about that these past couple of months and it's meant the world to me. It really has."

Slowly, she lowered herself to the closest bench and waited for him to continue, the rising lump in her throat making it difficult to speak.

"But what you have to know is that talking to me — for any reason — could get my sister shunned not only within the Amish community but inside her own home . . . *in front of* and *by* her own children." Jakob cupped his hand over his mouth only to let it slide down his chin to complete his thought. "My leaving after baptism caused

Martha enough pain. I can't cause her any more."

"And you think *I* want to see her shunned?" She heard the disbelief in her voice, saw the way it only served to deepen the lines around the detective's eyes. "Tell me you don't really believe that, Jakob. Because you can't."

He stepped toward the swings then doubled back. "I don't think you want to see her shunned, but the more people who are aware of what's going on between Martha and me, the greater the risk grows."

"I told you I wouldn't tell anyone," she protested. "And I'm insulted to hear that you would doubt my word."

"I'm not saying you'd consciously decide to sell us out." Jakob paced back and forth across the portion of the playground closest to the table. "That, I know you wouldn't do. But it's like anything in life. The more people who know, the greater the chance someone will slip — even innocently."

She could feel the anger welling up inside her chest alongside the urge to get up and walk away, but she resisted. "I could have slipped, as you call it, just this afternoon. With Esther. But alleviating her fears for her mother is on you, not me."

He stopped midpace and turned to stare

at Claire. "Esther is afraid for Martha? Why?"

"Because she's a smart girl. She sees the way her mother keeps sneaking off. She sees the way Martha acts all jumpy after coming back from her mystery trips. And she's putting two and two together and coming up with six."

Again, he swiped a hand down his face. "Six?"

"That's right, six. Esther thinks her mother is sick and that Martha is disappearing in the middle of the day to go to doctor's appointments. She thinks the worried look she sees in her Mamm's eyes is because of a life-threatening illness of some sort."

"Oh no . . ." Jakob muttered. "Are you sure?"

"Positive. She shared her worries with me today at the shop."

"And — and you didn't tell her the truth?"

A swell of anger she could no longer tamp down brought her to her feet. "I wanted to, but I couldn't. I gave you my word I wouldn't say anything, remember?"

He crossed to the table and dropped onto the bench across from Claire, the sadness in his eyes softening her anger a smidge. "Oh man . . . Claire. I had no idea. I'm sorry I put you in that position." Propping his

336

elbows on the table, he dropped his head into his hands and exhaled a breath of exasperation. "But see? This is why I'm keeping you at arm's length right now. Because I don't want to put you in an awkward position like that again and . . ."

She waited for him to reclaim the words he let fade into the night air, but he didn't. Instead, he simply cradled his forehead and mumbled words that made no sense. "Jakob, please, finish your sentence."

"Look, all I can say is that Martha has to be my focus right now. I knew how much my decision to leave my Amish roots hurt me, but I never realized just how much it hurt her. I have to make amends. I have to make things right. That . . . *and she* . . . needs to be my focus right now."

"And being polite to me changes that somehow?" The hurt in her voice was unmistakable but she didn't care. She was tired of hiding her feelings about everything where Jakob and Benjamin were concerned. She cared for them in a way that went deeper than friendship.

He lifted his head off his hands and pinned her with a pained expression. "I wasn't trying to be rude. I'm just trying to fix my past before I even think about moving on to my future."

■ ■ ■ ■

If it hadn't been for the light peeking out from beneath her aunt's door, Claire never would have knocked. But seeing as how Diane was obviously awake, she gave in to her need for the hug she knew was always waiting.

"Diane?" she whispered through the door. "It's me . . . Claire. Can I come in for a few minutes?"

The words were no sooner out of her mouth than the door swung open and the hug she so desperately needed was there for the taking. "Claire, dear? Is everything okay?"

She reached backward and closed the door while doing her best to strike a tone that would allow her to get through the conversation she both needed and dreaded. "I don't know. I've been telling myself for so long that I don't have feelings for Jakob but it's not true. I do. I'm not sure how deep they run, but they're there. Just as the feelings I have for Benjamin are there, too. But I can't explore those feelings for either one because I'm English and they're —"

"Jakob is English now, too."

If it wasn't for the fact that her heart was

breaking, she'd have laughed at her aunt's persistence. Instead, she simply shook her head. "But his heart is with the Amish. And right now, there's only room for that."

As the words left her mouth and headed for the dissection room that was her aunt's brain, Claire wandered over to the window seat Diane had adorned with throw pillows of every shape and size and sat down, pressing her forehead to the cool windowpane. "And for whatever reason, hearing him say that hurt terribly."

Diane hesitated a moment then stepped in behind Claire with a brush and some much needed tender loving care. Slowly, the woman moved the brush through her niece's hair, again and again, giving them both a few moments to think. "I can't speak for Jakob, dear, but I'll tell you what I think is going on and you can decide whether it holds any merit or not."

She gave herself over to the nurturing feel of the hairbrush and the certainty that somehow, someway, Diane was going to make things better. "Okay, let's hear it."

"Have you ever heard that expression about loving yourself before you can truly love another?"

"Yes."

"I think that is what Jakob is trying to do

right now."

Startled by her aunt's words, Claire moved her head away from the path of the brush and looked at Diane over her shoulder. "What are you talking about?"

"Jakob may have accepted his decision to become a police officer, but he's never accepted the loss of his family *because* of that decision. If he had, he'd never have left the NYPD to come back here. Why would he? It's not like he'll ever get much recognition in a town the size of Heavenly, especially when half the town won't speak to him."

She swiveled her body around so as to afford an easier view of the woman who'd been her most treasured confidante since childhood. "Go on . . ."

"Don't you see? He came back here to make himself whole again. Though I'll admit, until you told me about him and Martha, I'd have said it could never happen. But now, who knows? If they're careful and don't let the word out, maybe he can forge some sort of relationship with her again."

"Whole?" she whispered.

"Losing something that matters to you — something that helped make you who you are — has a way of making a person feel less whole. You know, like something important is missing from who you are. And with that missing part, it's hard to ever imagine truly being who you want to be in the future.

"Sometimes, that missing part is acceptance — either from one's self or someone else. Sometimes that missing part is a *connection* to something else . . . like a person or an event. Jakob's missing part is his relationship with his family. Whether that can be satisfied by simply reestablishing a relationship with Martha remains to be seen. But I suspect he wants to put his own heart back together again before he can truly give it to you. Just like you need to put your heart back together before you can truly give it to him or anyone else."

It made sense. It really did. But still, her heart ached. She didn't want him to shut her out while he made himself whole. Then again, if there was even a chance he was doing all of this for her, how could she judge when her own heart still held such a question mark when it came to Jakob?

And Benjamin?

"Give him a chance to make that connection, Claire. I suspect it will make all the difference in the world. For him and for you."

CHAPTER 27

She was tossing the day's trash into the Dumpster behind the shop when she heard the approaching *clip-clop* of a buggy in the alley. The telltale sound, coupled with the noon hour, meant one of the Miller brothers had arrived to check on Ruth and the bake shop next door.

On one hand, she hoped for Esther's sake it was Eli. Maybe then, she could take comfort in the Eli-induced smile Esther would surely wear in response. And then, with any luck, that same smile would help rid Claire — at least temporarily — of the guilt she felt where her friend's continued and needless worry over Martha was concerned.

On the other hand, though, she couldn't help but hope it was Benjamin. Her own heart, if not her psyche as a whole, needed that.

"Good afternoon, Claire."

She sucked in her breath at the indisputable effect Benjamin's voice had on her demeanor and turned around, raising a hand in greeting as she did. "Benjamin . . . hi."

He reached behind his seat and retrieved a hand-tied bouquet of wildflowers before stepping down out of the buggy.

"Oh, Ruth will love those," she gushed. "I always love looking out the side window of my shop and seeing the flowers she likes to put in her own window. They brighten my day. Esther's, too."

"I hope that is true." With an uncertainty that was unfamiliar to Benjamin's gait, he stepped forward and held the flowers in Claire's direction. "These are not for Ruth. They are for you."

She looked from Benjamin to the flowers and back again before waving his words away. "No. I wasn't hinting for you to give them to me when I said that about Ruth. I was just admiring how pretty her flowers always are."

The bouquet did not move. Nor did Benjamin's steadfast focus on her face. "I do not bring flowers to Ruth. She makes Eli stop the buggy each morning and she gets down and picks them herself." He took a step closer, his arm still out-stretched. "I picked these. For you."

Feeling her hands begin to tremble, she clasped them behind her back only to unlink them again and reach for the bouquet. "I . . . I don't know what to say. They're . . . beautiful."

A slow smile started at the left corner of Benjamin's mouth and grew until it encompassed his large blue eyes, as well. "I am glad."

There was so much she wanted to know. From Benjamin and from herself. Why had he brought flowers? Did he have feelings for her the way she suspected he did? And how could she go from feeling so blue over Jakob to being so elated over a gesture that could go no further?

Pushing the pointless questions from her thoughts, she brought the bouquet to her nose and sniffed. "Mmmm . . . they smell wonderful."

He scrunched up his face and shrugged. "I know they bring bees. Two, actually."

She had to laugh at his honesty. "I'll keep them inside, where only I can smell them. Well, and Esther, I guess."

"Is Esther inside?" he asked.

"She is." She inhaled the sweet smell of her unexpected bouquet one more time and then beckoned him to follow her to the shop's back door. "Would you like to talk to her?"

He remained rooted where he stood, glancing between Heavenly Treasures and the Shoo Fly Bake Shoppe as she waited for him to follow. "I would like to talk to you, Claire, if I may."

Again she waved him over. "Sure. C'mon inside. That way I can put these in water and you don't have to keep standing there with the sun in your eyes."

"In private. Please."

She paused her hand on the handle of the screen door and searched his face for anything that might indicate what he wanted to talk about, but there was nothing. Nothing beyond the fidgety hands that hung by his sides, anyway. "Is everything okay?"

When he didn't offer an immediate answer, she let go of the door and retraced her steps back to where she'd been standing when he offered her the flowers. "Something came up with Daniel or Isaac, didn't it?"

"No."

"Is Eli okay?" She heard the panic in her voice and followed it up with a silent prayer that everything was alright. Esther didn't need anything else on her plate.

"Yah. Eli is fine."

"Ruth?"

"Ruth is fine, as well."

She'd run out of reasons for Benjamin's request and was left with nothing to do but wait. After a moment or two, he pointed to the line of trees beyond Claire's shop.

"You want to talk back there?"

"There is a bench to sit on. Eli helped me make it two years ago when Mr. Snow first opened his shop here. It is not far."

She fell into step behind him as he led the way to the tree line that ran along the back of each and every shop on the southern side of Lighted Way. When they reached the edge of the woods, he used his hand to tuck a few low-lying branches from her path. "See? It is there."

"Oh, Benjamin, this is lovely," she mused as she stepped through the opening he provided and stopped beside the sturdy wooden bench. Looking around, she couldn't help but feel the quiet intimacy of their surroundings.

"Please. Sit."

When she'd situated herself on the bench with the bouquet still clutched in her hands, he leaned against a tree that afforded the best view of Claire. "I do not think Ruth must worry any longer."

"You mean Esther?"

"Esther does not worry. Ruth worries."

She considered correcting him, but let it go when she realized she couldn't. Not if she was going to keep Jakob and Martha's secret from yet another person. "Why is Ruth worried?"

"She worries for me."

And then she remembered. Ruth worried about Benjamin living out the rest of his life alone . . .

A sick feeling began to grow in her stomach as she realized what he'd just said. "And she doesn't need to worry about you any longer?" she repeated even as her mind started cycling through the various Amish women who may have staked a claim on Benjamin's heart. None of them, though, made any sense. Not when they'd been there all along and no one — not even Ruth or Esther — had ever mentioned them in relation to Benjamin.

"Seeing Jakob around town the past two months, I see such a life is possible. I do not know what I would do, but I am good with my hands. Because of that, I, too, can make a living."

"A living?"

"I could even run the store when there are children, too."

"Children?" she asked. "What children?"

"The ones we will have."

She blinked once, twice. "We?"

"Yah."

The flowers began to shake along with her hand as the reality of what Benjamin was saying finally began to seep into her thoughts, bringing with it a mixture of hope and dread as well as a reply she knew she had to give.

"Benjamin, you were baptized. You are Amish. You can't change that."

He pushed off the tree and came to sit beside her on the bench, his eyes wide as they focused on hers. "Jakob was Amish, too. He changed."

She set the flowers on the bench between them and searched for a way to address Benjamin's statement without giving away more of her tortured heart than she was ready to reveal. "He did, but at a great personal cost that he can never recoup."

Benjamin's brows furrowed beneath the brim of his hat. "He is not happy being a policeman?"

That she couldn't answer. She thought Jakob was happy, but now she wasn't sure. "I think he is," she said honestly, "but I can't answer for Jakob. What I do know is that he misses his family terribly and that's something he can never get back."

"I would manage," he said.

"You really think you'd be okay not talking to Eli ever again?" she challenged, even as her voice broke at the knowledge that she was deliberately trying to shut the door on the affections of a wonderful man. A man who listened when she spoke, a man who made her feel as if she was someone special, a man who brought a flutter to her heart she couldn't deny. "Because . . . I don't. And Eli needs you. He needs your direction, your support, your encouragement, your love."

Benjamin bristled at her side. "Eli would manage."

"And Ruth? What about Ruth?"

"She would not worry for me anymore."

"Maybe, maybe not. But she'd ache from missing you. She'd ache not being able to be a part of your children's lives. You know that as well as I do, Benjamin."

For a long moment, he said nothing, the pain in his eyes filling in where he had no words. When he finally did speak, his voice quickly mirrored his tortured expression. "If I do not leave, we can not be together."

"We can be friends. Like we are now." Yet even as she uttered the sentiment aloud, she knew the easy relationship they'd shared over the past two months had been forever altered by a bouquet of flowers and an impossible dream.

Claire was grateful when five o'clock brought both an end to Esther's shift and the chance to finally ponder the way her world had changed in the blink of an eye.

Twenty-four hours earlier, she'd harbored feelings for two very different men — one she knew she could never be with, and one who seemed to be pushing her away without so much as a second thought or an explanation of any sort. Now, thanks to a roundabout reason guessed at by Diane and a suggestion that simply couldn't happen, her friendship with those same two men was on shaky ground at best.

She tried to tell herself it didn't matter, that she was thriving in Heavenly long before either came into her life, but she knew it was a lie. Heavenly was special because of Diane and Esther. But it was *magical* because of Jakob and Benjamin.

"Miss Weatherly?"

She lifted her head from its resting spot atop her metal desk then sat up tall, the identity of the man standing in her office doorway sending an unexplained shiver down her spine. "Isaac?"

"Yah. It is me." He hooked the thumb of his right hand toward the door. "I knocked.

You did not come."

"I'm sorry. I was lost in thought, I guess." She scooted her chair back from the desk and stood, pointing at the leather-bound album in his left hand as she did. "What's that?"

He looked down at the album and swallowed. "It is for my father's wife. I think it might be best for her to have now that he is gone."

She took the album from his outstretched hand and gently fingered the cover. "It's a photo album."

"Yah."

"But the Amish don't take photos," she reminded.

"I did not take pictures. My Dat — I mean, my *father* sent them to me with his last letter." Isaac's gaze remained on the book even as Claire set it down on the desk and flipped the cover open. "They are pictures of his life. So I can know about him in a way I did not know."

She directed him to a folding chair resting against her office wall and then sat back down in her own chair once again. "He made this for you?" she asked as she stared down at a black-and-white photograph of Robert Karble as a baby.

"He did. With Miss Simon's help." He

opened the metal chair and positioned it alongside Claire's. "I have looked at it many times since it arrived."

Page by page she leafed through the pictures collected and arranged in a way to introduce a grown man to the father he never knew he had. "Why would you want to give this up, Isaac? I mean, he put this together for you. Don't you think you should keep it?"

He kneaded his eyes with his fingertips then let his hands fall to his lap. "I lost a father I did not know I had until four weeks ago. His wife lost a husband she loved for years. These pictures should go to her, not me."

She continued to flip her way through Robert's life, stopping at a picture of a twentysomething version of the man who'd been murdered behind the Schnitz and Knepp stand at the annual Amish Food Festival. Beside him stood a young woman with light brown hair and a smattering of freckles across the bridge of her nose. Here, like in all the pictures before, Robert smiled out from the picture with emerald green eyes that twinkled and sparkled.

"That is Mamm. On the night I came to be."

At the audible crack of the man's voice,

she rested her hand across his arm. "They look happy, Isaac."

"Mamm's life was hard because of me."

"Your mother's life was *wonderful* because of you, Isaac."

His head bowed forward beneath his hat but he said nothing. Instead, she peeked at the next five or six pages in an effort to ease the sadness that hovered around the man like a heavy storm cloud. "Oh, these are pictures of him at work." She pointed toward one on the right-hand side of the page that showed Robert attaching a set of wheels to a toy car. "I think it's neat that you gravitated toward the same work your father was in and you didn't even know it."

At his nod, she turned the page, her gaze falling on a photograph that depicted a company milestone of some sort, based on the cake and balloons in the foreground. She leaned forward in an effort to make out the words on a framed certificate to the left of the cake but gave up when she realized the writing was too small.

"I wonder what they were celebrating," she mumbled before turning the page to reveal even more pictures of the men and women behind the success of Karble Toys. The faces, of course, were unfamiliar except for Ann's and —

She sat up tall, pulling the album closer to her face for confirmation. "Oh my gosh, Isaac! Do you know who that is?"

Isaac leaned across Claire's arm for a closer look, the brim of his hat obscuring her own view. "That is Mr. Watson. The man who brings the tour bus to our workshop each day." Pulling back, he turned to look at Claire. "Why is Mr. Watson in my father's picture book?"

She refrained from answering until she could study the picture more closely, the name tag the man sported providing the only words she could muster. "He worked for Karble Toys."

CHAPTER 28

She looked from the picture to the clock and back again as she grabbed the phone and dialed her aunt's number. Beside her, Isaac continued to stare at the photograph while Claire began counting rings.

One.

Two.

Three.

Four.

"Come on, Diane. Please, please, please pick up the phone," she pleaded before launching into her request the second the call was answered by her aunt's cheery voice. "Diane, I need to speak to Ann. Now."

"Is everything okay, dear?" Diane asked.

"I'm not sure but I need to talk to her. Please."

A slight pause was followed by the sound of Diane moving through the inn and stopping outside Ann's door. "Ann?" she heard her aunt say. "Claire is on the phone right now and she says it's important that she talk to you."

A moment later, Ann's tired voice came over the line. "Claire? It's Ann. What can I do for you?"

"Do you know a man named Keith Watson?" It was a rhetorical question really, especially in light of the fact she was staring at a picture that also happened to show Ann in the same frame.

"I do. Why do you ask?"

She leaned back in her chair and looked down at the picture once again, the surprise at spying the familiar face inside Isaac's picture book slowly dulling into more of a nagging sensation. "He worked for Karble Toys, didn't he?"

"He did. He was the man Melinda replaced," Ann explained. "He was in charge of our public relations team."

Public relations . . .

Suddenly all of the little tasks Keith took on for the Lighted Way Business Owners' Association made perfect sense. He didn't raise his hand when Al was looking for someone to paint porch railings or pass out flyers about upcoming events. No, his interest was confined to getting the word out to the local media and painting the town in the best possible light.

"Why did he leave?"

"Robert let him go."

She bolted upright. "*Robert* let him go? Why?"

"Because he could get Melinda cheaper, although we had to sugarcoat that fact by saying it was due to company-wide budget cuts."

Before Claire could comment, Ann went on in almost rambling fashion. "But Keith was smart. He knew he was being pushed out for someone younger and cheaper. He just couldn't prove it thanks to the crackerjack law team we have at Karble."

"Okay . . ."

Ann's voice grew a bit louder as Claire imagined her moving the phone closer to her mouth. "Why are you asking all these questions about Keith? Do you know him?"

Yeah, I think he murdered your husband . . .

It was a thought she couldn't share aloud. Not to Ann, anyway. Instead, she closed Isaac's picture book with a thump and stood. "Ann, I've got to go. I'll explain all of this to you later." Then, without waiting for a response, she closed her cell phone inside her hand and met Isaac's questioning eyes.

"Isaac, I need to borrow this album for a little while. Is that okay?"

For one brief heart-stopping moment, she

thought he was going to refuse, but, in the end, he merely nodded, the sadness in his voice tugging at a familiar place inside her heart. "You will show Jakob, no?"

"I have to, Isaac."

"Is it for my father?" he asked quietly.

"It is." She tucked the album under her right arm and reached for Isaac with her left. "But it's also for you and for Ann, too."

She studied the whiteboard on the far wall of Jakob's office and noted how many of the suspects on his list had been present on her own, as well. Aside from the name of another Amish man or two with a vested interest in the notion of the Back to Basics line being manufactured in Heavenly, their lists were remarkably similar.

Except, of course, for the one name that had found its way onto Claire's list over the past two hours and simultaneously erased all others in the process. Suddenly there was no longer a need to worry about Sarah and her children if Daniel was guilty, because he wasn't. And there was no longer any concern for Isaac's brother and sister, because he hadn't done anything wrong.

Neither had Melinda, who was nothing more than an overachiever who'd tried her best to help Robert deal with the shock of unexpected fatherhood.

And Ann? She was exactly what she should have been — a grieving widow and nothing more.

Jakob drummed his fingers alongside the picture of Keith Watson, Robert and Ann Karble, and a host of other Karble employees. "And why didn't Mrs. Karble or Ms. Simon tell us Keith had worked for Karble Toys?"

"Because they never saw him. They had no reason to think he was here in town and therefore no reason to bring him up." She left the safety of her chair for the window that overlooked the field where Robert Karble had been murdered five days earlier. "I was so busy looking at the memo's impact on Daniel and Isaac that it never even dawned on me that others outside the toy realm could be impacted by its words, as well."

"Like Keith . . ."

"Exactly. Keith said many times that the tour stop at Daniel's place made all the difference in the world for his business. That it was the thing that set him apart from the other tour companies in the area. So Daniel and Isaac being forced out of the toy business stood to create a major ripple effect across Keith's livelihood, too."

"And when you consider that the memo basically pointed to cost as the reason behind manufacturing the new toy line in-house, it stands to reason Watson could have snapped." Jakob closed his eyes momentarily. "I mean, can you imagine losing two careers to the same company?"

"But the only thing that doesn't make sense is why he would have ransacked the Karbles' room," she mused.

"Actually, that makes perfect sense. The only thing missing was the toy plans Robert had gotten from Isaac. Without plans and without Robert, the likelihood of Karble Toys going ahead with a line Ann questioned to begin with was pretty much nil. Stealing the plans was probably Keith's way of making extra sure Heavenly Tours wouldn't be affected by Karble Toys."

She turned from the window in time to see Jakob holster his gun and pocket his cell phone. "I thank you for bringing this to me, Claire. Without this, I'm not sure we would have figured this out so quickly."

"Then I did the right thing." Avoiding his gaze, she pointed at the album, her throat suddenly weighted with the kind of emotion she wasn't ready to try and decipher. She knew enough to recognize it had something to do with the distance she felt between

360

herself and Jakob and the gnawing fear that it was only going to get bigger over time. "Do you have to hang on to that or can I take it?"

"Do you need it?" he asked.

"I don't, but I know someone who does."

Jakob studied her closely. "Oh?"

She inhaled slowly and deeply only to release the same breath from between pursed lips. "Someone who needs to feel connected to their past in much the same way you do, Jakob."

CHAPTER 29

There were many things Diane had said to Claire over the years that had propelled her to make major decisions in her life . . .

Leaving Peter.

Moving to Heavenly.

Opening Heavenly Treasures.

And keeping Benjamin from making a choice her heart may have wanted but her head knew he'd one day come to regret.

Along the way, though, other things her aunt had said had left an impact on the way she looked at things in general. Like what constituted a healthy relationship and the importance of connections with family and friends.

Connections made you feel whole, Diane had said, and deep down Claire knew that was true.

Her connection with Diane gave Claire a sense of safety and unconditional love. Her connection with Esther reminded her of the benefit of innocence and the importance of friendship. Her connection with Benjamin and Jakob helped her see that just because Peter hadn't valued her in the way she'd valued him, that didn't mean she couldn't hold appeal for someone else.

Each connection and its contribution to her life was different from the next, but they all worked together to make her feel whole. And because of them, she knew that one day, when the time was right, she would be ready to love again.

Ann Karble was a long way from being able to love another man the way she'd loved her husband. But just because she wasn't ready for a mate didn't mean she wasn't ready to love and be loved again. In fact, after their countless conversations over the past few days, Claire knew how badly the woman wished for the comfort and strength each glance at her husband's eyes had yielded during their years together.

Her husband's eyes.

Her husband's *emerald green eyes* that twinkled like stars every time he smiled . . .

Drawing her shoulders upward in an act of courage, she knocked on Ann's door with the one and only picture of Isaac Schrock tucked inside her sweater pocket. "Ann? It's me, Claire. Do you have a moment? I'd like to talk to you about something."

Ann flung open the door and pulled Claire in for a hug. "Claire! Claire! Detective Fisher told me what you did! He told me that Keith Watson was apprehended for Robert's murder because of you! I don't know how I can ever repay you."

When she felt Ann's grip loosen, she stepped back. "There's nothing to repay. I just put two and two together and now justice will take over."

"And I'm grateful." Wandering across the room, Ann plopped herself down in the middle of her mattress and drew her knees to her chest. "In some ways, knowing Robert's killer is behind bars paves the way for me to move on to the next step in the grieving process. But at the same time, I'm not sure I want to. I mean, for whatever reason, this is the last place I ever saw Robert. And the thought of leaving here is harder than I expected it would be."

"You miss him, don't you?"

"More than I can ever express."

She glanced down at her pocket and contemplated the various ways news of Isaac could impact Ann.

It could go either way and she knew that. But something about Diane's talk the other night gave her the courage to share what she knew. After all, Ann was without her husband and the child they'd hoped to share, and Isaac was without the mother who'd raised him and the father he'd been robbed of knowing.

"Remember what you said a few days ago? About wishing you and Robert had had a child together?"

Ann nodded. "If we did, I'd still have a part of Robert here with me."

Slipping her hand into her pocket, Claire retrieved the picture she'd taken with her camera and printed off her computer earlier that morning. She looked down at it one last time, the sunlight streaming in through the window of Isaac's kitchen making his eyes twinkle beneath the rim of his Amish hat. "There's a way you still can," she whispered.

She sat perfectly still as she felt Ann's gaze drop to Claire's hand. "Claire? Who is that?"

"His name is Isaac."

She released her hold on the photograph as Ann's fingers closed around its edge. "He — he has Robert's eyes."

It was now or never . . .

"That's because he's Robert's son," she whispered.

With hands that suddenly trembled, Ann stared down at the new, yet familiar face smiling tentatively back at her. "Isaac," Ann repeated. *"Isaac."*

"Isaac is why Robert came to Heavenly. He wanted to meet the son he never knew he had." Then, as Ann listened intently, Claire filled her in on everything she knew about Isaac and his recently discovered tie to Robert. When she was done, she took both of Ann's hands in her own and held them tightly until one by one, the tears Ann had managed to keep at bay began to fall, forging a steady path down both sides of her pretty face.

"He is so handsome . . . just like Robert."

"Yes he is." It was such a simple response, but considering everything that had been said already, it was all that was really needed. The only thing that remained was whether Ann would want and need the connection with Isaac that Isaac wanted and needed with her.

"I want to meet him, Claire. I want to meet my stepson."

Dinner that night was a quiet affair with Ann the only guest still remaining at the inn. But that was okay. Because sitting there in the dining room next to Diane, Claire couldn't help but feel as if she was witnessing a miracle of sorts playing out on the other side of the table.

How else could you explain two people who'd been without a family only hours earlier suddenly finding and forging one of their own? There were stories of Robert that made both Ann and Isaac laugh, and stories of Robert that brought tears to Ann's eyes and an awkward yet touching burst of compassion from Isaac toward his new-found stepmother.

It was like Diane had said in relation to Jakob, connections made a person's life brighter. And in return, set them on a course toward a brighter and more fulfilling future. Which in Isaac and Ann's case meant a second chance at a family for both of them.

"Claire? Would you mind getting that, dear?"

She swung her gaze to her left to find Diane studying her with a look she couldn't quite identify. "Getting what?"

"The door. Someone just knocked."

"Oh, sorry, I didn't hear that." Excusing herself from the table, Claire pushed her chair back and headed in the direction of the quiet yet persistent knocking she'd somehow missed amid the excitement that was Ann and Isaac's reunion. So much had gone wrong in the past few days her heart and her psyche had needed a healthy dose of joy.

Did she wish things could be different with Benjamin and Jakob? Of course she did. But even so, her life in Heavenly was good. The only way that would change was if she let it change.

Squaring her shoulders, she opened the door to find Jakob holding a plate of food in her direction while the smile she'd come to love crept its way across his handsome face.

"Claire Weatherly, I think it's high time you finally tried that Schnitz and Knepp you got cheated of at the festival the other day, don't you?"